I0687607

For my mum who always encouraged me to put my heart into everything I worked at.

For Sue and Ian Harrison; without you I would still be on the endless road to finding a publisher.

For Ken, my husband and inspiration; this story would never have been told without you. Thank you for believing in me.

Nargis Darby

'The distance between your dreams and reality is called action.'

Unknown

A DIFFERENT SHADE OF LOVE

NARGIS DARBY

APS PUBLICATIONS

APS Publications
www.andrewsparke.com

Copyright ©2018 Nargis Darby
All rights reserved.

Nargis Darby has asserted her right to be identified as the author of this work in accordance with the Copyright Designs and Patents Act 1988

First published worldwide by APS Books in 2018

No part of this publication may be reproduced, stored in or introduced into a retrieval system, or transmitted, in any form, or by any means (electronic, mechanical, photocopying, recording or otherwise) without the written permission of the publisher except that brief selections may be quoted or copied without permission, provided that full credit is given.

THE SECOND COUNSELLING SESSION

By the time of her second appointment with Charlotte, Mina had lost all hope of having the decision taken out of her hands. She had given up anticipating an epiphany each time she awoke from her slumber. What she did know, with more clarity than ever, was she and Justin were meant to be together.

The chair was exactly as she remembered it, soft and cosy enough to make her want to release her feet from the snug brown ankle boots she had been wearing for the past three hours..

Charlotte sat upright in her chair with her legs crossed at her ankles and said, "How are you today, Mina?"

A few seconds passed as she thought about the best way to answer and then opted for the reply she had used in the previous session, "I'm doing fine so far."

"Have you had any thoughts about what we discussed last week?"

"I still feel so unsure about what I'm supposed to do." She tensed her shoulders and placed her outstretched hands in between her knees. "All I know is that I can't live under my parents' roof much longer now and I can't tell them that I'm pregnant."

"How do you think they would react if you were to tell them?"

Mina immediately began to imagine that very situation...but all she could see was herself standing in the middle of the family living room, alone, hugging herself and crying as she looked around at the place she had called home for over twenty years. She was scared of being in this place where her future was so unknowable.

As Charlotte offered Mina a tissue, she found herself wanting to embrace this young girl to try and reassure her that it was going to be alright, but all she could do was give her time to talk things through and make the right decisions for herself.

"That's the worst thing...not knowing how they'll react. I wouldn't even know how to begin telling them."

Mina looked up at Charlotte and it was as though she could read her mind because Charlotte said, "What does the father of the child think?"

Mina shook her head. "I haven't told him. I need my head to be clear before that happens."

Charlotte's next few words would stay with Mina for a long time after the dust had settled. "Whatever you choose to do needs to be for you because only you can live your life."

"It really doesn't feel like that...I don't know if it ever will. If I choose to have this baby, how am I going to look after it...I don't have a clue how to bring up a child."

"You're dealing with new challenges and because of this you find yourself having to make decisions where the results are uncertain."

Mina nodded, relieved to have someone listening in the way she needed to be listened to.

Charlotte continued, "What do you think is the most difficult challenge you're facing."

Mina's eyes flitted around the room as she pondered the question. She looked at the picture on the wall depicting hope and then another depicting loneliness and finally said, "I might not be able to live in my family home anymore."

"Why do you think that?"

"It's all I've ever known. I haven't ever imagined what life would look like outside those four walls even though recently it has started to feel less like home every day." As she spoke, she pictured herself coming home every evening and instead of conversing with whoever might be in the living room, she would grab a cold drink and head upstairs to her bedroom to spend the rest of the night, partly on studying and partly on the phone to Justin.

"It sounds as though you're feeling disconnected from your home or your family. When did you start feeling like this?"

Mina looked up and seemingly through Charlotte as she tried to remember. "Can I have a glass of water please?" When it was handed to her, she took a sip, and a deep breath. "I've noticed it for a long time, but I've only started to feel affected by it...I'm not sure...I think it's been since me and Justin started seeing each other."

She re-established eye contact with Charlotte who said, "Why do you think your relationship with Justin has affected how you feel about your family?"

"Well I didn't think it had, until just now." There was no doubt in her mind about the effect Justin had had on her self-confidence, but she'd never equated that with feeling less connected to her family. "I know mum and dad work really hard for us and sometimes that means I don't see them when I get home, but I didn't think it would affect me in any way because that's how it's been for a while."

"When you give yourself permission to reflect on your feelings, your innermost thoughts come to the surface. When that happens, you may find that, subconsciously, your actions are a response to those thoughts and feelings."

"Are you saying I went looking for a replacement family and found Justin?" She sat back, relaxed her shoulders and considered what she'd just said.

"How do you feel about that?"

"I feel..." She searched for the right words, "...strangely comforted. If that makes sense."

"Why is that?"

"Well now there's a reason why I was drawn to Justin in the first place." She braced herself. "I can tell him I'm pregnant and trust him to support me."

This brought a little smile from Charlotte. "Do you now feel you can tell your parents too?"

Mina sat forward and placed her head in her hands. "I need to find out how Justin feels first so I'll know what my options are if they disown me." She looked down at her watch and realised that an hour had almost passed and the session would be over in just a couple of minutes.

Charlotte said, "You've made significant progress today. Shall I book you in for the same time next week?"

"No, the week after, please."

Mina stepped out of Charlotte's office and back into the problematic world she had left behind sixty minutes earlier.

BEFORE

In Weston with Tania

A much-loved sole child, Tania was the opposite of her closest friend in some ways. Mina had a strong mind but found it difficult to express her thoughts, whereas Tania had bags of confidence but didn't necessarily consider all her options before making decisions. Together they balanced each other...most of the time.

Tania had been a little jealous when Mina told her about moving down to Weston Super-Mare. It seemed like a fantastic idea and exactly the kind of thing she would have done herself if she wasn't already committed to her studies. The best she could do was show outward support and go with Mina on a weekend trip to get to know the area.

The two friends ended up finding a table overlooking the beach and Tania went to order their drinks. Approaching the bar, she saw a handsome looking man serving another customer. She noticed how toned his upper body was, hugged tightly by his t-shirt. She imagined how firm his chest would feel under her hands and unconsciously bit her lower lip. She smiled at him when he acknowledged her. "Hi. What can I get for you?"

"An elderflower fizz and a dry, white wine, if you don't mind?" she said, twisting a strand of hair around her finger.

The barman reached for a glass and said, "I don't mind at all. It's what I'm here for."

"That and polite conversation, I hope."

His smile widened. "I haven't seen you here before."

Tania raised her eyebrows. "Is that what you say to all the girls?

He carefully placed the elderflower fizz on the counter, adding a few raspberries and said, "Yes. If I haven't seen them before."

A deliberate tilt of the head. "There must be something else you could open with?"

"Well," he filled a wine glass. "It really depends on what kind of conversation the customer wants." A brief pause. "What kind of talk would you be comfortable with?" He looked at her, his lips smirking.

"I suppose I'd enjoy something that would leave me wanting more."

He shook his head.

"What?"

"I'm not used to being rendered speechless."

Tania paid for the drinks and said, "There's a first time for everything." She could feel his eyes on her as she walked away.

Mina wondered what was taking Tania so long; *she's not ordering for a party of ten*. She turned to try and see what her friend was doing and immediately realised the flirt card had been dealt, yet again.

The art of flirting eluded Mina. She really was clueless, which is probably why Tania got all of the attention when they were out together.

Tania set the drinks on the table and was clearly pleased with her accomplishment but turned straight away to more serious matters. "In all honesty, Mina, how long do you think you'll be able to make it out here?"

With a slightly surprised lift of her eyebrows. Mina said "I was expecting more positivity from my best friend." She took a sip of the refreshing elderflower fizz. "I plan on staying here."

Tania couldn't believe what she was hearing. She had no idea why Mina was so adamant about moving away from her family. If she decided to leave her own mum and dad behind they'd be lost without her. Her parents had invested so much in her education that she'd even started to feel guilty about partying with her friends. Not quite guilty enough though, when attracting the male attention she craved. Actually, she'd have a riot of a time if she lived so far from prying eyes. She shifted in her seat. "You mean this could be a permanent move? Seems a bit extreme in the name of finding yourself don't you think? I mean you could just move to Edgbaston or Harborne. You don't have to go hundreds of miles away."

"I've done nothing really since college so something has to change."

"How on earth are you going to manage? You've never lived away from home."

"Neither have you, Tania," Mina almost shouted back. "That's why I asked you to come here with me." Her voice softened. "I just need some moral support."

Tania couldn't look at Mina for a few seconds. "Fine."

Mina wasn't usually hot tempered, but the response made her blood boil. "Fine? Really?" She shot out of her seat. "I'm getting another drink."

Mina waited to be served. The bartender looked cute. She now understood why Tania had taken her time with him. She absent-mindedly tapped her fingers on the counter whilst she watched him serving another couple.

"What can I get for you?"

She rested an arm on the counter and used her free hand to play with her hair. "What I want isn't on the menu." *That sounds too desperate*. She placed both palms on the counter. "Sorry. Let me try that again...One elderflower fizz and a dry white wine please."

"I can definitely do that for you." He felt bad for this girl but it seemed better not to show it. He knew she was with the confident flirt he'd served a short while ago because he'd been glancing in their direction. "I was telling your friend I haven't seen her here before."

"Well, she's only here because of me so you'd think she'd be a bit more supportive." Mina looked straight ahead. The seating area behind her was reflected in the mirror behind the display of bottles. "She's supposed to be my best friend." She rested her elbow on the counter and her chin in her hand biting her lip.

"That's a bad habit."

She stopped and looked the bartender in the eye. "That's exactly what my mum keeps telling me." They exchanged smiles and suddenly she felt less agitated.

The bartender said, "She's right."

"Don't let her hear you say that. You'll be her best friend for life."

"Actually, I'd like to have a mum for a best friend." A sad expression appeared fleetingly and then he was smiling again.

In the mirror, Mina could see Tania looking in her direction and considered giving her something to think about. She took a deep breath and apologised. "I'm sorry, again, for what I said to you earlier." She felt her cheeks burning. "The thing is I'm just not very good at that kind of thing."

"In my experience, practice is the best way to get better."

She shook her head. "No. I'm too honest for that. What if I attract attention from someone who I have no interest in? What do I do then?"

His brow furrowed and he said, "You're really over-thinking it." He put the drinks carefully on the counter. "Do what comes naturally."

Mina nodded and they both laughed.

"Thanks...for the drink... and the pep talk."

"You know where I am if you need more of either."

A while later, the friends ordered some food when the tension they had both had a hand in creating eased. As the night drew on the bar bustled with people ready to start their weekend with a bang. The air filled with loud chatter and now there was music and a DJ announcing something about dancing the night away.

Tania's eyes widened. "That's my song." She grabbed Mina's hand and raised it in the air with a big, "WOOOOOOO. Come on Mina, let's dance!" Before Mina could protest, she was being dragged away from her comfortable seat to the altogether more uncomfortable standing position on the dance floor. Thankfully, there were a few other bodies around them; among them a trio of men who'd been looking their way earlier.

The next song was less to Tania's taste and she led the way to the bar. Waiting to be served she shouted over the music to Mina. "Cheer up. It's not every day you get to have a dance and a drink and not have to keep looking over your shoulder."

"It's getting late. We should go."

"What? Are you serious? The night's only just started." Tania looked left and right and gestured with both hands. "Not to mention all of the fit guys here. Even you might get lucky."

Mina cringed, unused to dealing with an intoxicated Tania on her own. They were just about to get served when Tania shrieked with glee. "It's another of my favourites." She started to dance around Mina. "I'm going back on the floor. Get my drink for me."

Mina contemplated returning to her seat outside but then caught sight of the cute bartender. She waved. He nodded in acknowledgement. A moment later and he was beside her, leaning over to take her order. She leaned forward too. He smelt enticing, in spite of the overpowering whiff of beer.

"Dry white wine?"

The feeling of his breath on her skin sent chills down her. She stepped back from him and shook her head. Then leant in again and shouted, "Vodka and lemonade."

They both stepped back, smiling. Mina closed her eyes as his smell lingered. Just because she was a rubbish flirt didn't mean she should deny she was enjoying the moment. She turned to try and spot Tania on the dance floor and saw her with her arms around someone's neck, dancing close. When her attention returned to him, the bartender was holding Tania's drink. She paid and mouthed, "Thank you."

Rather than signal to Tania that she had her drink, Mina squeezed through the gathering crowd and found a seat in a slightly quieter part of the bar. She put the drink on the table and looked back across the crowd of people dancing. She admired the fact that Tania didn't need to surround herself with people she'd had to coax into joining her but she felt safer where she now was. She didn't have to keep checking for creepy men trying to dance with, or worse, behind her and she needn't worry about sticky shoes from inconsiderately spilled alcohol on the floor.

Tania had now moved on to full mouth on mouth contact. When they both finally came up for air, they made their way toward the bar. Tania was giggling like a teenager her fingers interlocked with those of the man she'd hooked.

Mina stared down at the vodka and lemonade she'd brought for Tania and sighed. She picked the glass up and thought how disappointed her parents, her whole family, would be if she were to drink it. She examined the unassuming liquid in the glass and bought it up to her mouth. Her eyes widened as the pungent smell hit her nasal passage and as she felt the burn of the vodka down her throat, she grimaced.

"Oh, wow. How on earth do people drink that!"

Mina was talking to herself and was startled to get a male response. "That's another thing that takes practice." It was the bartender. He'd been collecting empty glasses and discarded bottles.

She smiled up at him. "I'm gonna have to make a list at this rate!"

"I'll fetch you a pen and paper."

Mina held up her phone. "I can type a list in here."

"I'll leave you to it then." Turning back, he added, "If I think of anything else for your list, I'll come find you!"

She hoped everyone else in Weston Super-Mare would prove as friendly; it would make her move a lot easier. She took another sip of the vodka and suffered the same pained reaction.

They had been in this bar a few hours now and Mina was ready to leave. Tania, on the other hand, clearly wasn't. She'd made herself comfortable on the lap of the guy she'd been dancing and sharing other things with. "Say hi to Luke," Tania implored.

Luke said, "You look lonely here all by yourself. I'll call my mate to keep you company."

"No, I don't think so." Mina stood up. "I'll give you two some privacy." She glared at Tania. "I'm going outside for some air."

She marched away from, fists clenched. The street lights lessened the harsh blackness in the sky and there was a gentle sea breeze. She found somewhere to sit and, almost immediately, there was a figure approaching her. She was rehearsing how she would tell Luke's friend that she really had no need for his company, when she realised it was someone far more welcome.

"I thought of something else for your list."

"Wait. Let me get my phone ready. Go."

"Knowing who your real friends are."

Mina's had started typing before she registered what she'd heard. She leant back in her chair and closely studied the bartender's expression. He said, "It seems to me your friend is only thinking about what she wants and how she feels. You'd be better off without people like that in your life."

How on earth can you think you know anything about my friendship with Tania, is what she wanted to say, but the truth was that she'd asked herself the same thing before now.

"We've been friends for years."

He held his hands up with his palms towards Mina. "All I know is if I was your friend I wouldn't be leaving you alone in a strange place."

"Thank you. I appreciate your concern." She stroked the cover on her phone, thinking he would return to work and, when he didn't, she was unsure what else to say.

"What time are you thinking of leaving?"

She wiped her hand over her eyes and said, "I'm ready now, actually."

"Shall I call you a cab?"

"No need." She shook her head. "I'm not too far from here."

Mina tried to locate her friend to tell her she was going but couldn't find Tania in the crush inside.

She walked back to her hotel with the bartender's insight very much on her mind.

Making Amends

The morning after the night before had Tania feeling let down by Mina and Mina feeling unsupported by Tania.

Mina considered ordering room service so she could stay cosy and warm in the large bed under the incredibly soft duvet, but then remembered they'd agreed to have breakfast together each morning of their stay. Grudgingly, she dragged herself out of bed.

She found herself thinking about exactly what she hoped to gain from moving away from home. She wanted to find out what the world, well at least Weston, had to offer her in the way of life lessons; she wanted to build her confidence around a complete bunch of strangers and see if she could hold a conversation without looking for a way to escape it; she wanted to feel as if her every move wasn't being scrutinised by people who were only interested in gossip and she wanted to learn how to look after herself.

As she stepped out of the shower and into the cold bathroom, she heard the sound of her phone. Tania had texted to say she'd be ready for breakfast in about twenty-five minutes.

Mina had decided what she was going to wear for the day so she'd already saved herself some time. She carefully applied the coconut body lotion she'd packed and paid extra attention to the feet she'd be exposing in a pair of green sandals. Then she reached for the white robe provided by the hotel and started on her ridiculously long hair.

It had been significantly shortened over the last few years, going from thigh length to waist high, but it was still awkward to handle. For today, she decided to wear it loose. She slipped on a pair of black denim jeans paired with black vest top and a dark green cardigan. Putting on her sandals, she took a quick look in the full-length mirror and went downstairs to join her friend.

She looked around the large, mostly empty dining room. The waving hand wasn't hard to spot. Tania had chosen a table two rows away from the enormous bay window, but still close enough to get a good view of the beach beyond the road. As Mina sat down, she saw Tania had already started.

"I hope you don't mind, I was desperate for a coffee."

"Of course not. I'd have done the same." Forced smiles were exchanged.

"So, what's the plan for today?" asked Tania.

"Well, do you remember the bar we were at last night?"

"I won't forget that in a hurry, trust me."

"Thanks, Tania. Neither will I. Anyway, I saw a sign. They're looking for bar staff, so I thought we could go back there and try my luck."

"With the cute bartender or with the job?" Tania grinned.

Mina's shoulders dropped. "I tell you what. I'll try for the job and you can try with the bar tender."

A hotel breakfast was something Mina was experiencing for the first time in her life and she decided she could get used to it. So many options to choose from; not like at home where it was your bog-standard cereal, toast and possibly a fried egg with a paratha. On Sundays Dad would make French toast or, as Mina called it, eggy bread.

Tania had already chosen a cooked breakfast and fetched herself another cup of coffee whilst Mina chose fresh fruit with natural yogurt and a glass of freshly squeezed orange juice.

As the friends sat down to eat, the sky outside turned grey and it began to rain lightly.

"It's a good thing we're both prepared for just such an emergency," Tania said, attempting to lighten the mood. Unimpressed, Mina stuck her foot out from under the table so Tania could get a look at her footwear.

Tania said, "We could head into the town centre and ask around in the shops too."

"Sounds good. And then I need to find somewhere to stay."

"You know," started Tania, "It might be worth asking some of the shop owners. They must know that sort of thing."

"That's actually a really good idea." Mina nodded in approval and took a sip of her juice. She shuddered and pulled a face. "Nope. I won't be drinking anymore of that."

As the friends ate their breakfast, Tania allowed herself to think what she dare not say out loud about Mina's future plans. *Why on earth would Mina give up the comfort of a free home with everything being done for her by a doting mother, to live miles away from everyone she knows?* She also had to admit to a touch of jealousy, masked so far by silly jokes and giggles. If any of Tania's friends had bet money on which of them would be first to move out of the family home, she'd be the favourite, by a long way. *Mina's way out of her depth. She doesn't have the conviction to get what she wants, or know what that might be*

"Oh my God, Mina. Look who it is." Tania almost choked on her breakfast when she spotted the bartender from the night before sit down a few tables away from them.

When Mina tried and failed to locate the object of Tania's comment, Tania flicked her head in his direction. Mina squinted and said, "Who's that?"

"Seriously? How could you forget that face?"

"Who is it already?"

Tania sighed at her friend's lack of recall. "It's the barman who served us last night."

Mina said, "I'll take your word for it."

Tania, lost for words, shook her head. "Right. Fate's at work here. I can feel it." She took a large sip of her coffee and stood up. "I'm going over there to introduce myself and see if I can make this weekend a lot more exciting." As Tania moved away, Mina wondered if she'd noticed the hurtful nature of the remark she'd just made.

Rather than dwell on that, Mina decided to get herself a second helping. This time she opted for a hot breakfast and poured herself a mug of tea. As she walked back she looked over at Tania sitting opposite the barman. Tania had her elbows on the table and was leaning in to show her apparent interest in whatever it was he was saying.

Mina sat down. As she did so the cute barman looked over at her, smiled and went back to the conversation he was having with her friend.

Mina stirred the teabag in the mug to draw out the flavour and then let it sit for a minute. She had to admit she was worried how long she was going to be able to stay in this picturesque seaside town. Such a huge change to her life would not be easy, but she felt only good could come from it. She added milk and sugar to her cup and sipped slowly.

The rain was easing off now and the sun was trying to find its way out of the clouds. There were families out there trying to enjoy themselves regardless of the weather. Small children were eating ice cream cones bought from the stalls on the promenade. Parents were trying, unsuccessfully, to stop them running in case their ice cream dropped, but they were too excited to listen. Mina finished the last mushroom on her plate just as Tania returned to the table, noticeably less excited than when she left.

"So," Mina said, cautiously, "What have you and the cutie got planned?"

"He said he's working all weekend. Can you believe it?"

"Yes, I can. I'm sure he has bills to pay like the rest of us." She added, with a hint of sarcasm, "At least you get to enjoy the rest of this fabulous weekend with your best friend." She gave Tania the best grin she could produce.

Tania didn't reciprocate. Instead she stood and headed toward the toilets. Mina was considering getting up for more food when a male voice said softly, "Hi." It was the barman.

"Oh. Hi. Tania's just gone to the ladies' room, but if..."

"To be honest, I've no interest in your friend, but I don't think she takes hints very easily."

Mina smiled and said, "No. The direct approach is always best when it comes to Tania."

"And what approach is best with you?"

She was stunned into silence, trying to figure out what he actually meant. Eventually she said "The direct approach usually works with me too."

"Right then..." He began writing on a piece of paper. "Here's my name and number. I'm sorry this is so rushed. I just don't want your friend to be more upset than she already is. Call me and we can talk some more." With that, he was gone.

Now Mina was totally confused. What had just happened? Why did he give me his number? What did he mean by "...we can talk some more"? Had she somehow given him the impression she was even remotely interested in him? She had so many questions, but no time to ponder them now with Tania making her way back to the table.

Mina consciously concealed the folded piece of paper in her hand. "Why don't you get yourself something else to eat and then we can go out?"

"I'm ready to go now." Tania turned leaving Mina to follow, carefully placing the note in the back pocket of her jeans.

She called after Tania, "I don't mind if you want to do something else instead of helping me look for work." Mina didn't mean that to sound sarcastic but it was too late to take it back.

Tania stopped walking and glared at Mina. "I have to get something from my room. Wait here for me." She marched off in the direction of the stairs.

Mina shrugged and made herself comfortable in one of the oversized armchairs in the hotel lobby. The reception area had a high ceiling adorned with two large chandeliers. She was sitting in the heart of the building; all of the other areas were accessible from here; she could imagine friends on a night out meeting here to greet each other before heading out to party the night away.

She remembered the unexpected interaction with the barman and took out the piece of paper he had given her. She turned it over in her hands and foolishly thought, *what if this is destiny is at work here?* She desperately tried to recall showing any kind of interest in him, apart from smiling. She suddenly realised the potential awkwardness that might arise if she made a job enquiry at his place of work. Let alone if she was actually hired.

There was still no sign of Tania and, when Mina checked her phone, she saw fifteen minutes had passed. She was in the middle of texting her when the lift doors opened and Tania walked out.

Mina didn't make a habit of it but she gave her friend a hug and said, "For a minute I thought you were going to become a hermit up there."

"I'm here for you, Mina. So, let's get started, shall we?" Tania looked serious despite an attempted smile and, as if she could read Mina's earlier thoughts, said, "We can still go and ask at the bar from last night."

Mina hugged her friend again. "Thanks. You're a star."

It took just one long morning for Mina's hopes to wilt. They had been into what felt like every single business in Weston when Tania had the crazy idea of asking at their own hotel. When the receptionist went to get an application form, the friends high-fived in relief.

"I know. I'm amazing!" said Tania.

"Right now, you most definitely are!" Mina hugged her. "But...it's not a job offer, is it?" Tania shook her head at such negativity, but Mina went on. "What if they want me to start straight away? I haven't found anywhere to stay yet!"

"Mina, calm down already." Tania stopped as the receptionist came back and handed the form to a hesitant Mina, who thanked her. Tania didn't let it go at that. "How soon do you want the vacancy filled?"

"As soon as possible really. We understand that the applicant may have to make arrangements if they're already working."

"She's not working so you wouldn't have to worry about that."

"Oh. Would you be available to start straight away?"

Mina was frowning with anxiety, but couldn't let Tania do all the talking for her, so she said, "Actually, I'm going back to Birmingham on Monday afternoon." She saw the look of disappointment on the receptionist's face and explained that she couldn't take a job until she found somewhere to live.

The receptionist beamed. "Today might be your lucky day!"

"What do you mean?"

"Accommodation at the hotel is part of the job offer."

Mina couldn't believe her luck and neither could Tania, who gave her a big slap on the back to congratulate her. "That's great." Mina had one last question. "If I fill in the form and get it back to you later, will you be able to make a decision before I leave on Monday?"

"As soon as you return the application form, I'll e-mail the manager and see what she can do. What's your room number?"

The Big Reveal

Tania's parents picked them up from the station and drove Mina to her house. She asked them if they wanted to come in, mainly for moral support, but Tania was tired and wanted to get home to rest.

Mina turned the key and when she stepped into the house, the unmistakeable smell of her mother's cooking lifted her spirits. Her mum loved to cook and Mina was sure that she had prepared her favourite dish, rice with mincemeat and spices – keema chawal.. She put her bags down in the hallway and opened the door to the room on the left.

"Hi, Mum." Mina headed through the living room and into the kitchen.

"Mina! You're back!" Mina's mum put down the big spoon she had been using to stir the rice and hugged her daughter as if she had been away four years, not four days.

"Something smells lovely." Mina stood with her face over the pot and breathed in the smell.

"I know. It's the perfume your dad bought me for my birthday."

The two women looked at each other and, after a couple of seconds, burst out laughing. Her dad was hopeless at remembering important dates.

Mina asked, "Have you got the night off work?"

"No, sweetie," her mum sounded disheartened. "There's a booking for twenty-five people so I'm needed tonight." Mina's mum was one of two head chefs in an established Indian restaurant in the city centre and she worked all kinds of shifts, mainly nights. Mina had only eaten there two or three times. Although the food was impressive, it couldn't stand up to mum's home cooking.

"What time will dad be home?"

"Same time he usually gets home."

"Ok. Well, I'm going to unpack. Where's Anisa?"

"She has classes until six o'clock." Mina was just about to comment when her mum said, "You can take that disapproving look off your face. We want your sister to have every opportunity to succeed in her education."

"Education isn't everything, mum."

Her mum didn't look up from what she was doing, "Maybe not to you, Mina, but we know how important it has been in your brother's life and that's what we want for your sister. We hope there is still time for you to change your mind."

She brushed her mum's comment away. "I'm going to unpack."

She took her shoes off in the hallway, picked her bags up and made her way upstairs to her room. She loved the way her bare feet sunk softly into the deep pile carpet on the stairs. With her mum's comments ringing in her ears, Mina was pleased she didn't have to share a room with her eight-year-old sister. Right now, she wanted to have time to reflect on her weekend and look forward to her future.

As soon as she opened the door to her room, she was hit with the ever so subtle smell of sandalwood. It meant her mum had been burning incense not long ago. She had a fairly good-sized bedroom with a fitted wardrobe on the wall behind the door. A single bed stood on the opposite side of the room and there was a small desk near the window which looked out onto the back garden. She dropped her bags, not too hard or she would have heard a shout from the kitchen below asking if she wanted the ceiling to fall on her mother's head!

She lay down on her bed and closed her eyes.

A few minutes later, she began unpacking, and as she did, she considered how much stuff she would need to take with her.

There was a knock at the door. Her mum poked her head around it and said, "I have a peace offering." She offered Mina a steaming mug.

Mina took it. "I need to talk to you and dad."

Her mum shook her head and placed her hand on Mina's shoulder. "Don't worry, we have plenty of time for that." She was out of the door before Mina could reply.

She sighed in resignation and took a long sip of the masala tea her mum had made...perfect, Mina was developing the theory that her mother always used food and drink to get her own way. She resumed unpacking and then got into her comfy pyjamas. As she was placing her jeans on the hanger, a piece of paper floated out of one of the pockets.

Mina bent down to pick it up and suddenly was transported back to Saturday morning in the hotel. The cute bartender, Mina smiled. She wasn't able to conjure up a memory of having actually read the note at the time. It was now or never. She sat down on her bed and opened the paper. There was a phone number, as expected, and a name, Justin.

Talking to Mum and Dad

Mina had been desperately trying to initiate a Weston-related conversation with her mum and dad for over a week and time was running out. Her mum always seemed to have an excuse to put it off; the family is coming around; she has to go to work; she's cooking. Mina went downstairs and as she entered the living room she saw, to her surprise, that her parents were both chilling out on the sofa. She knew she mustn't avoid it any longer. If she did, she would end up waving goodbye to a new adventure. She took a deep breath.

"I haven't seen you both together since I got back. This must be my lucky day."

Mina's parents gave each other a glance, implying they suspected what was coming. Her mum started to complain. "Mina, I'm trying to relax after a long week. Can't this wait?"

"Not unless you just want me to leave without telling you where I'm going and what I'll be doing." She surprised herself with her own abruptness, but sometimes her mother brought out the worst in her.

Her parents exchanged looks again but said nothing and, more crucially, neither of them got up. Mina took this as a good sign, but was now feeling very nervous.

"I'm going back to Weston Super-Mare on Sunday. I've been offered a job and somewhere to stay and I can start next Monday." She waited.

Her mum was the first to respond. "I don't understand why you are going to live so far from your family."

"I finished college months ago and I haven't done anything since. I think it will be good for me to explore other opportunities."

"Which magazine did you read that in?"

"I don't read magazines, mum." Mina was feeling agitated. "You might notice that if you showed a bit more interest in me."

As soon as she had uttered the words, she braced herself for the comeback. This time it was her dad who spoke. "Mina, the world out there can be cruel if you're not ready."

"I won't be ready if I stay cooped up in the house, dad." She was calmer now, thanks to her dad's measured response. "I'm trying to make a life for myself, be independent."

"How are you going to manage your finances?"

"The hotel I'm working at will provide me with accommodation until I find somewhere to rent." She paused to allow time for a further question, but when one wasn't asked, she continued, "I also have some savings that will keep me going until I'm paid."

There was silence for what felt more like minutes than the few seconds it really was. Mina had her hands clasped together in between her knees and her eyes were looking everywhere, except at the sofa where her parents were trying to absorb the information they had just received. She used the silence to reminisce to herself over the many events that had been celebrated in her home over the years' the countless birthdays and Eids that had been celebrated in her home over the years. On those occasions most of her cousins, aunts and uncles and those her mum adopted as family, would gather to enjoy good food and company. The house was usually full to bursting and that was just how mum liked it. Unfortunately, and for reasons unclear to her, such get-togethers had dwindled over recent years.

Her mum said, "You will be so far away from us. What will you do if you get sick?"

It was nice to hear her mum's concern. "Well, maybe you could make me a box of your traditional remedies just in case." She was sure that would go some way to appease her mum's anxiousness, although she was highly unlikely to use any of that stuff, recalling the last time she had toothache and was given clove oil to rub on her gums. "I'll make sure I register with a doctor's surgery straight away."

Her mother said, "So you are going on Sunday?" Mina nodded. "But you haven't given us time to organise a leaving party for you."

"You don't have to arrange anything. I'd be happy with all of us having dinner together." She suddenly remembered her elder brother. "I'll talk to Rehan, if that's alright."

Mina's mum nodded, rising from the sofa. "Tell him that we will have dinner here on Thursday evening." She crossed over to her daughter and reached down to hold her hands. "I don't want you to go, but if you think it will be good for you then you should go." She bent forward and gently kissed Mina's hands.

Mina had anticipated more of a battle, but her parents seemed alright with her plan. The thought of telling Rehan, however, still filled her with dread. Mina slept much easier that night.

Justin and Frankie

Justin and Frankie arrived a little early for the appointment. During the drive they had decided that whatever the outcome they would have lunch at their favourite canal-side, Italian restaurant. They had been there often enough they'd tried almost every dish on the menu, and on a sunny day the whole restaurant bathed in warm sunshine.

There were five other people in the spacious waiting room. The seating had been arranged to allow maximum privacy. There was a water cooler in one corner and a selection of snacks in the machine next to it. Unlike some surgery waiting areas, the walls were not covered with masses of information about every sickness known to man; the magazine rack had been kept tidy and the publications were solely about healthy eating, exercise, and mental health.

The receptionist told Frankie her she would be next.

"That's good." She turned back to Justin. "You'll be able to drive back to Bristol tonight then."

"Well, I didn't realise I was getting in your way." Justin crossed his arms. "I can leave now if you want me to."

"Stop acting like a child. I was joking." She patted the seat next to her. "Just sit down and stop pouting."

Justin sat down. If this is how she reacted to potentially stressful situations, he felt sorry for her work colleagues. Even though whatever happened in the consulting room would only directly affect Frankie, it didn't stop his stomach from twisting and turning. He felt physically sick.

Frankie was busy replying to texts from clients. It was as if she was waiting for a routine check-up. Justin wished it was; she had been feeling unusually unwell and had then discovered a swelling under her arm. Her GP had arranged a biopsy and a phone call had summoned her here for the results. It began to dawn on him that he was less worried about Frankie's reaction than about what he was going to have to do to support her; how he was going to react; how he was going to cope.

***

Antonio's was busy, as usual, even on a Monday afternoon but Frankie spotted a table out on the terrace, overlooking the canal. They squeezed their way through to it and when she finally sat down, she released a long sigh and dropped her shoulders, as though a big weight had been lifted.

"Now what?"

"You know what. You were there with me, little brother." Frankie started reading the menu. "More tests and when the oncologist knows the extent of what's going on inside me, I can move on to the next step."

Interrupting them, a waiter approached and took their order.

"At least the tests will be done by Wednesday...," started Justin, but Frankie cut across him.

"No. You need to get back."

Justin folded his arms across his chest. "I'm staying and you can't stop me."

Frankie groaned. "You're not coming with me when I have the tests."

"Stop being so bloody stubborn.".

"Really? How am I being stubborn? The tests are going to take hours. You'll have nothing to do." As an afterthought, Frankie added, "I'll ask them to run some tests on you whilst they're at it. You seem quite moody all of a sudden."

Their waiter came with the drinks they'd ordered. Frankie stretched her hands out on the table, palms uppermost, motioning for Justin's hands. Holding them she said calmly, "I know you're worried, but there's nothing you can do...except maybe letting me talk when I need to."

Justin shook his head so Frankie squeezed his hands tighter. "If I start to fall apart, I'm going to need you to help pull me back together."

The siblings enjoyed the rest of their lunch in the sunshine as talk turned to family.

***

The view from Frankie's apartment was incredible; you could see landmarks for miles; Pigeon Park cathedral, the Bullring and the tall, elongated blue mass of the Radisson hotel. Justin had been staring out onto a once familiar landscape for some time now. He was trying to clear his mind; trying not to think about what his sister would be undergoing at that moment. He felt like a passer-by who could only catch a glimpse of a significant event. Frankie had refused to change her mind and had even decided not to involve any other family members until the next set of test results had come back. He was fully aware of Frankie's need for independence cemented by their parent's death and witnessing its impact on him. She just couldn't bear the thought of putting other people through that sort of trauma. And that's why he wasn't by her side.

Justin was fighting to keep things in perspective whilst overcoming his own angst. He had contacted the few friends he had left behind when he moved to Bristol and four of them were meeting him tonight. He'd invited them up to Frankie's to eat before they made their way to the busy Broad Street bars. He searched the cupboards and fridge for inspiration and after ten minutes of indecision concluded that a takeout would be the best option.

Next, he went into the bedroom and chose the clothes he was going to adorn himself in. Whatever he wore would have to be perfect; after all, he might get lucky tonight. He settled for a pair of deep blue trousers, a matching jacket and a white shirt. The outfit would be finished off with a pair of navy shoes. It was an ensemble that, when previously worn, had attracted a fair amount of female attention. Justin nodded, revisiting his previous encounters with the opposite sex. He had never had a one-night stand - it was a practice that made no sense to him – getting drunk, jumping into bed with a complete stranger and then feeling ashamed the next morning. He preferred harmless fun; flirting, holding the waist of an attractive woman, dancing chest to chest; slow, passionate kisses. Those were the kinds of experiences to get his pulse racing. Which was not to say that he hadn't ever been in a serious relationship.

Justin had met Eve during a business conference. The physical connection was almost instant. The emotional connection had taken longer to develop, but neither of them seemed in too much of a hurry although Eve was a demanding woman, both in and out of bed. She took three hectic years of Justin's life.

Then, during another business conference, Justin discovered an unsuspected fact; that one man was not enough for her. After losing Eve at the hotel, he was thinking about taking the elevator up to their room and was gobsmacked, when the lift doors opened, to find her in a compromising position with a colleague. The incomprehensible part of the discovery was that Eve and this man hadn't even considered making themselves presentable for the doors opening in the foyer; it was obvious they had completely lost control.

The ensuing debate was short, but revealing enough for him to discover that the sex in the elevator was not the first incident of its kind in the time they had been together. He left the conference immediately. On the drive home, his mind was torn between shock at Eve's lack of faithfulness and arousal at her sexual exploits in the elevator; he would like to have had the courage to have done something similar with her himself, but he had always been too constrained to follow through. The result was that for the last few years, Justin had been more than happy to keep female admirers at arm's length.

He started the shower and began undressing when the phone rang. In panic he almost dropped the phone as he went to answer it. "Frankie; what's wrong?" He began to pace the bedroom.

Frankie said, "I'm not feeling so hot after the tests. I just needed to have a rest and something to eat. One of the nurses got me a room to rest in." Before he could get a word in, she added "Don't worry about picking me up. I'll make my own way back when I'm ready and I want you to get on with your night out."

Justin could hear that she had no intention of being argued out of her decision. "Okay" he said. "Take your time."

He put the phone down and flopped onto the bed. He knew that she was in good hands but he felt his power being drained away; he should be looking after his sister, the same way she had looked after him.

He spoke aloud to organise his feelings. "Be calm, there's nothing you can do. She doesn't want you there." He lay on the bed a few seconds more and then went back to the shower.

The Boys in Brum

Blaring music, cheap drinks and old friends; it was exactly what he needed. Considering men don't bother asking each other what they'll be wearing for a night out, the friends were obviously on the same wavelength, all sporting smart, casual suits and looking dapper. Justin, Darren, Alex, Marvin and Sam were the hottest group of chocolate-skinned men on Broad Street and quickly casting aside any cares about being out on a week night they bought their second round of drinks. Glasses were raised to old friends and to the concept of drinking on a Thursday night.

"Oh man. This is just what I needed." Marvin shouted, gulping down his drink and then slamming his glass on the table. The residue splashed onto Alex.

"Hey, Marv." Alex put his hands in the air. "Don't ruin my threads!"

"Sorry, mate," Marvin took a final swig of his drink, "I seriously need this night, guys."

"Hear, hear." They all joined in another toast.

As the night continued, four of them began bopping to the music and cutting some shapes on the dance floor. Darren, the only single man in the group apart from Justin, was busy making a move on a woman who had caught his eye.

As Justin danced with his friends, all thoughts of Frankie left his mind and the men were soon joined by a group of women. One of the women was dancing ever closer to Justin and his friends started making kissy faces at him. He put his fists up in a fighting gesture but kept to the beat. The next song was a slower jam giving him the perfect opportunity to test how close the woman would get. He turned to face away from his friends and caught her eye, and held out his hand. She took it. He pulled her towards him. She put her arms around his neck and his hands found her waist. They held each other's gaze and he let his hands slide down her back. He pulled her in closer so he could feel her body against his and they swayed to the music. She stroked the back of his head and pulled him down into a slow and passionate kiss. Behind him, he could hear Sam, Alex and Marvin cheering him on.

When he eventually left the dance floor, it was with his friends and a rather smug smile across his face, but not the sultry stranger he had been holding. "Damn, man! She was *fine*! It's no wonder you're still living the single life." Sam was in awe of his friend.

Justin shook his head and frowned as he picked up his whisky and coke. "Nah, Sam. It's good for the first few moments, but...," he pointed at Alex, "I want what you and Lauren have got."

Alex and Lauren had been together for five years and, whenever Justin was around, they seemed to be ridiculously blissful. Alex held up his glass and Justin met it with his. "Cheers to that, Jus. It's not easy though." They both downed their drinks.

Darren piped up, "Guys, guys, guys. I thought we agreed, no talk of women."

Sam laughed, "Yeah. That's only because you got rejected!" The whole group laughed except for Darren, who lowered his head bashfully. Sam continued to rib him. "You should follow Justin around. He'll show you how it's done."

"Nah, I've got a better idea." Marvin waved his finger around. "Justin should write a guide so he can share his knowledge with the world." He made an invisible globe with his hands and held it there for a few seconds, until the others roared with laughter and high fived him.

"More drinks?" Justin stood up. "What are you all having?"

Darren said, "I'll help carry them" and accompanied Justin to the bar, secretly hoping for some tips on getting to second base.

As they approached the huddle around the bar, Justin put his hands on Darren's shoulder. "There's a woman with short red hair, one person down."

Darren looked carefully to his left. "Okay. What about her?"

Justin tutted. "She's watching you, fool."

Darren straightened his back and stuck out his chest. "Right. What do I do?"

"The guy standing in between should get served next. That's when you make your move. But whatever you do, don't let her order before you."

Darren looked confused. "Why not?"

"Because that's what she's hoping you'll do. I'll see how she reacts when you don't let her order before you."

"Okay then. Nothing to lose." He looked in the redhead's direction and said, "If she slaps me, I'm never taking advice from you again."

The person in between was paying for his drinks and Justin was massaging Darren's shoulder in supportive preparation. Obviously nervous, Darren had always believed that in most situations it should be ladies first. The bartender finished taking the other man's payment and looked up. Darren gestured that he was next, trying not to look at the woman now standing right next to him.

"Five Southern Comfort and lemonades and five sambucas," Darren said in one quick breath.

"She's not pissed. Make a move."

Darren turned to the woman and said, "I'm so sorry, were you before me?"

The red-haired woman said something back to Darren in a low voice that Justin didn't catch so he put his hand on Darren's back and whispered, "Tell her that you'll see her on the dance floor in ten minutes."

Darren did as he was told. As they made their way back to their waiting friends, Justin patted him on the back. "Well done, mate. I know that was hard for you."

"Thanks, but nothing happened."

"Don't fret about that. Just get on the dance floor in ten minutes and see what goes down."

"Like your choice of words." Darren grinned. He placed the tray of drinks on the table. All of them picked up a shot glass and Darren made a toast, "To good friends and good times."

There was a unified, "Cheers," and they all downed the sambuca.

Alex raised the next glass and made another toast. "To the women in our lives." He gestured in Justin and Darren's direction. "And to the women soon to be in our lives."

Another resounding, "Cheers," followed and once more they all downed their drinks in one.

"Ok lads, let's get back out on the dance floor and show Birmingham what it's been missing." Justin stood and the others followed.

They were doing their version of dancing, which included some strutting and pulling faces, when Justin spotted the red-haired woman moving through the crowd towards them. Twenty minutes later, the group left the dance floor, without Darren.

Marvin yawned and said, "It's getting late. I need to get going."

Sam and Alex agreed, but wouldn't leave without saying goodbye to Darren. They split up to look for him. Two minutes later, Marvin texted Justin to tell him he'd found Darren on another table across the bar. "I'll tell him we're going."

Justin found them easily enough with Marvin's directions. As he approached, the redhead looked up and Darren followed her gaze. Justin said apologetically, "We're all off now. But you can stay if you want."

Although he looked gutted at the thought of having to leave this perfect moment, Darren decided he should. Justin went back to wait with the others while he said goodbye to the redhead, pulling her into a deep and passionate embrace. When they finally left each other, Darren bounced back to his friends who all congratulated him. Turning to Justin he gave him a bear hug.

"What happened with you then?"

Darren proceeded to explain the appreciative gesture as the friends made their way outside. "Thanks guys."

There were hugs all round and Justin said, "It won't be so long till we next meet. I'll be back pretty soon, for Frankie."

"Gimme the heads up when you're back up and you can all come round to mine," Marvin said.

With a final round of goodbyes, Darren, Alex, Marvin, Sam and Justin made their separate ways home to their individual realities.

***

Frankie had taken the next morning off to give herself time to fully recover from the tests. She was still asleep when Justin woke up. He made himself a mug of mint tea and wrote down a shopping list; he wanted to fix lunch for her before she went into work. In the lift on the way down to the ground floor, he scrolled through some of the texts his friends had sent him over the course of the night; some were jokes and one or two had a more serious tone to them, letting him know they were on hand to support him in any way he might need. He'd forgotten how close they used to be. All their parents had, at one time or another, made the same comment that as boys they'd lived in each other's pockets.

The lift pinged and Justin stepped out into a modestly chic reception area. The warm breeze through the open front doors made him think about the Bristol estuary breezes and that he'd be getting back to some sort of normality this time tomorrow.

The supermarket aisles were quiet, which made shopping a far more relaxing experience than in the weekend chaos. The menu he'd fixed for lunch, was steamed fish with Moroccan couscous and some flavoured water he decided to experiment with. All items paid for, he made his way back to the car, his stomach already yearning for the scrumptious repast he was now ready to make. His phone buzzed for an incoming message and when he opened it he half laughed and half shouted aloud. It was a photo message from Darren of himself and the redhead from last night.

The message supplanted the thought of food in his mind as he drove back to Frankie's. If Darren and the redhead stayed together long enough, he would be the only single one in the group. In itself that didn't fluster him; he enjoyed the thrill of meeting someone new, a new face, a new body; but was becoming increasingly aware of the value in what his friends had.

He had only been gone an hour, so when he opened the door to Frankie's apartment and found a note on the kitchen worktop, his heart sank. The note read;

> Hey Justin, thanks for letting me sleep in. I feel a lot better this morning. I'm sorry that you weren't here when I left, but I had to rush. Love Frankie
>
> P.S. I've got a dinner reservation with a client at 6pm so I won't see you before you leave for Bristol.

Justin found Frankie's aloofness exasperating. He scrunched up the note and threw it into the bin. Then he looked at the shopping he had just done and declared to himself, "Well, big sis, you're getting lunch whether you like it or not." He began to steam the fish and cook the couscous. The kitchen filled with Moroccan flavours and, thirty minutes later the meal was ready. He carefully placed the food in an airtight container and filled a clear plastic flask with raspberries, pieces of watermelon and a few fresh mint leaves before adding water.

Before taking the surprise lunch to his sister's office, Justin sat down at the breakfast bar to eat his own portion. He tried to take his time and appreciate each mouthful, but he found no reason to stay any longer than necessary. He rinsed the used crockery and cutlery and put them in the dishwasher, packed up his things from the bedroom and bathroom, picked up Frankie's lunch and left the apartment.

DURING

High Hopes in Weston

Her dad dropped her off at New Street, handing her a rather large amount of cash. "It's from me and your Mum so you won't have to dip into your savings too much."

Mina had conflicting thoughts about this: weren't they worried that they were making her even more vulnerable by giving her a large amount of cash but, hey, at least her parents had actually discussed how they could support her decision.

She read the printed email she had received from the hotel manager with directions to the hotel from the train station. During the short journey Mina felt like a small child eagerly awaiting the moment where she could unwrap her birthday presents. From the moment she had made her final decision to leave home, the one location in her head was the seaside. The resort she had visited most often was as a child was Blackpool; the illuminations were a yearly highlight. She remembered the way her stomach did back flips, threatening to exit through her mouth as she and her family made their way past the rollercoaster cars to the child friendly rides. Choosing Weston Super-Mare over Blackpool had been a no-brainer; no memories to get in the way of...she didn't quite know what, but at least here she only had to look after herself.

Arriving at her destination, she took a moment to stand back and look at the place she was going to call home before entering the building and heading straight for the reception desk.

"Hello. I'm Mina and I start work here tomorrow."

The male receptionist responded with an ear to ear smile. "Hi. I'm Dan." He offered his hand. "Rachel told me you were coming. She asked me to show you where you'll be staying and she will be here..." Dan looked up at the large clock above the desk, "...in around half an hour."

Dan left the reception desk to a woman called Sarah while he escorted Mina to her room. The small talk during the lift ride to the fourth floor, was mostly Dan talking. He asked about her journey and if she had ever been to Weston before. She told him about her visit the fortnight before and when they reached the room at the end of the corridor, he opened the door and let her in. Before she had time to comment Dan gave her the room key and said, "I'll ring up when Rachel arrives." Before leaving he added, "Me and a few others are going out for drinks after work tonight. You should come, it'll be fun."

Mina frowned. "Thanks for the offer, but I don't drink and I think I'd like to rest tonight." Seeing the obvious disappointment on Dan's face she said, "Maybe later on in the week?"

Dan smiled. "You bet," and he closed the door behind him.

She looked around at what would now be her living space. It comprised a basic hotel room with just the bare essentials. She supposed that at the interview, she should have asked to see where she would be living but why argue? A familiar saying used by her dad popped into her head, *Don't bite the hand that feeds you.* She walked towards the window, which was directly opposite the door, started about three feet off the floor and reached the ceiling. She breathed a sigh of relief: she had a view of sorts of the beach to the front of the building. She observed the goings on outside for a few seconds before moving over to the bed.

She slipped off her shoes and removed her jacket, hoisted herself all the way onto the bed and leant her back up against the headrest softening it by wedging pillows behind her. Now she was able to soak in a clear view of her living quarters. Directly in front of the bed was a dressing table cum desk with a flat screen television, to the right a chest of drawers slightly shorter in height and, sitting on top of that, a tea tray. She had a wardrobe further right and then the doorway into a tiny bathroom. She found the room's colours calming; lime green, deep purple and magnolia; they made her reminisce about the countless Eid outfits her mum had bought her over the years.

Ten minutes later, Mina was downstairs filling in paperwork with her new boss. They discussed her working hours which would be either earlies, starting at six in the morning or late shifts from four in the afternoon. She was also provided with her uniform and details of meal arrangements and wage payments. As the conversation progressed, Mina pushed aside any hesitancy; she was fully aware of how desperately she needed this to work out.

When Rachel had finished with her, Mina made a quick detour to the reception desk. Dan spotted her before she reached him. "Mina! How's it going?"

She wondered if he was this cheery all the time. "Okay. I've already met Rachel and I start tomorrow."

"Fantastic. Let's celebrate!"

The comment exasperated her. It seemed Dan had stored their earlier conversation in a file labelled *Not important enough to remember* but she didn't have the energy to challenge him. She found herself agreeing to go out later.

Dan said, "We'll be meeting in reception at eight o'clock."

She wasn't much concerned with what she was going to wear because she honestly didn't take any pleasure in dressing up and plastering her face with inexcusably expensive make-up. As long as her hair had been washed everything else would fall into place. What did worry her was having to force herself to look forward to meeting new people in a new environment. She couldn't shake the nagging feeling that this adventure would become an epic quest that would slowly unravel to reveal her true level of immaturity.

"Pull yourself together, Mina," she scolded herself out loud.

Loneliness was creeping in and she needed someone to talk to. She opened the contacts list in her phone and scrolled through the favourites. Mum, dad and Anisa were all out of the question: they would tell her to get the next train back to Birmingham and then whisper quietly to each other that they had told her so. Rehan might be better but she couldn't guarantee he wouldn't let something slip to their parents. She finally stopped scrolling. The one person she could talk to was Tania. After all, they had recently spent a weekend together. Mina pushed the call icon and waited for an answer. When Tania picked up they spent the next half an hour catching up and Mina eventually managed to unload most of the pressures that had built up since her arrival.

The Wait is Over

Sunday evenings were generally quieter than Saturday, but there was a steady flow of people to Sunset Strip, which occupied a prime location across the road from the beach. The bar was aptly named because at the right time of day, if you were a patron eating or drinking alfresco style, you would be awed by the sun setting over the water.

Justin had been in the back office for around an hour now catching up on mundane paperwork, but he had also been speaking to his older sister. During their daily chats he and Frankie had developed a keen avoidance of uncomfortable topics; one of which was Frankie's illness. Their talks usually ranged from five to thirty minutes: this time it had been slightly longer. He was helpless as far as her physical wellbeing was concerned, but had assumed responsibility for her emotional state.

The situation was worsened by the distance between them. Occasionally, after these conversations, he would feel like a total disgrace for leaving his sister alone. Their parents had passed away when he was still a teenager and their aunt and uncle had opened their homes to both of them but all they really had was each other. However, Frankie was considerably older and had her own home. She was adamant that Justin should live with her and Justin's gratitude was grounds enough for his current sense of guilt.

Although Frankie loved her time with Justin, she had no desire to be a parent and had chosen to focus on her career. She had never knowingly coaxed her sibling to follow a work-driven life, so she was ecstatic when he landed a job managing a highly reputable chain of hospitality outlets. He believed though that without Frankie his life would be unrecognisable.

Justin pocketed his phone and walked out into the main hub of the bar. At a quick glance around he guessed there were around thirty-five people in the bar: it was a skill he had gradually developed over the years. As he was about to speak to one of his staff, a group of eight entered the bar. He thought that he recognised one of them but thought nothing of it and continued with the task in hand.

Justin made a point of making himself a visible and useful part of his team and wasn't afraid of helping with absolutely anything he could expect them to do. He often served drinks behind the bar, believing it an excellent way of getting to know the people who had chosen to spend their money with them. It was entirely typical that he should step across on this occasion as a new customer approached.

"Hi. What can I...get for you?" his words trailed off as his eyes met the those of the brown-skinned beauty on the other side of the bar. There was complete silence for a few seconds.

Justin felt a nudge from one of the other barmen. "Uh. D'you want me to take the order?"

Oh, my goodness, it's Justin, Mina thought, but all she could manage was a smile.

She's smiling at me, thought Justin. He was finally encountering the woman from the hotel a fortnight before and the excitement he was feeling was wholly unexpected.

In all the panic and excitement of leaving home, Mina had completely forgotten about Justin and his note. She began to feel uneasy but also excited. Maybe something would come of this now she didn't have to compete with Tania.

With his gaze still on Mina, Justin replied to his colleague. "No, it's alright. I've got this."

Just then Dan waltzed up. "What're you doing, Mina?"

Justin repeated her name in his head as Dan continued to scold. "If you think I'm letting you buy a drink on your first night out, you've got another thing coming, young lady."

Justin already knew the man who had taken up the spot beside Mina. "Ah, Daniel. How are you?"

"All the better for seeing you. Can you rustle up some drinks, and a special for the new recruit here."

"Congratulations on the job, Mina." Justin smiled at her and then nodded at Dan. "Don't worry about him. His bark is worse than his bite." Dan lunged forward pretending to maul Justin. It was obvious to Mina that they knew each other well. No wonder this was Dan and his friends' favourite watering hole. When Justin said her name though, she felt all strange inside. While Dan was talking to him, she had a good look at the man on the other side of the bar. He was much taller than she was and probably two or three days into growing his beard. He was wearing a white polo shirt with a black logo, not too tight. Randomly, she imagined running her hands up his arms and down his back.

Justin placed a tray on the counter and started preparing the round Dan had ordered. There was nothing for Mina to do so she excused herself and went back to the table.

Justin said, "I'll bring the drinks over." He wanted to spend as much time around Mina as possible, but needed to do it under the guise of work. He finished the preparation and moved around to pick up the tray. He was a man in his early thirties who suddenly felt like a big kid experiencing his first childhood crush. Mina had taken a seat facing the bar and her heart began beating faster as she saw him approach the table. He called out the drinks one at a time and handed each one to the right recipient. With the last drink he looked at Mina and said, "This is on the house for the new recruit."

As Mina reached for the glass, their fingers lightly touched and she wondered if he was feeling the same thing. She said, "Thank you." Some of the others went "Oohh." She couldn't bring herself to watch as he walked away from the table.

"OH MY GOD. He likes you!" Dan was beside himself with glee.

"Shut up. No, he doesn't."

"We come here A LOT, you know."

"Well, I might have to find somewhere else to drink." The smile spreading across her face told a different story.

***

As she woke to the sound of her alarm, she momentarily forgot where she was, and then it dawned on her. Snippets of last night came flooding back: Justin and the brief brushing of their fingers. She felt her cheeks burn up with embarrassment but she had the feeling this was not the last she would see of him.

When she checked the time, she saw she had eight hours until her first shift on the job. As she got into the shower, she felt more optimistic than yesterday. She was looking forward to work and making new friends. She dried herself, put some clothes on and began to tackle the mass of hair on her head. It was going to be a major trial trying to tie it up before work each day. Her mum had agreed she could trim the split ends, but it was still so long that she felt like a Muslim Rapunzel. It would be a good idea to practice how she would keep her hair out of her face, and out of customers' food. She opened a small zipped bag and dumped the contents onto the bed. It took another ten minutes to find a comfortable, and flattering, style. As soon as she was happy with her hair, she put on a pair of black and white trainers, grabbed her purse and phone and headed downstairs to the restaurant. She opted to walk down the four flights of stairs instead of taking the lift. She had a spring in her step enhanced by the clear blue skies she could see through the windows. She had already decided what she was going to have for breakfast; a bowl of cereal to start with and then a cooked breakfast with a strong cup of tea.

As she walked out onto the ground floor, a voice behind her made her jump. "Morning, Mina!"

"Oh my God. You scared me."

Rachel chuckled. "Oh, I'm sorry. I suppose I shouldn't sneak up on you like that!"

"Don't worry. I was in a world of my own. Well, thinking about breakfast actually."

Rachel nodded. "I don't feel right without a good breakfast. You've got your uniform already but you'll have to come to reception for your badge."

Mina's face lit up. "That's great. I'll be going into town to buy some tights and shoes a bit later." When Mina was given her uniform, and realised it was a skirt, not trousers, she had taken a long, deep breath. She had never owned a skirt and her college friends had often called her a tomboy. The challenges were coming thick and fast.

"Enjoy your breakfast and I'll see you before you start your shift."

Mina continued to the restaurant. She recognised the waitress as Louise; she'd been in the group last night. Louise spotted Mina and started waving frantically. When Mina got close enough, Louise welcomed her with a hug.

She was not used to having people in her personal space and she didn't feel comfortable hugging back. Louise didn't seem to notice. "Did you have a good night last night?"

"It was fun," Mina said, hiding the truth about her awkwardness around strangers.

"We go there every weekend. There's a DJ and small dance floor."

Mina raised her eyebrows at the thought of dancing. She said, "I won't be able to come with you this weekend. I'm working the late shift."

"Oh no. That's too bad," Louise looked genuinely sad.

Mina's stomach began to rumble and she sneaked a glance over into the restaurant over Louise's shoulder. Louise took the hint and apologised. "Sorry. I'm keeping you from breakfast. Go straight through."

Mina chose to sit at a table near the wall with her back to the entrance of the restaurant. She thought about what her loved ones would be doing in Birmingham: Mum, dad and Anisa would be having breakfast and then dad would take Anisa to school; Rehan would already be on his way to work and Tania would still be in bed because she didn't have any lectures until two o'clock. She wondered what she might be doing if she hadn't decided to leave home: watching television, cleaning and cooking seemed likely. She didn't rush her first meal of the day and after around forty minutes, she couldn't eat anything more.

***

On the way back from the shops, Mina collected her badge. Entering her room, she carefully placed her bags on the bed, and slumped down in the chair near the window. She had managed to deposit the cash her dad had given her into her bank account and then bought the items she needed to complete her uniform. There were still four hours until the start of her shift. She began thinking forward to tomorrow: *how was she going to occupy her time before work?*

Determined not to let negative thoughts taint her mood, she busied herself trying on her uniform. The skirt was black and knee-length and the top an emerald green, button-down blouse. She studied her reflection in the mirror on the wardrobe door; the tights and shoes she had purchased earlier were a perfect match. The finishing touch was her name badge. She nodded and smiled at herself. This would be the first skirt ever to make it into her clothing collection. She picked up her phone, took a photo and sent it to Tania.

She was just going to slip off her skirt when she heard her phone: Tania had sent a picture of herself wearing pyjamas and a message wishing Mina good luck. Mina sent back *thank you*. Out of the blue, she found herself picturing Justin in his snug polo shirt and black trousers. Then her body remembered the feeling she got when their fingers brushed. *It couldn't do any harm to have lunch at Sunset Strip one day soon.* An immediate afterthought, was not to divulge this to Tania: she would be livid if she found out Mina was showing an interest in someone she had made advances to, even though she'd been rejected.

Mina knew exactly what she wanted to do, but she couldn't help feeling he might think her desperate. It would help if she could find a colleague to go with her, but she didn't know anyone well enough yet. *Maybe I can order food to takeout? That way I'm not there for too long.* She considered it for a second and realised they probably wouldn't do take-aways. *It isn't that sort of place. Just go there and see what happens. He might be there, he might not be there. Either way, it makes no difference because I'm only going for lunch.*

She did a quick reflection check and marched out of the door like a woman on a mission.

***

The aromas of hot food from Sunset Strip invited Mina in to explore. When she looked around, there were plenty of other people inside who'd been enticed by the smells. The specials board just outside the terrace was showing a lunch deal for two people, so she didn't bother reading the rest. As she walked inside, her eyes darted around the bar, but Justin was nowhere to be seen. A big part of her was pleased; she was getting a bit cocky having only been in town for twenty-four hours. She picked a menu up off one of the tables and scanned it for something appetising. It was printed in landscape, rather than the usual portrait format, and was coloured in hues of orange, red and gold, the colours of a sunset. She went to the bar and placed her order. "Where do the stairs go?"

"Up to the first-floor terrace."

"Can I take my food up there?"

"Of course, you can. I'll have it brought up to you if you'd like." He gave Mina her order number painted on a large S made of carved wood.

"That would be great."

When she reached the terrace, the uninterrupted view took her breath away; she could see for miles in front and she even thought she could see another island of some sort. She put everything she was holding onto the table and sat down. Now this was something she could get used to.

***

Justin was in the kitchen at Sunset Strip, having a chat with his head chef and also casting his eyes over proceedings. The food tickets had been coming through at a steady pace and there were three plates of food ready to be served. One of the bar staff picked up two plates and Justin took other plate. On the way, he collected cutlery and a basket of condiments.

James was on his way back to the kitchen to collect the last plate, when Justin called over to him, "I've got table twelve."

"Thanks, boss."

As Justin walked up the stairs he mulled over his activities for the rest of the week: most of it was business, but on Thursday he'd be travelling to spend the evening with Frankie. It was a regular part of his weekly routine. They would take turns choosing a movie and ordering takeout. On the odd occasion, if they were both up for it, they would head to the local cinema, and eat out afterwards.

From the top of the stairs, Justin spotted the wooden S with number twelve on it. A table on the other side of the terrace. He had just started thinking about how, on a day like today, the addition of the terrace to the building had been an excellent idea, when he froze in his tracks. He knew he would see Mina again, but not so soon and he hadn't expected to be serving her lunch either. About a hundred different thoughts raced through his mind, one of which was that she might be making the first move, except that he didn't think that was in character for her, although he had no idea what her character comprised. Another thought *She's having lunch with a friend, but then why only one food order? Stop assuming and go and find out,* he said quietly to himself.

***

From the corner of her eye, Mina saw someone coming towards her with, what looked like a plate of food. She moved a few of her things onto the chair to make space on the table.

"I didn't think I'd be seeing you again so soon." Justin was standing beside her table.

Mina closed her eyes. Her heart began pounding at a hundred miles an hour. She took a deep breath and opened her eyes. He was standing on her left-hand side holding her food. She looked up at him and was relieved to be wearing her sunglasses because she was sure he'd be able to read her expression.

"My work friends speak highly of the food here." She said, hoping to sound disinterested in his presence.

"Well, when you've finished eating, you can judge for yourself."

"I have to start eating before I can finish and you're still holding my plate."

"Sorry about that." He placed everything he was carrying down on the table. He wasn't standing particularly close, but the smell of whatever aftershave he was wearing wafted in Mina's direction and tortured her some more.

Justin remembered that he was a mature man and so put himself on the line. "Would you mind if I sat with you?"

Mina, startled by the question said, "Shouldn't you be working?"

"I'm due a break soon anyway." He wondered how far he could push before Mina pushed back.

"I would prefer that you didn't." She had never been in a position like this before. "You see, I want to eat and you'll want to talk. It would be awkward for both of us."

"That's fair comment." He pulled out a chair anyway.

Mina panicked. "Don't blame me if you get told off."

"Nothing to worry about." He waved her comment away. "One of the perks of being the manager is that I get to take a break whenever I want one."

Did she hear what she thought she heard? *Did Justin just tell me that he manages Sunset Strip?* She was rendered speechless. It was a good thing that she hadn't started eating yet or she would probably be choking on her food right about now.

"You really should start eating before it goes cold."

She couldn't tell if he was being cheeky or was genuinely concerned about her food going cold. She didn't want him to believe she would do whatever he told her to, but she really did need to eat. *Maybe I should get this put in a takeout box and eat it back at the hotel?* She tried to think of a way to ease herself out of the situation.

Just before excusing herself she remembered how eager she wanted to be to embrace new challenges. *Surely this is just one of those challenges?* On the other hand, was this really a challenge she could handle? She didn't have the benefit of any real experience of physical relationships; her cultural background giving her limited physical closeness with the opposite sex. Her heart had won the fight and she remained seated. After all, Justin hadn't been rude, he had simply taken her by surprise.

"You're right." She took a sip of the elderflower fizz she had come to enjoy. "I can't take too long. I start work in a couple of hours."

She placed the glass on the table and picked up half of her panini. It was still hot and when she took a bite, the cheese oozed out onto her chin. Justin held out a napkin and Mina took it without looking at him. She seemed to be proving herself a professional in self-humiliation. The oozing filling aside, the panini was good and tasty: the combination of cheddar, mushroom and red onion worked well.

"I need to ask a question." It was something which had been plaguing Justin. "Don't worry about offending me, but why didn't you call me after I gave you my number?"

She finished chewing and took a sip of her drink. "I was only here for a long weekend." She decided to follow that up with a question of her own. "Don't you think you run the risk of putting me off you by being so forward?"

"Not at all. You told me you prefer the direct approach."

Mina looked at Justin and said, "What? When did I say that?"

"At the hotel, just before I gave you my number." Justin grinned, feeling his confidence grow. His gaze was steady on her face as she sifted through her recollections of that moment.

She ate more of her panini and sipped her drink. She couldn't allow a total stranger to get the upper hand, so she defended herself. "I had a lot going on at the time. I came here for several reasons and your phone number wasn't one of them."

Sensing the tension in her, Justin said, "I've never given my personal number out to anyone." He leant forward, inching closer to Mina. In response, she pushed her sunglasses onto her head. Now they were both searching each other's eyes as Justin continued, "So now that you're finally here in front of me..." Mina was beginning to feel something she couldn't describe. "...I'd like to see what develops."

Mina swallowed down the rest of her drink, sat up straight and stretched her legs out, crossing them at her feet. "The view from here is amazing."

Justin refrained from telling her the view from his apartment would put this one to shame; he was sure she would get up and walk away. "That's what makes this place so special."

Returning to the point before she shifted the conversation to the view, Mina said, "I haven't even started my first shift at work. I don't know that I would be able to juggle...," she shrugged as she tried to find the right words, "...whatever this is."

"Look, you work at the hotel down the road. I'm here five days a week. We can meet just for a coffee, or a meal and talk."

"Where are you the other two days?"

Justin's eyes lit up at Mina's show of interest in his whereabouts. "I go to see my sister on a Thursday evening and I'm there until Saturday morning."

Now, she had another question, "What were you doing in the hotel that Saturday morning?"

Justin recalled spending the whole of the previous week with Frankie after her diagnosis. They had talked, with each other and with her specialist. They had informed their extended family about Frankie's diagnosis and then were inundated with visitors to her apartment.

"Are you okay?"

"Sorry...." He wasn't ready to share those parts of his life, just yet. "I'd just got back after a week with my sister. She's going through a difficult time at the moment." A brief silence fell enabling Justin to recompose himself." Anyway, I have breakfast there if I can't be bothered to go back home."

"I have to get back." Justin stood up with Mina and she picked up her phone and bag. *If you're going to do it, do it now*, she thought. She held out her hand and said, "It's nice to meet you Justin. I'm Mina."

Justin took her hand and this time she knew he was definitely feeling the same things she was. "It's good to meet you too, Mina. I hope we can do this again, soon."

***

Justin remained on the terrace as Mina left and watched her walk away, smiling like a cat that's had the cream. He found himself pondering over all the smallest details from the last thirty minutes; the words they had spoken, the short silences and, the most vivid memory of all, how he felt when they held each other's hands. Justin had not been expecting any kind of physical contact, so when she offered her hand, he'd have fist pumped the air if it wouldn't have made him seem foolish. He hadn't felt this excited to meet someone in a long time. Mina was like a breath of fresh air and a much-needed distraction.

Downstairs, he placed Mina's glass on the counter and headed towards the kitchen. The lunch crowd had dwindled and James greeted him in the doorway.

"Where've you been all this time, boss?"

Justin shook his head. "Firstly, you know I don't like being called boss..." James grinned knowingly. "...and secondly, I was making sure the customers on the terrace were being looked after."

"You were ages."

"I struck up an interesting conversation."

James raised his eyebrows. "So, what did you and the dark-haired beauty talk about?" Justin smiled and shook his head. "You mean you didn't even notice we'd been on the terrace looking after the customers too? Shame on you!"

James was right: for a moment, or thirty minutes to be precise, Justin had forgotten he was at work. He was setting a bad example and that had to stop. Justin had to get James off his back, "I found out she works at the hotel with our Daniel."

"So, we'll be seeing her again? I wonder if she's as rowdy as the rest of them!"

"Only time will tell, James."

***

Mina left the bar with a spring in her step. She pondered all the details from the last thirty minutes: finding out that Justin was the manager at Sunset Strip, the smell of his aftershave as he placed her food on the table and, most vivid of all, how she felt when they held each other's hands. She was certain she had surprised Justin when she had offered him her hand and she shuddered as she remembered the touch of his skin on hers.

She was bursting to tell someone what had happened, but who? Tania was out of the question, at least for the time being. "Dan!" She shouted out when she spotted him walking into the hotel. She frantically waved him over.

"Mina!" Dan waved back and changed direction. "Are you on the late shift this week too?"

"I am. Are you?"

"Yeah! I'm so glad."

Dan put his arm around her as they entered the hotel. "Why? What happened?" he excitedly enquired.

She blushed, looked around to make sure nobody was listening and whispered, "Justin happened."

Dan stopped walking. His eyes were wide and he looked as though he was ready to catch a fly in his mouth. "Shut up!" he said, playfully shoving her.

"Ssshhh." She looked around again.

"Let's go to the staff room and you can dish the dirt."

She didn't like the sound of that; there would more than likely be other people there and she wasn't ready to air her dirty laundry in public. "We could go up to my room." Unless the room was bugged, no one else would be privy to their conversation there.

"Right, I'm putting the kettle on." Dan announced as they entered Mina's room. "You just sit down and tell me everything."

She detailed as much of her encounter with Justin as she was comfortable sharing. Dan was engrossed. He kept her going with sudden outbursts of, "NO!" and "So what did you do?" When she finally finished, Dan said, "Wow. He's not wasting any time, is he?"

"I know! If this is what happens in my first twenty-four hours away from home, I'm scared for the rest of my time here!"

The alarm clock on the bedside table told Mina that she now only had three quarters of an hour until the start of her shift. Dan had become absorbed in his phone so she excused herself and changed into her uniform in the bathroom. After talking like this, she felt a weight had been lifted off her. Unfortunately, she already knew Dan liked to talk so, from behind the closed bathroom door, she shouted, "I don't want anyone else to know about this, Dan."

After a pause, Dan shouted back, "You should have told me that before."

Mina was horrified. She gently banged her head against the bathroom door before going back in, cleared her throat and stood with her hands on her hips and a frown on her face until Dan looked up from his phone. She said, "Who have you told?"

He pursed his lips together and prolonged an answer. "I was only joking. I haven't told anyone."

Mina grabbed a towel from the bathroom and threw it in Dan's direction. He stretched his arm out to catch the incoming object and then commented on her uniform. "That colour really suits you."

"I see what you're doing. You're trying to get on my good side again."

Dan watched her fighting to put her waist-length hair up in a reasonable style. Then he asked impatiently, "What's next for you two?"

She shrugged her shoulders nonchalantly. "I told you, we'll just chat and maybe get some lunch."

"Lunch? You two should be ripping each other's clothes off by the sound of things!"

She raised her hand to cover her eyes and shook her head. "I've only just set foot here. The last thing I want to do is rush into anything."

"Alright. But if you ask me, you two should be together."

Mina sat down to finish her tea and, once again, replayed her enticing encounter with Justin.

***

Twisting her neck from side to side to loosen it up, Mina calmly climbed the stairs back to her hotel room. She could feel the effects of her first night's work making their way through her inexperienced body. She quickened her pace looking forward to the comfort of the soft, warm bed, and a decent mug of tea three more floors above.

She had become intrigued by the variety of people she had met at the hotel during her first night; predominantly, families with young children and a sprinkling of senior citizens to balance out the ages. She had been shadowed for a significant part of her shift. It was like wearing a headset to receive instructions from your team, only the team was Rachel and she was clearly visible. Mina was given a tour of the hotel, which was more extensive than she would have guessed. She now had a general idea of the location of the laundry room, the staff room and the kitchen, but there were other places, like the stock room, that she forgot pretty much as soon as she was shown. The tour conjured up memories of her first few weeks at secondary school; she pictured herself back then standing in the enormous playing field on her first morning, looking up at the five-story giant building she, and a few hundred others, were about to enter.

She swiped her key card in the panel on the door too quickly. Red light. She tried again, a little slower. Red light. She clenched her fists and tried again, even slower. Success! She changed into her pyjamas and crept into bed, checking she had set her alarm to go off in eight hours' time.

In fact she woke up naturally, lay on her back and thought about where she was. Her first day of independent living had been a success - by her standards anyway; she had met some new people, whom she hoped to make lifelong friends and had earned her first day's pay, although she wouldn't see it for two weeks. She wriggled further under the duvet and then groaned as the drone of the alarm clock sounded. She hit snooze and snuggled down again.

She made a mental note to call home today and let her parents know how she was getting on and to find out how, and if, they had explained her disappearance to the rest of the family. The pressure to run each and every decision made by any one of them past all the members of her extended family was, in her opinion, unnecessary and time consuming, but it was a practice maintained by the older generation. She could picture the confused looks on her aunts and uncles' faces when they eventually discovered she had travelled alone over a hundred miles from home, to work in a hotel. Then the

41

gloating would ensue; *Aftab is doing so well at his restaurant. He is hiring four more people to work with him, Tasleem will be finishing her medical degree in two months. We are so proud,* and so on and so forth.

Good riddance to that, she thought and slid out of bed. She put on a pair of black tracksuit bottoms, a dark green t-shirt, which she thought complemented her skin tone, and a pair of green trainers. She combed out her hair and loosely tied it in a bun. Finally she took herself downstairs for breakfast.

Mina's family members weren't the only people floating around in her mind; Justin was there too, but in a different room altogether and they would never meet, rather like the arrangement of the sexes at the Muslim weddings she had attended with her family. The men and women would be escorted to different areas to celebrate the same thing. The women's room was generally filled with chatter about their children, grandchildren, nephews and nieces, the next big wedding, or in some cases, the last funeral, and the hottest topic would likely start, *Well. I heard that [fill in blank space with name here] daughter is having a baby/ has left university/ is seeing a white man,* or whatever else might be going on in the life of the unfortunate woman who was the subject of discussion and, more than likely, not present in the room at the time. She supposed that the men wouldn't be talking about religion either, but instead showing off their latest gadget and giving a detailed breakdown, or better than that, a tour, of the slick new set of wheels parked outside amongst the competing mass of other slick new sets of wheels.

Mina had come away from meeting Justin yesterday, with a sense of excitement and as she had an entire day to do as she pleased, she gave serious consideration to a follow-up visit. *Or would that make her seem over interested.* She walked outside the hotel into the warmth of the sun and let her feet take her where she needed to be. The shops scattered along the promenade were filled with everything a young beach lover could possibly need; buckets and spades in all sizes, moulds of starfish, octopus and sea shells for sandcastle building and a plethora of inflatables in a host of shapes for those venturing further than the shoreline. In between beach supplies shops were more than a handful of places where patrons could readily spend their coins in arcade machines promising soft toys and a return on their cash. The most wonderful thing about the walk though was the aromas emanating from the cafes and stalls; sweet and sticky candy floss and toffee apples and fish and chips doused in vinegar. Mina was transported back to the family trips to the Blackpool illuminations.

Aunts, uncles and cousins came together in four or five cars for this annual day trip and, along the way another two cars crammed with more remote family members joined them. In those days, all Mina and her siblings had was each other for entertainment so the journey was filled with games of *I-Spy* and *How many red/ blue/ white cars?* Their mum would always be the first one asleep and dad would have tuned in to weird Asian radio station on the AM wave. After they had had enough of the games, they would start on the supply of snacks lovingly cooked by mum.

She felt as though she had hijacked those times from someone else's memories. The only way of confirming the truth of those trips was when the photo albums were bought out of hiding. She was saddened by how quickly things changed without you noticing.

She looked up to her left and saw the familiar building from the day before. She breathed deeply and walked in. It was much busier today but eyeing up the outdoor area to find somewhere to enjoy the glorious weather she spotted one free table. It was surrounded by four others, all busy with groups of friends drinking and talking. It would be less cluttered, and more private, inside.

Mina ordered her food and chose a mango juice to wash it down.

"You're back," said James, who had served her the day before and who, unbeknown to Mina, had spotted Justin with her.

"I guess it's easier to stick with what you know."

"Will you be sitting outside?"

Mina shook her head. "No. There are too many people out there." She glanced around for somewhere quieter. "I'll be over there," she said pointing to a table behind her.

She was unsure whether she should ask for Justin or just wait and see what happened. She opted for the latter; she could do without questioning looks or embarrassment. While waiting, she took out her phone and dialled home.

"Assalamu alaikum?"

Mina smiled as she heard her mum's voice. "Hi, Mum. It's...".

"Mina beti! How are you beti?"

"I'm really good mum. Everything is going well. How are you? What have you told everyone about where I am?" She braced herself for her mum's response.

"Oh, me and your dad are busy with work, as usual...and Anisa is spending a couple of days at Rehan's."

There was a brief silence. True to form, her mum had avoided Mina's second question. She tried again. "That's good. So? What have you told everyone about me?" She gripped the phone tightly so she wouldn't drop it.

"You shouldn't worry about that. It's not important." Mina could picture her mum waving her hand about as she spoke.

"Mum, it is important. You raised me to respect other people's opinions so please tell me what's been said." She expected something upsetting, but not what came next.

"Mina, you have put your dad and me in a very difficult position. If you come back home this weekend, nobody has to know anything." Mina couldn't believe it; her mother still believed her decision was foolish.

She stared at the phone with eyes wide and mouth agape. "Oh my God. You still don't support me. You're ashamed of me." She tried hard to hold back the tears that were building up. "I haven't asked you and dad for anything except your understanding. What you've just said...," she took a deep breath. "I don't know what to say. I'm not coming home this weekend, or next weekend, or the weekend after that." Mina was shaking her head. "Bye, mum."

She put her head in her hands and cried, until she remembered where she was. She wiped her eyes with her sleeves and then searched her bag for a tissue and was gracelessly blowing her nose when her food arrived. She thanked whoever had brought it, without looking up. She was so disappointed. She allowed her mind to fill with torturous thoughts of where it had all gone wrong for her. Was it when she hadn't passed her eleven plus exams? Was it when she failed to get a place at university? Or was it simply being born the middle child? Whatever it was, she had always believed that a parent's support should be unconditional. She supposed that whatever she did now would be of no consequence to anyone but herself. She could feel herself losing track of why she was here; after eating, she would call her older brother who had a way of seeing things rationally.

The smell from her plate woke her out of self-pity and brought her back to reality. As she tucked in to her jacket potato and veggie chilli she began to feel better. She looked across to the bar and saw a welcome distraction, Justin waving casually to her. He finished what he was doing and came over to her. Mina noticed he walked with strength and confidence. He smiled at her and looked years younger for it.

"Do you mind?" He pulled out a chair, a look of concern growing over his face when he saw her red eyes. "Are you okay?"

"I'm fine. Thank you." She wasn't but that wasn't his burden. "How are you?"

"Busy. I have to be at a meeting in an hour."

Her heart sank, so much for the distraction. "That's too bad. Anything interesting?"

"Yes, actually. We're opening a new branch and there's a lot to plan. Are you sure you're alright?"

A trickle of tears rolled down her cheeks and she couldn't stop them. Justin reached out and covered Mina's hands with his own. She felt incredibly vulnerable and...stupid. She wiped her eyes and nodded her head. "I'll be fine. I've just had an unpleasant conversation with my mum."

"Want to talk about it?"

"Oh, gosh no. Anyway, you've got somewhere else to be."

"Hmm, I know. Look, how would you feel about me taking you out sometime, away from here? Then we can get to know each other a bit better."

Mina looked up at Justin with red eyes, wondering if that would be such a good idea. Surely, she shouldn't be giving her parents reasons to mistrust her. She never had before now, but somehow, they had found something. Then in spite of her reservations she agreed. "I'd like that."

Justin straightened up. "Great. Meet me here tomorrow at...say twelve o'clock."

"Tomorrow?"

"If that's not good for you, we can do it next week?"

She had plenty of time and no excuses. "Tomorrow at twelve sounds good."

"Oh, by the way..." Justin had a glint in his eye. "You should wear that colour more often. You carry it well."

***

Mina had gone from feeling disappointment with her mum's words, to anger, and a conversation with Rehan had been far from helpful. He seemed sure their mum was trying to protect her, but she told him, in no uncertain terms, that their mum only cared what other people were going to say. It was the closest she and Rehan had ever come to an argument.

She was too preoccupied with family to really appreciate the small amount of time Justin had spent with her, but she remembered one thing clearly; the feel of his skin on her hands. A small part of her, deep inside, hoped, there would be more of that tomorrow. But, before then, she had a night of hard work to get through.

First Date

She had the radio playing in the background and the music lifted her mood. Dan had been on hand for a quick chat before they started work and he gave her a much-needed shoulder to cry on. One thing she discovered she had in common with Dan, was disapproving parents. She hated herself for even contemplating the idea that the colour of Dan's skin meant he could have whatever he wanted, without any fuss and she gained a new respect for her friend.

She wrapped her hair in a towel whilst she picked out what to wear, remembering Justin had thought green suited her. She only owned two tops in that colour, so she picked the one he had not yet seen her in; a V-neck top with three quarter length sleeves which hugged her in all the right places. Before getting dressed she sprayed herself with the perfume Tania had given her as an eighteenth birthday present. Then she got to work on her hair; tied it back in a ponytail, twisted it and pinned it up in a claw clip.

***

Justin was reading through the final plans for the new venue, but he was thinking about Mina. He reflected that Mina didn't flinch when he had placed his hands over hers and then decided that she was probably too upset to have noticed. He finished his tea, sent an email to head office regarding the plans, and then grabbed his jacket and went through the kitchen into the dining area. Everything was under control, with lunch orders picking up pace. He made sure there was nothing that needed his urgent attention and then went outside to wait for Mina.

***

Justin nervously checked his watch. It was almost midday. Then suddenly Mina was there beside him.

"Hi. I see you took my advice." She had listened to him and his confidence rose.

"I was going to wear this today anyway, so don't flatter yourself." She felt that was a convincing enough lie. Her eyes were drawn to his chest. "I love the colour of your shirt." She wanted to reach out and feel the fabric, like she would have if she was out shopping for her next Eid outfit with her mum and Anisa. Fabrics and designs fascinated her, as did the efforts shop owners would go to in order to close a sale, opening previously untouched packets so their customers could see an outfit in a particular colour, and how disheartened they could appear when told *We'll keep looking and maybe come back.*

"Thanks. I'm parked over here." He gestured toward the parked cars and Mina followed. They stopped at a blue Audi. He opened the passenger side door and Mina got in. Justin made himself comfortable in the driver's seat and entered some information into the navigation system.

"So, where are you taking me?"

Without looking up from the screen he said, "There's a place about ten minutes from here I think you'll like."

"I suppose we'll see about that then."

He drove the length of the coastline and Mina saw the spot she and Tania had reached when job hunting, just a few weeks ago. She was careful to keep her arms close to her body to minimise any accidental contact with Justin. She was starting to feel flustered, which wasn't helped by the heat outside, so she looked around for the button to lower the window. Justin beat her to it. "I wouldn't want you to accidentally fire the rocket launcher." He kept his eyes on the road while still making it obvious that he could tell what Mina was doing. Her nerves were clearly radiating and he was undecided whether to play on it or not.

"Oh, I had no idea you were a secret agent. Is Justin even your real name?"

"If I tell you that, I'll have to kill you."

"Not if I get you first!"

Justin laughed. "I'd like to see that!"

He was unwinding after a long spell of being under pressure, and it felt good. His sister apart, Mina was the first female he had spent this much time with since Eve. This wasn't a quick fix in a club or bar to fill the void that had developed in him over the years and he understood the importance of making a good impression this afternoon.

As Justin slowed down, Mina took in the glorious view from the cliff top. Her eyes scoured the panorama, trying to absorb all that she could see; the sea reaching to the city on the other side. She could make out the outline of some of the buildings and wished that she had a pair of binoculars.

The sea breeze was a welcome break from the growing heat. Justin switched off the engine and was about to climb out, but then saw how mesmerised Mina had become. He hated to bring that to an end. "There's a whole lot more inside." He got out of the car and before he could open the passenger door for her, Mina followed suit.

"Whoa, careful." He jumped back to avoid being hit by the car door.

Mina gasped as she realised what she had almost done. "I'm so sorry. Are you alright?" Before she knew it, she was reaching out to take Justin's arm to steady him. His hand promptly settled on her arm.

Neither of them let go of the other. "It's a good job I parked away from the edge." He let his fingers stroke Mina's arm and searched her face for a reaction. She met his eyes in silence.

"I'm so sorry." She almost pulled away from his touch, but she couldn't help savouring the moment.

"I'm not." He used this opportunity to take a really good look at the woman who was making his head spin. "Shall we go inside?"

She nodded but kept her eyes fixed on him. "I think that's a good idea."

In the months to follow, they would both debate who let go of whose arm first, each trying to get one up on the other.

The building they were about to share their first lunch in, was like something Mina had seen in one of those self-build television shows; the outside unassuming, but the inside a stark contrast. There were floor-to-ceiling windows all along one side of the building and in the middle, the doors opened out onto a decked area with enough seating for at least thirty people. Everywhere she looked, bright, uplifting, mood enhancing colours surrounded her. She smiled again and not for the last time that afternoon.

Justin was leading her out onto the decking. "I'd like to sit inside, if that's okay with you." He let her choose the spot to sit and she settled for a curved booth with a high back and deep seats. Each individual panel was coloured differently and when she sat down, she ran her hands over the velvety fabric.

"What do you think?" Justin picked up a menu. "Was I right in thinking you'd appreciate this?"

The biggest smile he had ever seen appeared on her face. "You were right. This is wonderful!" She pushed herself back onto the deep seat so her feet no longer touched the concrete floor. "You play a good game, Justin."

"Mina, I assure you, this isn't a game." He put the menu down and leaned in. "I wanted us to spend some time together in a place we'd both be comfortable in." He moved a little closer to her and started perusing the menu again.

"You've been here before then?"

He sensed what she was implying but was determined not to get defensive. "I come here when I need some space. It's been a while, actually."

"So why've you brought me here?"

48

"You enjoyed the view from the terrace at Sunset Strip, so I guessed you'd like it here." He turned to face her. "Is there anything else on your mind?"

Mina shook her head. She deserved that. He was being thoughtful and it was she who was creating unnecessary tension.

"Look, I want you to know I haven't been in a relationship for over three years now. You're the first person I've taken out for lunch in all that time." There was no point in avoiding the subject. Hopefully, she would start to understand. "Remember, I don't give my number to just anyone."

The sudden realisation that the harmless flirting of two weeks ago had the potential to develop into something more, and the upsetting conversation with her mother the day before, became unbearable. "I'm making a huge change in my life right now, totally unsupported by my parents who think I'm making a big mistake and that I should get on the next train back to Birmingham." She put her elbows on the table and rested her chin in her hands. "So, long story short, there's a lot going on in my head."

One word jumped out at Justin. "You live in Birmingham?"

"Yeah. Why? Do you know the area?" She had no idea of his connection to her home town. He was about to explain when a waiter brought their meals.

"This smells good." Mina picked up her cutlery and started to dig into her fish pie. "I'm still waiting for an answer though." The morsel on her fork was steaming, so she blew on it to avoid a burnt tongue. "So?"

"I lived in Birmingham until four years ago. That's when I moved here. Frankie still lives there."

Mina began thinking of all of the ways they might have already passed each other on the street, or in the supermarket. Then she abandoned the idea. Being two very different people, meeting would be improbable, but... *we're sitting here now, so perhaps not so improbable at all.*

"What're you thinking? Your face is all scrunched up."

"I was just thinking how unlikely it would have been for us to have met in Birmingham."

"Why?"

"I don't think we would hang out in the same places and...you know, Birmingham is such a big city." Mina quickly shovelled more food into her mouth to stop herself saying something she might later regret.

Justin allowed a moment to pass before speaking again. "So, we've lived in the same place for years and never met. You've been in Weston for three days and we've met, what...four times?" Justin picked up his glass and, holding Mina's gaze, sipped slowly. "How do you explain that?"

"I guess when you make one change in your life, you become ready to accept other possibilities."

Justin raised his eyebrows. "I'm a possibility? You might be surprised to learn that, since I met you, I'm also ready to accept new...possibilities."

Mina's heart raced at how Justin was making her feel. She wanted the heat between them and she wanted to luxuriate in thoughts that would make the Birmingham Mina blush.

They finished their food, deep in the same thoughts. She looked up occasionally at other couples scattered around the restaurant; some holding hands, some with their arms around each other. As the table was being cleared, she excused herself and took temporary refuge in the ladies' room. Staring in the mirror, she gave herself a good talking to. *This is insane, but it feels right. How is this going to work? Why does he have to be so bloody thoughtful? Why do I feel like I need a wee again?* She smoothed her clothes, regaining her composure. *You came here to change your life. So, go out there and change it! Whatever happens, happens.*

When she returned to the table, she made a point of sitting closer to Justin. "It looks so peaceful out there." Her eyes focused on the sea view. "I can imagine not worrying about anything, if I was out there."

"Mina, I want us to do this again, and again, and again. I thought I'd experienced all that I could, as far as relationships were concerned, and then you walked into my life." He reached for her hand. "I know we should take things one day at a time. What do you think?" He felt her fingers tighten around his.

"One day at a time." She moved yet closer, letting him put his arm around her waist.

Justin and Mina spent the rest of that afternoon together in almost complete silence. They were both in unchartered territory, unwilling to force the next move, choosing instead to let intuition be their guide.

Justin pictured the looks on his friends' faces if they could see him now. They would be wondering why he hadn't put the moves on this woman, but then they didn't know Mina. He sensed the conflict brewing in her life, and knew the wise thing to do would be to allow her space to make her own mind up about the pace of their relationship. He could easily sit with her in his arms for the entire afternoon and well into the evening. She had a way of calming his busy mind and helping him float away from the stresses he faced; Frankie's illness and her reluctance to share her feelings as well as the development of the new venue.

If Mina were to picture the looks on the faces of her friends and family they would carry appalled expressions. She had not been raised to behave in this way and she would be marched out of Justin's arms and told, in no uncertain terms, that she was shaming her family. Regardless of this, she was the happiest she had been for months. She was becoming her own person, creating an identity to match her hopes and dreams instead of living an unfulfilled life that only served others.

Before getting out of the car and going back to work, they agreed to see each other on Monday evening to have dinner in the Italian situated in the heart of Bristol.

Justin and Frankie

Two weeks into her treatment, Frankie remained as stoical as the day she received her diagnosis. The nature of her work meant more often than not, she could operate from almost anywhere, as long as there was internet access and a good phone signal. If she was having a bad day, she would simply stay put in her apartment where there was no one to ask questions she had no intention of answering.

Today she had prepared for Justin's arrival by comfort cooking; curry goat with rice and peas. Frankie hardly ever used her kitchen for anything except her early morning coffee. Ironically it had been the kitchen which sold her on the apartment – or the view from it to be exact. On a clear day, she could see people making their way around the city centre, on foot and in cars. Having lived here for fifteen years, she had witnessed at first-hand the continuous changes to Birmingham's infrastructure and she was a stone's throw from both the Paradise Circus redevelopment and the recently completed Grand Central.

She was putting the finishing touches to the meat, which had been marinating for twenty-four hours and the smell reminded her of Saturday evening dinners at home when they were still a family. She looked at the framed photograph of her mother and father she had placed on the kitchen wall. Their death had had a tremendous impact on her life choices.

She and her then partner's views on starting a family conflicted; he felt they both had so much love to give to a child whereas Frankie couldn't see past the pain for any children they had if anything were to happen to them. In the end they were unable to reconcile their differences and, after two years together, went their separate ways.

Despite her fears she showed no hesitation in becoming the fifteen-year old Justin's guardian. After all he was already making his way to and from school by himself, so all Frankie had to do was make sure she was home in the evenings to help with his homework and make sure he was eating properly. She was proud of the man he had become and thought that one day he would make a devoted father and husband.

"Something smells good!" Justin put his bags down and walked into the kitchen. He lifted the lid off the pot and inhaled the aroma, which took him to the same place it had Frankie.

Frankie shouted from the bedroom. "Don't you touch it until it's ready."

"Yes, mother." Justin quickly replaced the lid, but not before dipping a spoon in to taste it.

Frankie came out of the bedroom and the siblings embraced. Frankie held onto Justin longer than he had expected and he tightened his grip too. "How are you doing?"

She sighed and then pulled away. "The chemo's going okay, I suppose."

"I asked how you're doing, not the chemo."

She looked at Justin and said, "I'm alright. I'm not feeling as tired as I have been, so I can get a lot more work done."

"Happy to hear that." He gestured toward the kitchen. "I didn't think you were going to keep up your end of the bargain. During the drive, I kept thinking about where we might possibly be having dinner tonight."

"Ah, yes. I've delivered, but have you?"

Justin place a carrier bag on the kitchen counter top and opened it to reveal a pot. "Rice and peas, as promised." He lifted the lid and the contents made Frankie clap as if a magic trick had been performed.

"Go and get yourself settled in and I'll make us a drink."

In the second bedroom Justin unloaded his bag, put his toiletries in the en-suite and placed his shoes in the slide out wardrobe rack. As he unpacked, he considered whether to tell Frankie about Mina; they had only been out once and he wasn't ready to answer some of the questions Frankie would ask.

Over dinner, they discussed work. Frankie was fascinated with one of her current client's lifestyle; Amanda owned properties in four different locations around the world and never stayed in one of them longer than four weeks at a time. Amanda had flown Frankie out to each of her homes so she could work her interior design magic by sourcing local businesses to help with furnishings. That was one of the perks of her job; she needn't worry where to book her next holiday because her clients were always flying her from one end of the globe to another. That was another reason Frankie chose not have children, but Justin would always say it was more an excuse than a reason.

Justin had brought along details of the new venue H&B would soon be ready to open and Frankie looked them over. She was unimpressed, but that didn't bother him.

"If you were offered the opportunity to manage this place, would you?"

He tapped his fingers on the papers. He had asked himself the same question a few months back, but things were different now. "Having spent so much time away, I don't know if I'd want to live so close to you again!" He held his hands in front of his face as if expecting to be attacked. He peeked between his fingers and looked at Frankie.

"You're lucky to be sitting far enough away or you'd have got a smack upside your head!"

"That's why I'm sitting here. I've had that smack before."

Frankie sat uncomfortably in her seat. "Well, we're both older and wiser now, aren't we?"

"Older, yes. I'm still working on the wiser." *Perhaps Mina would help me with that.* He stood and walked over to the fridge. He helped himself to a beer and poured Frankie another glass of red wine. He hesitated, multiple thoughts racing through his mind and, as one of them crossed the finish line, he said, "I've met someone."

He set the drinks down on the coffee table in the lounge, afraid to look directly at Frankie, dreading the course the conversation would take if she voiced any kind of doubt.

"What's her name? Tell me about her. What does she do? How did you meet?" Frankie believed these to be questions Justin could, and should, be able to answer without breaking into a sweat.

He sat on the sofa opposite her and said, "Her name is Mina. She works at the Royal Weston Hotel near Sunset Strip and we met when she was in Weston for the weekend."

"So, she doesn't live there?"

"She does now."

Frankie looked surprised. "Did she move for you?"

Justin shook his head vigorously. "No, no. She moved because she wanted to explore life on her own terms."

"Are you something she's exploring?" Frankie raised her eyebrows questioningly and he looked away embarrassed at the suggestion.

Rather than answer, he skirted around the question and said, "We've decided we'll take it one day at a time."

The conversation that followed was brief but comfortable...until Frankie, said, "I'm coming to spend a few days with you next week."

Justin's head shot up. "So you can check up on me?"

"That's not the reaction I was hoping for."

"I'm sorry. I didn't mean it like that." He panicked, sensing the irritation in Frankie's voice. "It's just I thought that...because I haven't told you much about Mina, you wanted to come and see for yourself. I mean, you wouldn't be disappointed, but...you can be critical."

Frankie was used to being perceived as uncompromising and in the space of the evening, her younger brother had had a couple of digs at her. "I'm going to let that one slide, but only because I'm in a good mood." She stood and gazed out of the window with the direct view of Colmore Row. She had lost count of the number of newly opened restaurants and bars that had managed to find another empty old building to reside in, until they themselves became redundant, and the cycle continued. Despite her scepticism, she had been to each of these establishments with clients and colleagues for lunch or evening drinks and, at the end of each visit, she left feeling glad that, so far, these stunning buildings had not succumbed to permanent closure and redevelopment.

"I've already booked my train tickets. The train leaves New Street at six on Wednesday evening." She turned to face her brother, her expression changing. "This is me reaching out, Justin. Don't knock me down when I'm being more open. Isn't this what you want from me?" Frankie felt herself wavering and she was doing all she could to control her anger, pain and sadness, until Justin put his arms around her and hugged her tightly.

As Frankie cried, Justin felt huge pangs of guilt about the things he had said. "Frankie, I'm so sorry. I've taken you for granted and I'm sorry." He stroked her hair and she began to quiet. "I love you so much and I've been such a complete idiot."

Frankie put her head on his shoulder and Justin rocked her gently. "I love you too, Justin. I know I'm not easy to get along with, but I'm trying."

Drying her eyes Frankie sat down on one of the two blue sofas. She slipped off her shoes and pulled her feet into herself. "This chemo must be zapping away my hard exterior."

"That's a good thing."

"Not if it means turning me into a blubbering wreck." She took a long sip of the hot, black coffee Justin had made. "That's so much better." She decided to get an early night after finishing her coffee. She kissed Justin on the forehead and left him to his own thoughts.

He took another beer from the fridge and opened the doors onto the small balcony. It was a humid night and the streets of the city below were brought to life by the amber glow of streetlights and the sounds of people and trains, taxis and buses. He picked up a stool from the kitchen and sat down with his feet up on the balcony rail. As he sipped, he thought about Frankie's behaviour; he had never seen her with her guard down, even when it the time came to make arrangements for their parent's funeral. Not even when she split from Grayson, her former partner.

Second Date

Dan had become someone she easily opened up to, more so than with Tania. She didn't feel like she was in competition with him and he wasn't judging her. He had even helped choose what to wear tonight and how to wear her hair. He offered to braid it for her and, seeing the doubt on Mina's face, pulled out his phone and showed her photographic evidence of his work, as modelled by his sister.

Mina had received a single text, from Rehan, asking if she was okay and saying Mum and Dad were asking about her. Mina replied that she was great and they could call if they wanted to. A week into her new life and she wasn't going to let pressure from her parents change her mind. Anyway, it would be Eid in a few weeks and that would be a good excuse for going to visit.

Straight after her lunch, she was back in the hotel restaurant. There appeared to be more people today and they seemed friendlier than last week's patrons. Mina had to learn to engage in small talk, another reason she had accepted the job offer - it would force her to interact with strangers and build her self-confidence. Since leaving college, Mina had felt everyone else was moving on with their lives leaving her stuck; overlooked by a university-educated older brother and a gifted younger sister. There were countless occasions when Mina felt as though other people were speaking for her and when it time came for her to speak for herself, she would often trip over her tongue in the rush to get her words out. Each time she talked to Justin she hoped the awkward Mina would stay hidden long enough for her to make a good impression.

"Excuse me."

Mina woke from her daydream to find a woman standing beside her, pointing to something on the menu. She said, "How can I help?"

The woman was the same height as her grandmother and Mina assumed she must be of a similar age. "I can't seem to find baked trout on this menu." The woman's hands shook as she raised the menu up so that Mina could read it. "Can you see it? I had it the last time I was here some time ago now."

Mina remembered Rachel telling her that amendments were made periodically to the menu. She smiled and said, "I'm sorry, we're not serving the trout because it's out of season but I can recommend the halibut."

"Oh, I see. Thank you, young lady." The woman turned and went back to her table.

For the next ten minutes, Mina kept looking toward the elderly woman's table, thinking what could possibly have led up to the point where she was eating lunch in a seafront hotel, alone. She hoped the opposite for herself.

***

"Sorry, Dan."

"What? Again?" Mina had been to the toilet three times since Dan started braiding her hair twenty minutes ago. "I think you should see a doctor about that!"

"I don't know why I'm feeling like this. I mean, it's not like we haven't been out together." Mina sat down in front of the mirror and Dan continued where he left off.

He spoke to Mina's reflection. "Maybe you're ready to speed things up with him. You know..." When she looked up at him, Dan winked and made kissy faces.

"Stop teasing and get on with it."

Mina looked in the mirror and thought about how she had reached this point in her life. The heel of her right foot was bouncing restlessly on the floor and she felt she needed to empty her bladder again. The last time she was in Justin's company, she had given herself permission to feel his body closer to hers. He had a genuine desire to be with her and he listened to her go on about her troubles without making false promises. *But what do I want?*

"Dan."

"Mina."

"Am I doing the right thing? There could be so many problems for us if we're together."

Dan stopped braiding and placed both hands on Mina's shoulders. "Are you happy when you're with Justin?"

She nodded. "Then don't think about what *could* happen and enjoy what *is* happening. Doesn't that make sense?"

"Yeah. I'm just being silly."

"No, you're not." Dan finished her hair. "I know what it's like when you don't have anyone to turn to. All done." He held up a mirror behind Mina's head so she could get a look at the length of her hair.

"It looks amazing. Thank you."

"I'm not doing this every time you go out on a date you know. Have you ever thought about cutting a few inches off?"

"Oh, this isn't long, trust me."

Dan gathered up his things and said, "Right, I'm going to let you get ready for your big night and I look forward to hearing all about it." He stroked her back. "You'll be fine."

She was passing through the hotel lobby when she was approached by one of the receptionists. "Justin left a message to say that he'll have to meet you at the restaurant so he's sent a taxi for you." The receptionist walked her to the waiting car. "Have a good night."

Mina wondered why Justin hadn't called her to let her know and then realised that he could only do that if he had her number. She set a reminder in her phone to make sure that before the night was over she gave it to him. Then she had a different idea. She took out the piece of paper he had given her, almost a month ago, entered the number into her phone and prepared a message thanking him for the taxi and saying she was on the way. Looking at the draft and then at the send button, it dawned on her; she was creating an invisible connection. She was about to initiate contact with him so he could call or text her whenever he wanted and she could do the same. It felt a huge step. Once the message was sent, there would be no going back. She inhaled. A took deep breath and hit the send button. Exhaling slowly she sank back into the seat.

Mina scrolled through the other messages she had stored in her phone. After Justin came Dan, then Rehan and then Tania. The last time they had been in touch was on Mina's first day at work. Mina opened the messages and sent a short text to her Birmingham friend.

Wow, Tania, that was quick, Mina thought when her phone buzzed to indicate an incoming message but when she checked, it wasn't from Tania. She read and re-read the message as the taxi slowed and stopped. She placed her phone in her bag and stepped out of the car.

Inside the Italian restaurant, Mina was greeted with warmth and, to her, new aromas. She looked around, unsure who to talk to and what to say. Then a waiter acknowledged her. "Good evening, madam. How can I help you?"

Mina was about to answer when she heard Justin say, "It's fine. She's with me." He offered her his hand. Without hesitation, she took it and he led her to their table. As they walked, Justin said, "I was beginning to worry you might never use my number."

She reached into her pocket and showed Justin the paper. "It's a good thing I kept this then."

His face lit up and he laughed softly. "I can't believe you still have that!" He reached for the paper, but she pulled it away.

"No, no. This is mine. You gave it to me, remember?"

"I did, didn't I?" Mina could feel his eyes on her as she pulled her chair into the table. "I don't think you've given me anything yet."

She couldn't help but smile. "I've actually given you something I can't get back." Their eyes locked and she said, "My time."

Béchamel, fettuccine, linguine - alien words to Mina. As far as she was concerned, anything that wasn't spaghetti was just pasta but the rest of the menu's descriptions were easy enough to understand. She avoided pizza because she wrongly thought it couldn't be much different to the frozen pizzas she was accustomed to eating. "So, the ricotta and spinach are wrapped inside the cannelloni?"

"Yes. Then it's topped with cheese and baked in the oven."

"You must think I'm such an idiot." Mina hid her face behind the menu, hoping to become invisible.

Justin lowered the menu and said, "No, I don't. There are foods I haven't tried."

"Really?" She sat up straight. "Like what?"

"Indian food."

Mina's mouth fell open and she stared at Justin with wide eyes. "You've never had curry?" He shrugged. "Guess where we go next time?"

"I've no idea what a good Indian restaurant looks like. I wouldn't know where to start."

She wagged a finger at him. "Don't think you can get away that easily. I'll find the restaurant."

"First playful, now assertive." Justin bit his lower lip. "I can't wait to see what the rest of the evening has in store."

She looked everywhere but straight at him. She took a sip from her glass. She felt her cheeks becoming flushed. She knew exactly what he meant. If she had any hope of maintaining her confidence, she was going to have to give as good she was getting.

Their conversation turned to discussion of family. Justin asked whether Mina had spoken to her mum since their last conversation and she asked if he'd a good stay in Birmingham. He told her how he and Frankie had made the deal to each cook part of a favourite meal and suddenly realised he hadn't told her anything about Frankie's health or about his parents. He stopped talking in mid-sentence and rubbed the nape of his neck. He took an unusually long sip of his drink while Mina mentally urged him to continue talking.

"There are things I haven't told you about my childhood and my sister." He saw her face change. "Don't worry. It's nothing bad. It's just...I don't talk about them with anyone." Another sip. "I'd like to talk about them with you, if that's alright?"

"It's more than alright." She smiled awkwardly, trying to stop her heart from beating out of her chest.

"When we've finished eating, we can sit in the lounge area." Mina's eyes darted around the restaurant, like a meerkat on the lookout for predators. "It's at the back of the room, through a door on the left."

"Why do they need a room at the back? What exactly goes on in there?" She sat back in her chair with her arms crossed. "And you want me to go back there? With you?" When he nodded and grinned, she couldn't hide the shock. She shook her head and said, "Uh, uh. No way." She reached for her glass and Justin took her hand.

"I'm joking, Mina. It's only open to customers. It's full of sofas and comfy chairs for talking over coffee. It's usually busy, so we wouldn't be alone, if that's why you're looking sideways at me."

From then until the end of the meal, they exchanged random glances, each trying to read the other's thoughts. Mina was fixated on what might be waiting in the mysterious lounge at the back of the restaurant. Meanwhile, Justin was gearing himself up to reveal information that he had only ever shared with a select few people in his life.

A feeling of serenity grew around them both, despite the buzz of people coming and going. Mina had no idea how much time had passed, but the darkening horizon told her sunset wasn't far off. The freshness of the situation began to reveal itself; it was her first time out in the evening without Dan or others from work, or without Tania; it was her first time trying Italian food and it was the first time she had used Justin's phone number. Looking across at her companion, her heart quickened and she crossed and uncrossed her feet unconsciously.

The distance between them seemed unnecessarily prolonged so she cleared her throat and said, "That was delicious." She pushed her plate away. "I don't think I can even manage dessert," she lied. "And that's unusual for me."

"So, you'd eat here again?"

"Are you planning on bringing me here again?"

"You answer my question first and I'll think about answering yours."

Mina faked careful consideration and said, "Yes, I would."

He put his elbows on the table, locked his fingers together and rested his eyes on Mina, and then, for what seemed hours to her, stayed silent.

"I'll order another drink while I wait for you." She scanned the room for a waiter.

One came over to ask Justin, "What can I get for you, sir?"

Mina said, "Oh, he won't be needing anything. I can't let him get distracted." She made a point of smiling at the waiter and said, "He has an important question to answer. But I'll have a latte, please."

Returning with her coffee the waiter asked, "Has he answered the question yet?"

She shook her head. "I think he needs more time."

"Good luck."

Mina sipped slowly from her mug making sure to focus only on the drink, and not the man, in front of her.

"I'm ready with my answer now."

Mina put her mug down on the table.

"I am definitely bringing you back here." He looked triumphant, as if the answer had just won him the cash jackpot on a television game show.

Mina Meets Frankie

The world she had once known seemed so far away now. The nothingness beyond the sea was all she could imagine as she sat on the warm sandy beach. She burrowed her uncovered feet further into the sand in an effort to protect some part of herself from the cruel events she had borne witness to. As if in response, a chill ran through her body and she instinctively wrapped her arms around herself, despite the warmth in the air. With her head between her knees, Mina exhaled and released her tears. She cried and thought. Then she thought, and cried some more. Her teardrops were leaving their own marks on the sand below her body, marks that would eventually be covered by the incoming tide. The idea that not only could people forget her, but that nature would soon wash away the imprints she had been responsible for, filled Mina with an immense sense of abandonment. Much like anyone who had experienced, what she considered, a betrayal, Mina questioned how on earth she had allowed this to happen. She had always believed herself to be sensible and clever, yet she been unable to see this coming.

She and Justin had shared their first telephone conversation, the day after dinner at the Italian. He had arranged a time and place for her to meet Frankie and she was beginning to feel part of something bigger. She had developed a group, albeit a small group, around her that she could call her Weston family. It made her feel like she belonged. She found it incredible that one single act, perpetrated by a member of that family, could leave her feeling as though she was hanging on to her sanity by a thread. When she added to that the effect it would have on her Birmingham family if they were ever to find out, her body became heavier, the thread close to fraying.

Mina closed her eyes and lay down. She was being beckoned by the darkness and she felt her body sinking deeper into the sand.

"Mina!"

The voice got closer. "Mina!"

She recognised the voice. It was friendly and it caused her to open her eyes. When she looked around, she saw the figure headed in her direction. "Mina is that you?"

She closed her eyes and whispered, "Leave me alone."

A hand touched her arm. When she opened her eyes, she saw a welcome face. "I got worried when you didn't come back." Dan lay down beside her and held her hand. "We shouldn't be here, you know. There'll be sand coming out of us for days."

"You don't have to stay."

"Of course, I do. I'm your friend, and I think you need a friend right now."

They lay in silence looking up at the clear blue sky.

"What am I gonna do, Dan?"

Dan sat up and looked down at her. "Come back to my place. I'll make the best mug of tea you've ever had and we can talk it all out."

"I like it here."

"You shouldn't stay here. You need to go somewhere different. Put some distance between you and Justin."

Dan stood up, brushing sand off himself. He held out a hand and, after a few moments, Mina sighed and accepted it. Before they started off, she looked behind her at Sunset Strip. Seeing she was getting emotional again, Dan linked his arm through hers and nudged her along.

She had never seen so many colours in one room before. The living room walls had been painted a dusky grey and everything around it, from the sofa to the hanging artwork, was a mish-mash of teal, lilac, mint and pale blue. Mina's experience of living room colours stretched through the entire spectrum of creams and browns, with an occasional splash of red, and patterned wallpaper, sofas and rugs were rife in Mina's cousins' houses.

"Make yourself at home. I'll go and put the kettle on."

She spotted the largest beanbag she had ever set eyes on and decided she was going to make herself at home on that. It was so large she was able to almost lie flat on it.

Dan brought in a tray and the sight of Mina lying on the beanbag stopped him in his tracks. "Ah, look at you!" He sat on the large, mint sofa. "Help yourself to milk and sugar. I know how particular you are."

"I can't help it if I know what I like." She frowned. "Even if it doesn't like me back!"

"Stop whining. I'm sure it's a misunderstanding."

Her attempts to raise herself off the beanbag were accompanied by grunts and puffs before Dan stepped in with a helping hand. Mina said "Sorry. It looks like I didn't get all of the sand out of my clothes."

"That's okay. You can give it a quick vac before you go!"

"Alright."

Dan looked at her and whistled, waving his hand above his head to indicate his joke had gone right over her head but she was paying attention to her tea and didn't see what Dan was doing. She sat down on the other side of the sofa with her mug. "I'm supposed to be meeting his sister tomorrow evening. How am I gonna look at him without thinking about what he's done?"

"You need to talk to him before then."

"What am I supposed to say? Who's the floozy I saw you cuddling up to last night?"

***

Thanks to Dan, Mina was able to get a good night's sleep so she could at least go to work with a clear head. Every time she saw a couple hugging or kissing, her mind raced back to last night at Sunset Strip. She knew Dan was right; she would have to speak to Justin and whether or not she would actually meet his sister would depend on his response. To prevent herself backing away from the situation, Mina had sent him a message earlier that morning to say she needed to talk to him.

Her lips would be sore tomorrow if she didn't stop chewing them. She kept telling herself to stop. Justin had asked where they should meet, but her mind had gone blank so they kept it simple, meaning unfortunately Mina could no longer avoid Sunset Strip. She had the feeling the people sitting nearby were looking over and willing her to stop being miserable.

Mina was starting to lose count of how many times she had ventured into unknown territory since her arrival in Weston. She felt a hand on her shoulder and almost jumped out of her chair as Justin sat down opposite her. "Should I be worried?"

Mina feigned a smile, but couldn't bring herself to look him in the eye. Instead her she fixed her gaze on his strong shoulders, continuing to torture herself by picturing him holding the strange woman in his arms. She shook her head to try to rid herself of that image. "Me and Dan were here last night."

"Oh, I didn't see you."

"No, we didn't stay for long. I could see you were busy."

"If I had known you were here I would have made some time for you." He reached for her hand under the table but she moved it.

"I'm just gonna say it…I saw you with another woman last night and you looked more than a little friendly." She watched Justin's expression change.

Finally, he said, "Hopefully, you're talking about Frankie. You are talking about Frankie aren't you?"

"Justin, I haven't met Frankie. I don't know what she looks like! I just know that I saw you with another woman last night and you looked happy and I had to leave." She put her head in her hands, determined not to cry.

"Mina," Justin said as he took her hands, "The only woman I was with last night was Frankie." He took his phone out of his pocket. "Let me show you a photo." He searched through the gallery on his phone until he found one. "Is this her?" He moved his chair next to Mina and gave her the phone.

She looked at a photo of Justin with Frankie. It had been taken as they were giving each other a high five. She thought back to last night. The enormity of her insecurity was beginning to dawn on her. She gave the phone back. Now, instead of feeling betrayed by Justin, she felt she was the one who'd betrayed him.

"Hey. What's wrong? Come here." Justin moved so their knees touched. He held her hands in his again and said, "You thought I was seeing someone else?"

The words refused to come out and all Mina could do was nod weakly. The confirmation seemed to set Justin back a little and he took a long exhale. Then he pushed his chair back and placed his legs either side of Mina's. "I want you to do something for me." He put his hands just above Mina's knees. "All I want you to do is come to me if you ever need to ask me anything. Remember what you told me about the direct approach working for you? Well, it works for me too, so I don't want you to ever feel like you can't talk to me...about anything."

She put her hands back on top of his. "I'm so sorry for not trusting you. This is all so new to me and I guess...I'm just over thinking everything." Before she could stop herself, she had thrown her arms around him.

"No, I'm sorry. I should have shown you Frankie's photo."

Mina felt the warmth of his arms travel up her back and instantly, was blissfully oblivious to her surroundings.

Justin whispered, "This is nice."

She shivered as his breath touched her skin. She was the first to pull away. "Are you still okay about introducing me to your big sister?"

"There's no turning back now. I've asked her to be on her best behaviour!" Mina got the cheeky smile she liked so much. "Right," he stood up, "I need to get back to work now, unlike some of us who can relax the rest of the afternoon."

"Excuse me. I'm gonna be a nervous wreck for the rest of the afternoon!"

She stood to leave and Justin asked, "Are we okay, here?"

Mina said, "We're more than okay."

***

With the time for the two most important women in his life to meet drawing ever closer, Justin could empathise with Mina. He was glad to have a busy afternoon to keep him occupied. He had just recruited a new assistant manager and two more front-of-house staff, so he had to ensure they were given a formal introduction to the rest of the team, which usually meant drinks and food at the bar after hours. He'd also been following the development of the new venue closely and was aware he would soon have an important decision to make. He'd often wished he didn't have the luxury of a few months before having to make that decision but now his life was changing, he could feel it, and Mina was a huge part of it. He was sure she had no idea of how important she was to him, especially after their earlier conversation.

Each time they were together she would surprise him with a comment, or something spontaneous, like hugging him. He enjoyed the limited physical contact they shared. It gave him an opportunity to connect with Mina in a way he was unaccustomed to. He was consciously letting her control how much contact she wanted because it would give her time to develop her confidence and, hopefully, she would realise how attractive she was to him.

Since their night out, they had called each other twice. He tried to understand her struggles with her family and was certain her apprehension was due to concern about what would happen if they found out she was seeing someone like him. He would try to support her independence without being overbearing or expecting her to forget about what they might say, or think, or do.

When he got home, Justin thought he was walking into an empty apartment. He hung up his jacket and bag and opened the doors to the balcony to let in a much-needed breeze. He looked around but Frankie was nowhere to be seen. He checked his phone to make sure he had read her last text message correctly; she should be here. He knocked on the door to the second bedroom and then opened it carefully, so as not to startle her if she was in. She was but she was sound asleep, until he went to close the door.

"Justin?" she mumbled from beneath the covers.

"Hi, sis." Justin went to the bed and sat down next to her. "How're you feeling?"

Frankie stretched and sat up. She rubbed the sleep out of her eyes and said, "I think the last two days is catching up with me."

"We could have done this next week, you know."

"Yeah, but I've been looking forward to meeting Mina and I didn't want to cancel."

"Oh. You wanted to see Mina, not me? I can make myself scarce if that's how you feel!"

Frankie pushed Justin off the bed.

"You've still got some strength left in you." He straightened up. "Shall I make you some herbal tea?"

"Mmm. Yes please."

As Justin put the tea onto the bedside table he asked Frankie if she could manage a night out and a short while later called Mina to tell her where to meet.

***

Mina asked the driver to let her know when they were five minutes away and then called Justin. When she got out of the taxi, he was waiting for her. She looked around at the surrounding buildings and was clueless as to where they were going.

"Look at you. Come here." He pulled her into him. "I never realised how short you are until now."

"I've been told good things come in small packages." Mina pressed her face into his chest. He kissed her forehead and held her a little longer. He was enjoying their closeness, and trying to delay the news he was sure would unsettle her.

She was impatiently curious about where they were going. "So where is this place?"

"Well. About that." He kept Mina close to him as he continued. "Frankie's absolutely shattered and we decided it would be better if she didn't have to go out tonight."

"Is it only me and you then? Not that I mind."

"Well, she still wants to meet you...so we're having a takeout." Justin shut his eyes and grimaced waiting for her response.

"Let me get this straight. We're not going out to eat?"

"No."

"We're getting a takeaway."

"Yep."

"We're getting a takeaway to eat in your apartment."

"Yep."

He felt her head droop and tried to say something to make her feel better. "It was gonna happen sooner or later."

They walked into the building and towards the elevator, hand in hand.

"How far up are you?"

"Two floors from the top."

"I think we should go up in separate lifts." She pressed the button to call the elevator. "It's a punishment for being sneaky."

"Fair enough. I accept my punishment." He bowed his head. Then he grinned and put his arm around her waist. "I'll be all alone with nothing to do and nobody to keep me company."

She moved his hand away. "Maybe next time you'll be straight with me."

He put his arm around her again. "I was only thinking of my sister's health."

Mina couldn't continue pretending to be mad at him. She said, "I guess I can let you off with a warning this time."

In the lift, Mina put some distance between them, the perfect opportunity for Justin's mind to wander. She wasn't immune from the same thoughts and, if he had been aware of that, perhaps he wouldn't be so far away. "That was the most fun I've ever had in a lift!" he said.

She frowned. "But nothing happened."

Justin's hand reached out to move her hair out of her face. His voice was low and slow as he said, "But it's what could have happened that made it fun."

Mina's eyes widened as she realised what he was implying. Justin had the sudden urge to kiss her and never let her go. He admired her innocence and because of it knew he'd have to make the first move. Right now, however, there were more pressing matters. He led her to his apartment. "Let's go meet Frankie." He squeezed her hand. For the first time they were experiencing shared apprehension, even though for different reasons.

Justin called out, "Hi Frankie."

Frankie appeared. The first thing Mina noticed was her stunning hair; it was short and black and had streaks of silver running through it. Frankie's face seemed to soften as she looked from Justin to Mina and back.

Frankie said, "You must be Mina. It's lovely to meet you." She reached out and hugged Mina like they were old friends. "I've heard a lot about you."

Justin said, "Don't worry, it's all been good."

Frankie led Mina into the living room, asked if she'd like a drink and instructed Justin to prepare one. From the kitchen he watched the two women in his life and the fear he had harboured until now, dissipated. Frankie was great with people. She met so many different kinds in her line of work. He was sure she would be nothing but hospitable and friendly. The first signs were good.

Breaks in the conversation were an opportunity for Mina and Justin to exchange reassuring looks. They phoned out for food and talk continued to flow. Justin listened and watched intently as Mina told Frankie about her family and why she'd left home. This was a rare chance for Justin to observe her from a distance. Earlier he'd felt a change in her confidence, and now he could see its consequence. He was interrupted by an intercom buzzer; their food had arrived. While Frankie fetched plates and cutlery, Mina was drawn to the view from the balcony.

Justin's soothing voice whispered behind her, "The doors aren't locked." He opened the doors for her and she stepped out. "The sun will start setting in an hour or so." His breath on the back of her neck sent shivers down her spine.

Back in the kitchen Frankie said to him "You've done good, little brother."

"Thanks. I'm glad you like her."

"Try not to ruin her."

"What? How can you say that?"

"It's what mum would have said if she was here. It's what she said to Grayson when I introduced him to her."

"Hmm. I never got to introduce anyone to mum."

Frankie touched her brother's arm and reassured him. "She would love Mina. I'm certain of that." She kissed his forehead.

They ate and for a while the clink of cutlery on crockery prevailed above the hum of distant traffic through the open balcony doors. Mina felt comfortable around Frankie; she was nothing like Justin's description of her, but then he had grown up with her and she'd only known her an hour or so. She didn't blame Justin for exaggerating Frankie's character traits. She would probably do the same if she was describing Rehan to Justin. How long until she would have to? For the time being it didn't matter; her Weston family knew about Justin and she was perfectly happy to leave it at that.

Frankie hardly touched her food. Justin asked, "You lost your appetite?"

"It seems so." Frankie put her fork down. "I'm getting tired again, too." She smiled at Mina and said, "I'm sorry but I need to get some rest." She hugged Mina and then her brother and apologised again. "I'm glad we could spend a little time together."

"Me too. It's been lovely meeting you."

Frankie closed the bedroom door behind her and then it was Justin and Mina, alone.

"Why don't we finish eating out on the balcony? I'll just wrap this up for Frankie." Mina didn't need to be told twice; the night was still warm and, as Justin had said, the sun was setting. "I can't believe how well you and Frankie are getting on!"

"I know, right? Especially since you kept telling me how difficult she could be."

"I really should stop that. She's got my best interests at heart really."

"It's so nice up here. I can't wait to get out of that hotel room and into my own place." This had occurred to her on more than one occasion since spending time at Dan's house and now she could visualise the freedom she would gain in her own place.

"It can get lonely sometimes."

"Not if you've got company."

He held her hand to his mouth and kissed it. "Thank you so much for tonight. I had no idea what to expect."

She bit her bottom lip and felt exposed. "Yeah, especially since you tricked me into it!"

"Oh, come on!" Justin clasped his hands together and knelt down in front of Mina. "What can I do for you to forgive me?"

She folded her arms and contemplated the question. "I'll have to think about it."

He sat on the table at eye level with her, lowered his voice and said, "I have a suggestion, if you'll hear it."

They were close enough to feel each other taking long, deep breaths - anticipation of what was about to happen. Justin put his arms on the chair Mina was sitting on and inched closer. "What do you suggest?" Her voice was barely audible.

Justin leaned in and kissed her. He stopped, their foreheads touching. He kissed her again and this time she responded, wrapping her arms around his neck. Justin's hands gently held her. Day became night and the summer breeze wafted around, and in between them, as they shared their first truly passionate kiss.

"You should stay the night."

Mina shook her head. "I should not stay the night." She sat upright. "We'll see each other tomorrow."

Justin held her face and said, "Tomorrow's so far away."

She had to exercise all the self-control she could muster, conscious of how easy it would be to agree to anything Justin might suggest now. She reached out and put her hands on his thighs. "It's getting chilly. Can we go inside?"

He took her hand and led her to the sofa after closing the doors behind them. She slipped her shoes off and was about to do something she did naturally at home. Then she remembered she wasn't at home and stopped.

"Go for it; but I thought you weren't staying?"

"How does putting my feet up on the sofa mean I'm staying the night?"

"Well, what's going to happen now is I'm going to sit with you." Justin sat down. "Then you're going to put your head on my shoulder and we're not going to move for the rest of the night."

Mina lay back and rested her head on Justin's shoulder. Her phone beeped to notify her of a text message. Justin wrapped one arm around her waist and his other hand stroked her hair. Mina's phone sounded again. She hated having to move but it might be important but first things first. "Can I use your bathroom?"

"It's straight through there." Justin pointed through the open bedroom door. "Whilst you're up, I'll make us another drink."

When she returned he said, "Your phone went off again. It seems like someone is desperate to get in touch with you."

She picked her phone up. "Oh, shit!"

"Mina! You said a bad word!"

"You might have a few bad words to say yourself when I tell you I can't see you tomorrow, or the rest of the weekend."

"Why? What's happening?" Justin brought the drinks around to the opposite side of the breakfast bar and sat down.

"Tania's coming to stay." Mina wanted to slam her phone down but didn't want to break it.

Justin smiled. Mina frowned at him.

"Now you have to stay the night."

"Justin! Tania's coming. She doesn't know about us."

"So, tell her."

She shook her head, rehearsing the lies she'd be forced to tell Tania. Her timing couldn't have been worse. *I could text back to say I've been asked to work? She'd probably insist on coming anyway.*

"I can't do that." Mina sipped her drink. "Ooh, this is lovely!"

"Thank you!"

"Anyway, if she finds out, who's to say she won't tell my parents."

A long silence followed. The moments they had spent alone together were being veiled by the reality of her current, and future, predicament; the revelation of their relationship to her own family. They drank in silence, trying to read each other's minds. Mina folded her arms on the counter and put her head down. Justin mimicked her movements and they looked over at each other.

"What do you need me to do?"

Tania Comes to Weston

Mina had insisted on a taxi; her Justin-free weekend would start with immediate effect. She ran her tongue across the inside of her lower lip; it felt like a pothole-covered road. Sleep was the only way to halt the agony she was feeling, but sleep was playing hide and seek. Each time she closed her eyes she felt the touch of Justin's lips, the strength of his hands, saw the glint in his eyes. Then she opened her eyes and Tania's imminent arrival flooded her mind. It threw up scenarios she hadn't yet considered let alone prepared for.

If there was anything positive about the upcoming weekend, it was that Tania had booked to stay in a different hotel so at least they wouldn't be in each other's pockets for the entire weekend. Anxiety turned to guilt; Tania was her best friend, they had grown up together, she had helped secure Mina's job here.

When Mina finally won her game of nocturnal hide and seek, it was on her side with the covers pulled right over her head.

Justin-free Saturday encountered its first hiccup when Tania suggested lunch at Sunset Strip. Mina tried, and failed, to divert Tania's interest elsewhere; she obviously had fond memories of the place or an unwillingness to relinquish the man who turned her down, wounding her pride.

And of course, there Justin was at the bar. Tanya was almost salivating, watching every muscle in his body tense and relax as he stretched up high and bent low preparing the cocktail she had ordered. Maybe this time around she would leave with more than just a memory.

Tania pulled her V-neck top down a little and straightened up, pushing her chest out. She wanted him to get a good look at what he had declined to take up first time around. Justin was about to place the glass on the counter when Tania took the glass from his hand, deliberately touching his fingers in the process. She put the straw to her mouth and watched him.

"So how have you been since we last met?"

He didn't register her face and Tania could tell.

"Breakfast at the hotel? I asked if you wanted to spend some time together. You told me that you had better things to do. Not those words exactly, but more or less."

Justin nodded and said, "You were here with your friend." He busied himself wiping the counter. "How are you?"

"Well, I wasn't happy that you didn't make time to see me."

He knew would either take his rejoinder as a compliment, or it would offend her. "I'd have thought a girl like you would have a line of men wanting to be with you."

She ran her finger along the edge of her glass. "The trouble is I don't always want to be with them."

He took a couple of orders from other customers and looked around for colleagues, non-verbally communicating his desire to handover bar duties to someone else.

Tania raised her voice to be sure she couldn't be misheard. "You should know I find you extremely attractive."

He stopped what he was doing for a brief second and sighed. He didn't want to upset her; they may well be seeing each other again, under different circumstances; but it would be wrong to continue to allow her to think she had any chance with him.

"Listen. I'm flattered, I really am. The thing is..."

Tania interrupted. "Oh, God, don't say what I think you're going to say." She held her hand up in front of her face.

"It wouldn't be fair on my girlfriend if I didn't say it. I've been seeing someone for a few weeks now." The words left his mouth with the ease of breathing and he felt proud to be able to say it.

It certainly silenced Tania, although she'd get over it rapidly. She consoled herself by imagining awful things about his girlfriend. She tapped her fingers on the counter and mumbled, "Hurry up, Mina." Finally she removed herself from the bar to awaited Mina's arrival at one of the tables. She contemplated both her successes and mistakes with the opposite sex; the most recent of the latter stung like a paper cut.

Tania understood, as did Mina, the unwritten rules in a family which still practiced arranged marriage. Their parents would always have the final say; prospective husbands would need a steady career, a solid income and, most important of all, share the same religion. She even had friends whose parents wouldn't agree on a husband or wife from a different caste, never mind religion. Tania wanted to believe she could be the exception to those rules with an arranged marriage as a mere back-up plan to give her someone to share a future and life's many experiences.

"Hi, stranger!"

"Hi to you too!"

They hugged fiercely and Tania said, "I've missed you." She held Mina at arms-length to study her. "You've changed!" She walked around her. "Something's changed about you. What is it?"

Mina had no intention of disclosing the truth, so she shrugged. "Nothing's changed. I'm still the same."

"I ordered lunch for us. Hope you don't mind. So, how have you been? Tell me everything!"

Mina gave Tania a detailed account of her new job and living accommodation. She told her she'd made some friends and they liked to go out at the weekend, depending on shift patterns. "In fact - you'll love me for this - I told them I wouldn't be available because you were coming, so they've invited you out too." What she deliberately failed to mention was she had asked Dan to help keep Tania occupied in an effort to keep her relationship with Justin under wraps. Dan had shaken his head in disbelief, but empathised with Mina's predicament and said he was happy to oblige.

Tania was thrilled. "Fantastic! I could really use a night out."

When their food was served, Mina refused to look up for fear of seeing Justin and letting her emotions show. Instead of leaving after putting the plates down, the waitress was searching for something in her pocket. She pulled out a pair of turquoise earrings and offered them to Mina. Her heart skipped a beat. She'd left them at Justin's last night. *What is he playing at? How am I going to explain this away?*

"I think you left these here yesterday."

"Are you sure?" Mina hoped to convince the waitress she'd made a mistake.

"Someone saw you take them off and leave them at the bar." The waitress pushed her hand in Mina's direction again. She was just going to have to accept the earrings which were a pair of her favourites. "Oh, yeah. Thank you."

Tania had picked up her cutlery with every intention of using it, but was intrigued that her friend might be hiding something. *What was she doing here last night and, crucially, who was she with? She shouldn't be seeing someone already; that's not why she moved here.* When they were alone, once more, Tania asked, "What's going on, Mina?"

Mina hesitated. "Nothing's going on." She quickly took a mouthful of food and chewed slowly.

Tania put her down her knife and fork and glowered sternly at her friend. "Really? First you tell me this place has closed for a refurb." She spread her hands out and looked around. "Which it clearly isn't. Then your earrings are being given back to you because you left them here last night!" Tania puffed. "Something's up and you should be straight and tell me."

Mina kept eating, dragging out the silence. She looked at the earrings, still on the table. She couldn't help smiling, remembering how it felt to kiss Justin for the first time. *I'd give anything to be with him right now.* She couldn't share the truth about her new-found independence. "Okay. I'll be honest with you." Mina picked up her condensation covered glass. "It's harder out here than I thought it would be." When she drank from the glass she avoided eye contact with Tania.

"You knew it would be difficult." Tania had trouble understanding how it could be that difficult living by the calm, clean sea and with people who seemed to be loving every minute of their coastal experience.

Mina used a question she already knew the answer to that would keep Tania talking. "Have my mum and dad asked you anything?"

"Actually, they haven't." Tania finished chewing the last mouthful of pizza. "But your mum did give me something to give you."

"What is it? What did she give you?"

"It's your mum. What do all Indian mums worry about?"

They looked at each other and grinned together as, in unison, they said, "Is my bachari beti getting enough food!" They burst out laughing and Tania almost brought back up the food she'd just eaten. As their laughter subsided, they both wiped the tears from their eyes and arranged the rest of the day's activities. Mina was off the hook for now.

***

Dan was thoughtful enough to recommend a bar in the city centre where Mina would be able to relax, not worrying about bumping into Justin. Tania blended seamlessly into the group, they were her kind of people; loud, game for a laugh and partial to a few alcoholic drinks now and again, which left Mina wondering how she had managed to relate to them.

The place they had come to was heaving with bodies, most of them scrambling to the bar. Mina could feel the music course through her body, the bass competing with the steady beat of her heart; she had never experienced anything quite like it. There were people on what she believed to be the dance floor; but then again, there were people dancing wherever they could find the space. Seating was limited so some of the group had squashed and squeezed their way into the middle of the dance floor, Tania and Dan included.

In spite of herself, Mina found she was having a good time, sitting on a stool, tapping her feet to the music, some of which she recognised. She hoped there would be no further need to lie to Tania for the rest of her weekend. She picked her phone up and was about to start scrolling idly though it, when she saw she'd got a missed call from Justin. Her pulse started racing, imagining his voice in her ear. She was about to return the call, but stopped herself. She turned the phone over so the screen was out of view and gave herself two choices. First she could return the call and cancel the Justin-free weekend by suggesting something ridiculous, like sneaking away to meet him right now or, second, she could fight that urge, enjoy the night and build anticipation for their next meeting. She tapped her fingers on the back of the phone in sync with her feet following the music. She put her phone into her bag and reassured herself she was doing the right thing.

Eid in Birmingham

Almost as soon as she stepped out of the taxi, Mina wished she was back in Weston Super-Mare. This place seemed full of repressed memories. She would be getting together with her extended family for the celebrations and there were sure to be questions asked and, of course, conclusions jumped to.

At least the drive had been interesting; she had found the strength to stay awake during the entire journey talking to Justin and admiring the views from the passenger seat. They had arrived in Birmingham an hour later than anticipated, simply because they couldn't keep their hands off each other. It had become normal for Mina to greet him with a long, slow kiss. He often told her she was spoiling him, but would find a way to live with it, and return the favour.

She dropped her bags and fumbled for her keys but they weren't in her handbag. Rather than open her case in the middle of the street, she rang the doorbell and tried to look happy. The door opened and the smell of food went straight to her nose. Then she saw who had opened the door for her.

"Mina, baaji!" Anisa jumped into Mina's arms. "I missed you sooo much!"

"I missed you too Anisa." She kissed her forehead and said, "It looks like you've grown. You'll be taller than me soon!"

In the hallway, she could hear more than one voice. She asked Anisa, "Who's here?"

"Shazia baaji, Rukhsana baaji and Uncle Qasim."

At least she was dressed appropriately. She left her case in the hallway and followed her sister into the living room.

"Eid Mubarak!" She greeted her relatives.

There were shouts of, "Kher Mubarak, stranger," and "Oh, my gosh, look who it is!"

They all took turns with the traditional two-hug greeting and then she found her mum, in the kitchen. "Eid Mubarak, mum."

Mina's mum stopped cooking and hugged her daughter. She could tell that she was crying and said, "Stop it or you'll start me off." By the time the finished the embrace, they both had watery eyes. Mina started wiping away the mascara from her mum's cheeks. "It's good to be home."

"It's good to have you back..." she scrutinised Mina's face. "...even if it is only for a couple of days."

Rukhsana joined them in the kitchen. "So, tell me all about Weston Super-Mare." Rukhsana was five years older than Mina. She had finished her studies and was currently engaged, with the wedding set for next August. Her sister, Shazia, was Mina's age and in the second year of a multimedia design degree.

They all had a good shared history but Mina doubted they would understand if she told them she was in a relationship with an older black man.

"It's great. I love being so close to the sea." She took some mugs from the cupboard.

"What about your job?"

"It was hard at first, but now I really enjoy it." She filled up a pot with water, put it on the cooker and added tea leaves, cinnamon sticks and cardamom pods. "How's wedding prep coming along?"

She listened to her cousin as she discussed the finer details; the outfits she had chosen to wear on each of the three days of a normal Muslim wedding, the trouble she was having finding accessories, the amount of people her parents were inviting, and suchlike. She could remember Rehan's wedding; insanely huge, expensive and full of people introduced as relatives who she'd never laid eyes on before or since. It had been her mum and dad's proudest moment though, seeing their only son get married and settle down.

"Mina, you need to get ready. Rehan and Leila will be here soon and then we are all going to have dinner at your naani's house."

***

Mina hadn't seen so much food since Anisa's birthday party in January and she hadn't seen so many people in one place since her night out with Tania and Dan. Luckily, all the aunties were too busy making sure everyone had plates piled with mountains of food. She sat next to Rehan in the oversized lounge. "You look different," Rehan said as she decided how much food could sensibly be crammed on her spoon.

"Really? Tania said the same thing." Mina let some food spill back onto her plate and then filled her mouth.

"How's work?"

She chewed slowly and thought. "It's not bad. The night shifts were hard, but not so much now." She moved the spoon around the plate and added, "What's hard is living in that hotel room. I have to go to the staff kitchen when I need to heat my food, or cook."

"Why don't you try finding rooms for rent? Some of my uni friends did that. It worked out cheaper than living in halls."

She told him she had had the same idea; she would have so much more space, and company.

The following day was a big family day out; fifteen of them went to the movies, went bowling and then finished with a meal at their favourite restaurant. Mina slumped in a chair and rubbed her stomach; she had eaten excessively for two days. *Oh, I miss the food in Birmingham.* She looked around at her family, at how much they were enjoying each other's company. The conversation never stopped, everyone seeming genuinely interested in what the others were saying.

"So, Mina, when are you going back?"

She looked at her uncle and said, "Tomorrow. My train leaves at five in the evening." *Tomorrow, I'll be in a hotel room preparing to meet Justin and his friends for a night out.*

Looking down at her luggage, Mina noticed she was taking back almost as much food as personal belongings. At least her weekend munchies problem was sorted.

The two days in Birmingham had rushed by so quickly and she and her mum had stealthily avoided being in the same room for too long. More than once, deep in conversation with a family member, Mina spotted her mum watching her; the strained expression on her face, as though she was trying to lip read their words. Shazia admitted how much she admired Mina for being brave enough to make such a drastic change to her comfortable life. She confided in Mina her daily anxiety about what her future would look like once she finished her degree; she doubted her reasons for studying, worried about landing a decent enough job – one that was related to her degree subject - and absolutely had no desire to get married like her older sister.

Unlike Shazia, Mina was less forthcoming with personal ambitions and fears for the future; she was still family after all and family had to remain oblivious to her activities. Despite two days filled with careful avoidance of sensitive information and a lack of time spent with her parents, Mina was relaxed, thankful for a break from Weston, which she would deny needing, should anyone ask. She said goodbye to an empty house, did a final check of the locks and stepped into the taxi.

Three Sides to the Story

Justin:

Wherever he went, he was followed by the sensation of floating on air, there was no obstacle or human emotion with the capacity to prevent him being blissfully happy. At work, a recently employed member of staff had been signed off sick indefinitely, but rather than swear and curse, he just placed an advert in the local paper and in the shops, and the position was filled within three days.

The following day, he got a puncture on the way to an important meeting, so he called a taxi and returned to change the tyre after the meeting. Normally, his reaction would have made him fit seamlessly into a scene from Fawlty Towers, becoming loudly frustrated at the thought of the task, not having enough time, and of his clothes being ruined. Not that day. For two whole weeks Justin had been serene, positive and unfazed.

The people important to him knew about Mina and, by the end of the night, they would have met her too. The initial bewilderment of his friends upon hearing he was about to present the woman in his life to them, increased threefold on the night of their formal introduction. When the men were alone, Justin was bombarded with questions.

"How did you two hook up?"

"How long have you been seeing her?"

"Do you really think this is a good idea?"

Sam had meant no malice in this last question, he only wondered if Justin had considered how potentially tricky being introduced to Indian parents could be. Justin had corrected Sam, telling him that Mina was Muslim, not Indian.

"Shit, Justin! What are you playing at?"

Even Alex was shaking his head. "She must mean a lot to you."

Justin turned to Alex and nodded. "I don't know how our future is going to pan out. All I know is when I'm with her, nothing else matters."

Yes, the last two weeks had been quite marvellous. Now, however, as he and Mina stood hand on waist, and face to face with a glaring Tania, he had the sinking feeling that the next few days were going to provide a stark contrast.

Tania:

If that uptight snob thinks she can look at me as if I'm a piece of gum stuck to the bottom of her cheap shoes, she's got another think coming. I didn't come in here to be insulted so I follow her out and see her smooching one of the few sexy men in the place, typical. Well I'll just have to put a stop to that. I finish my drink and put the glass on one of the podiums as I walk toward my friends.

The girls are appalled when I tell them what happened in the ladies' room. "I mean, can you believe she had the nerve to tell me to move!" Of course, this isn't true, but it's what she was thinking!

I don't usually go out looking for trouble, it just seems to find me. The worst thing is, me and the girls come here every weekend and now this snob thinks she can push me out. I grab Jodie's bottle, take a swig of water and clear my mind.

Now, where is he? I have to stand up to get a better look. The room spins and the lights play havoc with my head.

I turn back to the table and pick up a glass. "Top me up girls. I've got some business to take care of."

I steady myself on the strangers around me as I make the short walk towards the hunk who's going to give me what I want.

"Oh my God!" I bump into him, spilling his drink everywhere. "I am sooo sorry!"

"Damn it! Are you alright?" He puts his enormous arms around my waist and pulls me closer.

He smells amazing. "New shoes," I say and lift my foot to show him.

I snatch a tissue out of my handbag and begin dabbing at his top. "I've ruined your gorgeous jumper." I let my hands rest on his muscular chest. I smooth my hands slowly up his chest and onto his shoulders, pretending to be worried about his clothes. There are a few inches between us when I feel my arm being pulled.

"You need to walk away right now!"

I stare into the eyes of the bitch I've been looking for. "You had better take your stuck-up, scrawny little hand off me!" I pull my arm out of her grasp and shove her.

Her lame friends crowd round her to pull her away. She doesn't even try to put up a fight. As the group disperse, I spot two familiar people holding hands, consoling their friend. Maybe I have had too much to drink coz that looks likes Mina but she's miles away. Anyway she wouldn't be seen dead in a place like this without me!

Each step forward messes up my belief where Mina should be and what she's doing. They're staring right at me. They! How is this even possible? What the fuck is she doing with him? Try as I might, there was no way to calm myself down before I reach them. Oh, now things are going to get interesting.

Mina:

Mina had been thrilled not having had to say goodbye to any of her family. It would have made her feel guilty lying to them. This was a big night and the last thing she needed were thoughts of family invading her confidence.

In the two weeks since Tania's visit, Dan had commented on a change in Mina's attitude and personality. She was shedding the layers of her old self-effacing ways, making way for someone with a fresh perspective, a risk-taker. Her heart beat as fast a sprinter running the one hundred metres each time she and Justin kissed. Each kiss was full of potential; their bodies pulled in close together, their breathing in sync. Shivers ran through Mina's body and reminded her that she had to be ready in twenty minutes.

She filled her hand bag with essentials and winced over her feet in her new shoes bought especially for the dress she was wearing. Justin had asked if it would be alright for him to buy her a gift and she had ended the phone conversation more than a little confused until he turned up the following day with the dress. He had rambled on about hoping he'd picked the right size, and if not, then not to take it personally. Mina told him to relax, sizing would not become an issue and he told her he didn't want to see her in it until she was wearing it for an occasion.

She turned back to the full-length mirror in her room. For an instant, she had trouble recognising her own reflection. She turned to the left, then to the right. She moved her head around, as if that would help. Instinctively, she held out the sides of the dress and swivelled again. She adored the colour, plum with white floral patterns. It was a halter neck and fell between her knees and ankles. After a couple of minutes of self-admiration, it dawned on her; she remembered she'd seen this same dress in one of the shops she dragged Justin into for a spot of window shopping. He really was someone special.

She walked over to where Justin was waiting until he gestured for her to stop. His eyes were scanning her body, so she turned around, deliberately slowly. He crossed the last few feet to meet her, held her face in his hands and kissed her.

The introductions were smooth but brief; she supposed she would have the rest of the night to get to know more about each of them as the night went on.

After the meal they moved on to somewhere more energetic to work off the stresses of their week. During the short walk along Broad Street, Mina learned that Marvin was the eldest of the group and had been married to Chloe for seven years. She noticed the others asking his opinion on a variety of issues and she noticed his disapproving look when they got a bit too loud for their surroundings so, she wasn't surprised to learn that he was a father to two young children.

They were lucky enough to find seats for all of them while the partners got drinks from the bar.

"My feet are killing!" Lauren, Alex's partner of five years unbuckled the straps of her heels.

"Bad idea, Lauren. It's gonna be a hundred times worse when you put them back on."

"Darren's bringing the rest," Justin said as he put the drinks on the table. Darren's girlfriend got up to go and help. A few moments later they were alerted to trouble by the loud gabble of raised voices. As the crowd drew back, Darren, his girlfriend and another woman were revealed. Marvin and Alex sped over to help. When they returned a few moments later, questions and comments flew at Darren.

Mina stood next to Justin and asked what had happened, but he only kissed her and told her not to worry. She put her arms around him and, as they shifted their position, noticed the other woman involved in the ruckus with Darren, looking in their direction.

"Are you seeing who I'm seeing?" Justin asked, his hands finding Mina's.

"Hey, you both!" Sam put a hand on Justin's shoulder. "Come sit down." Failing to get a reaction, Sam whispered in Justin's ear, "Why aren't you talking to me, Jus?"

"Sorry mate," he said, without turning around, "We'll be there in a minute."

Mina's initial reaction was to loosen her grip on Justin as Tania approached, but found herself doing the opposite, either for comfort, or as an act of defiance, she couldn't be sure which. She decided that she was going to have to play on Tania's drunkenness; she had seen other people do it. It should be straightforward.

"Let me handle this," she said to Justin. "You go back to your friends."

She knew she would have to put a little distance between herself and Justin in order for her story to be remotely believable, so began walking to intercept Tania. As she closed in, she waved vigorously and shouted "It is you! What are you doing here?" Mina hoped she sounded sufficiently surprised.

"Never mind me. What the hell are you doing here?"

"I'm out having a good time with friends. Is that alright with you?" She would have to fight fire with fire.

Tania glanced over Mina's shoulder. "Depends who you're with."

Mina tried to speak above the music, "Let's go outside. I can't hear a thing!" She shook her head and covered her ears. She took Tania's hand and led her to the covered outdoor area, the smoker's hangout. She felt Tania swaying as she followed behind. Tania shook Mina's hand off and pointed in the direction they'd come from. "What are you doing here with him?"

"With who? I'm here with some friends."

Tania put her hands on her waist and said, "I've never seen those friends before!"

"You haven't met all my friends."

Tania's shoulders slumped and she went quiet. "So why did he have his arm around you?" She straightened up and glared at Mina.

Mina considered all of the possible answers to the question and then opted for straight denial. "I don't know what you're talking about!"

Tania put her head in her hands and started pacing. "You're lying to me, Mina! Stop lying to me!!"

"And you're drunk! How can you be sure what you saw?"

Tania was shaking her head. Mina could see she was mumbling something to herself. Tania's friends joined them and Mina hugged each of them. They commented on how sexy Mina was looking and that they didn't know she had it in her. As the small talk flowed, Mina saw Tania looking straight into the club, probably re-enacting what she thought she had seen.

One of the girls grabbed Tania by the arm and said, "We're getting out of here now. It's been great seeing you."

As Tania walked out with them, she turned back to Mina and said, "This isn't over."

***

No news is good news is what some people claim but most people spend too much time checking their phone to maintain their connection with outside events That's not how Mina went through the next few days; she started to leave her phone in her room, rather than in her locker, to prolong the inability of her family, or Tania, to contact her. It was easy enough to ignore her brother, but when Mina saw a missed call from her dad, she knew she had to act.

With Justin in Birmingham, Dan invited her to his place for moral support while she made the dreaded phone call. He made them both a hot drink and she picked up her phone. As she searched for Rehan's number Dan asked "Do you know what you're going to say?"

"Do you know how to make me a perfect mug of tea?"

"Ha ha, very funny!"

"Sorry." Mina sipped from her mug. "I did mean it though."

Dan threw a tea towel at her and made her spill tea down her front.

"Daniel!"

"You started it, don't forget!"

"Alright. We'll call a truce," she said as she using the tea towel to clean her shirt. She took a long sip from her mug and said, "Here goes nothing."

For the first few seconds, they shared the normal greetings, and then Mina said, "So why did you want me to call?"

She looked at Dan and frowned as she listened to Rehan. He said "Tania's been round to mum and dad's. She claimed she saw you in a bar on Broad Street with a man the same night you were supposed to be travelling back to Weston."

"And you believe her?"

She began pacing the length of the kitchen as Rehan continued. "Why would she lie to us, Mina?"

Mina threw her hand in the air. "Maybe because she was drunk!" She turned back towards Dan and realised she had just implicated herself.

"So, she did see you in that bar!"

She closed her eyes and paused to gather her thoughts. "Yes. I was there." When she opened her eyes again it was to see Dan staring at her nonplussed. She walked over to him and closed his gaping jaw.

"And who is this man you were all over?"

"What?" Now she would have to pull out all of the stops to make this convincing. "I wasn't all over anybody. I was with a group of people, men and women." She had to keep herself talking. "They were friends I've made in Weston. They were coming down for a couple of nights and offered to drive me back."

She looked at Dan for a sign that she had said the right thing. He nodded.

"So why did you tell us that you were getting the train back? Why didn't you just say that you were getting a lift?"

She sat down opposite Dan and thought about the question. He was right. She could have said she was getting a lift with friends. She had probably made this worse. But now she had started, there was no going back.

"Well, they were meeting some other friends before going back and they invited me. I didn't think you or mum and dad would have liked that idea." She pictured Rehan shaking his head in astonishment at his little sister's actions. She was also fully aware of his need to be out all night with the lads, and ladies, during his university days. Something she could possibly use to her advantage. When he didn't respond she said, "I only wanted to enjoy myself before going back to work." More silence. "You can understand that, can't you?"

She heard Rehan take a deep breath. "Yes, I understand. But it was different for me."

"Why was it different for you?" She was about to get her answer, but realised what it would be and said it for him. "Because I'm a girl." She began to pace again. "You know as well as I do how unfair that is. I can make my own decisions. I mean, I'm a hundred miles from home because I decided to make a change!"

"It's not only about that...Tania told us about the man you were with."

She stopped pacing and leant against the kitchen counter top. She shut her eyes and lowered her head.

"She said he was black. Mina, is that true?"

She wished for strength to continue the deception. It came in the form of a fresh mug of tea. She looked up to see Dan's smile. He placed a reassuring hand on Mina's arm and went back to the table. She sipped from the mug and was surprised to find that this time he'd managed to find the formula for her perfect mug of tea. She gave him a thumbs up and he responded with a bow.

"I was with a group of men and women and yes, some of them were black. But some of them were white."

"Just be honest with us next time. Alright?"

"I will." She hung up, picked up her mug and joined Dan as her phone started ringing again. "Thank goodness, it's Justin."

Dan left her to it.

Justin and Frankie

He had already made the phone call to Sunset Strip before calling Mina. From the moment he saw Frankie, he knew he would have to extend his stay; she had been for chemotherapy the day before and now she was hardly able to lift a glass off the table. She had no desire to stay propped up in bed all day so, with Justin's help, she made herself comfortable on an armchair in the living room and Justin propped her feet up on an ottoman. He made them both a lemon and ginger tea and sat opposite her.

"I'm staying a few extra days, until I think you'll be alright by yourself."

She strained to reach for her tea, so Justin crouched down beside her and handed it to her. As she took the mug, she placed her hand over his and said, "You're getting stubborn in your old age!"

"I learnt from the best!" He kissed her forehead and went back to his seat. "Mina hopes you feel better soon."

"Tell her thank you. When are we going to meet for dinner again?"

"It's her birthday in a few weeks and I wanted to do something special for her. We haven't talked about it yet, so I'm not sure if she's planning on celebrating with her family."

"If she's coming to Birmingham, we can go out for a birthday dinner."

"Sounds good. I'll speak to her about it." He hoped she would agree, but after the run-in with Tania, she might want to avoid going out in Birmingham altogether. He was unaware of any other fallout from the weekend and she seemed in good spirits, so he hadn't asked.

Justin picked up a pen and paper and started writing down a menu; it helped him organise a shopping list for the next few days to make sure Frankie was avoiding processed foods. He asked her what she might like to eat and added his own ideas.

"What are you doing?" Frankie had lowered her feet off the ottoman.

"I can't go shopping dressed like this, can I?" She cruised carefully around the furniture, towards Justin.

Rather than argue, Justin walked Frankie into her bedroom. Some fresh air and a walk might be good for her. She emerged wearing a black and white head scarf to match her trainers.

"I just need to let Alan know I'm on the way down."

"Who's Alan? And why does he have to know?"

Frankie pressed the button marked services and spoke to Alan. "He puts a stool in the lift for me."

When the elevator arrived, sure enough, there was a stool in one corner with her name on it. They were greeted by a man in his fifties, wearing a black suit and tie, crisp white shirt and black, shined-this-morning, shoes. Frankie took the hand he offered and stepped out of the elevator.

"Thank you. Alan. This is my brother, Justin. Justin, this is Alan." The men shook hands and Justin thanked him for the gesture of support made for his sister.

The supermarket was a short distance from Frankie's apartment, so they walked discussing the non-stop restructuring of the city centre and when it was likely to ease. Frankie was glad she didn't have need of a car; not only was navigating the roads a challenge, but parking seemed in short supply. If she needed to travel out of Birmingham, the train was her first option. Unlike her, Justin avoided public transport at all costs. He loved the freedom of his car, being able to go where he wanted, when he wanted and with companions of his choosing.

Thanks to a concise shopping list, they were in and out of the supermarket within fifteen minutes. They decided on chicken and vegetable soup with brown rolls for dinner. Justin made enough so they could have it again for lunch the following day. His passion for cooking had grown stronger due to the nature of his job; although not required, he would cook alongside the chef when a new dish or menu was being introduced. His method of cooking was more precise and measured than his mum's; he was a sucker for detailed recipes, whereas she had had a knack for judging by eye how much spice or other ingredient to throw in. Preparing meals for one person was sometimes arduous, and the ensuing pile of washing up would generally put him off, but he had mastered a host of one pot recipes that made the whole process almost relaxing. The soup he and Frankie were going to eat was one of them.

Frankie sat at the breakfast bar reading and responding to email. Justin noticed her movements had become stronger since their walk and took comfort in having the flexibility to leave work behind for a few days at a time if she needed him. Comfort was soon replaced by guilt; Mina mightn't mind him being away a few days longer than anticipated, but since they had grown closer, he ached being so far away from her.

He washed the vegetables and imagined stroking her fine, dark hair as she rested her head on his shoulder. He added the seasoning and recalled the scent of her fragrance on her neck. He browned the chicken and remembered how incredible she looked when he saw her in the dress he'd bought for her.

"Penny for your thoughts," Frankie said.

Justin sighed and absent-mindedly stirred the pot's contents.

"You're pining for your woman. Is that it?" Frankie said without looking up from the laptop.

"Something like that."

Frankie cleared her throat and said, "On the subject of pining, have you given any more consideration to the job you've been offered?"

Justin sighed again. "No. I need to weigh up the pros and cons."

"You need to get a move on. When do you have to let them know?"

"Beginning of July. So that's about three weeks' time." He replaced the lid and took a stool next to Frankie. "What do you think I should do?"

She closed her laptop and turned to face him. "You know very well it doesn't matter what I think. You're the one who will have to make peace with whatever you choose." Before resuming work, she asked, "Have you told Mina about the offer?"

He shook his head. "I was going to this weekend, but it'll have to wait until I get back." He was finding it difficult to be objective, but only because he seemed more concerned how either decision would affect Frankie or Mina rather than himself. At times like these, there was one person he could depend on for advice. Justin turned the heat down under the soup, picked up his phone and stood out on the balcony to make the call. "Marv, my man! How are you?"

The friends talked for half an hour, by which time dinner was ready and Frankie had put the rolls in the oven. Justin ladled soup into two bowls and Frankie put the warmed rolls on a plate on the breakfast bar.

Justin said, "A toast." They each held up their glasses. "To good health."

Frankie added, "And wise decisions."

The following morning Justin woke to an empty apartment. Frankie had gone back to work. After making himself poached eggs with mushrooms, he switched on the television and flicked through the guide until he found an interesting cooking feature. An agenda for the day began to form in his mind. The building had a gym for residents and their guests so that would occupy a couple of hours before meeting Alex for lunch.

The gym was spread over two floors, halfway up the building. It was one of Justin's preferred places to work up a sweat. Large windows bathed the entire area in natural light and looking out as he started up the treadmill, helped de-clutter his mind. He connected his earphones, selected his gym playlist and began. If anyone were to ask what he thought about as he gazed along the skyline, he would probably give them the answer they wanted, rather than the truth; this was the one place where he could truly relax, unhampered by the outside world, controlling every movement. He concentrated on his breathing and felt the tension of the steep ascent build in his calves. Two minutes later, he was on the gradual descent to where he first started. He wiped the sweat from his face and took a few sips of water.

When he went in to shower, he fought to keep thoughts at bay of Mina and how much he missed her. Dressed in dark jeans, a navy blue and white spotted shirt and dark blue trainers, he applied moisturiser to his face, did a quick check to make sure he hadn't forgotten anything and headed out to find Alex.

***

"She asked us to call you. She's through here."

The man in the suit ushered Justin in to a large room with a sofa and a handful of armchairs; Frankie was lying on the sofa. Justin rushed and knelt beside her. He took her hand and said, "How long has she been like this?"

"About forty minutes." The man in the suit stood in the doorway awaiting further instructions. "Is there anything I can do?"

Justin lowered his head and closed his eyes to think. "You can get her some water."

When his lunch with Alex had been interrupted by a call from Frankie's office, he instinctively thought the worst. Now, looking down at his usually strong, active and energetic sister, lying seemingly unaware of her surroundings, his heart began pounding rapidly.

He rested on his knees and stroked her hair. "Frankie. Frankie, it's Justin."

Frankie's eyelids fluttered open. She squinted as her eyes adjusted to the light. The man in the suit opened a bottle of water and handed it to Justin. Frankie lifted herself into a sitting position.

"Here, have some water."

Frankie accepted the bottle, but found she couldn't hold it, so Justin tilted it for her. Her smile was alien in its weakness.

"How're you feeling?"

"Really tired. I knew...I knew I needed you here. So, I asked Imran to call you." She looked over at the man in the suit and said, "Thank you." He acknowledged her with a nod.

"I need to get you home. Do you think you can walk?" He had no other ideas.

Imran said, "We have a wheelchair. We bought it after the last time."

"What? This has happened here before?" Justin glared at Imran, but this was not the time to start asking questions or placing blame. "Okay. Bring it through."

They lifted Frankie onto the wheelchair and Imran collected her belongings. Frankie eased herself slowly onto the passenger seat of Justin's car. Imran folded the chair and went to store it in the boot.

Justin said, "Thank you for looking out for her."

"I'm glad to have been some help."

They shook hands and Justin drove back to Frankie's apartment. When Justin wheeled Frankie into the foyer , Alan's initial look was one of real concern.

"Is Ms Granger alright?"

"Hi, Alan. She's exhausted." Justin offered a reassuring smile.

"Please let me know if there is anything I can do."

"I will. Thank you."

Justin placed three large pillows on Frankie's bed and helped her onto it.

"I don't know what I would do without you." Frankie lifted Justin's hand and kissed it.

"No need for that."

As he closed the door behind him, Justin rubbed his eyes, wiping away the incipient tears. He sat on the balcony with his head in his hands and a bottle of beer on the table. He thought about what Imran had said. She had passed out at work before. *Why didn't he know this?*

Last night's conversation with Marvin replayed in his mind. He desperately needed to talk to Mina, but had to do it where he could see her and touch her. But there was no way he could leave Frankie by herself.

He heated up the remaining soup and took it through to Frankie. "You should eat. You need to get your strength back." She opened her eyes and stretched. Justin placed the tray on her lap and she dipped a piece of bread in the soup. He watched her slow, laborious movements and then told her what he'd decided to do.

Justin and Frankie travelled down the M5 that evening. She had brought three large lever arch files, each dedicated to a different client, as well as her laptop; "I'm fatigued, not incapacitated." He helped Frankie get settled before returning to the car for the luggage. His phone rang.

"Alex! Sorry, mate. I'm back home."

"Nah, don't worry. How is she?" Justin explained what had happened. "She just came with you? No arguments?"

Justin cradled the phone using his shoulder as he lifted cases out of the boot of the car. "Yeah, I know. I was expecting some resistance but nothing. So here we are."

"What do you think about what we discussed? Does it sound okay?"

He closed the boot of the car and walked to the elevator. "Alex, it sounds like you know what you're doing and I'm happy for you."

"Awesome. I'll see you both next weekend?"

"You will. Good luck."

Not so Happy Families

With the events of the past few hours, Justin had forgotten Alex's news; he was going to propose to Lauren, after five years together. The first time Lauren was introduced to the group, Eve was beside Justin. He suddenly remembered how physical Eve had been during dinner; he was busy listening to how Alex and Lauren had met when he felt Eve's hand stroking his thigh, and any thoughts of an early night vanished. He called Mina and asked her over to talk. When he opened the door, forty minutes later, Mina didn't have a chance to utter a word before Justin had his arms around her. He held onto her as if they hadn't seen each other for weeks. He nuzzled her and said, "I missed you so much." He kissed her neck, her face, her lips. Any resistance Mina thought she might have, faded. She put her arms around him and responded. He moved her back against the wall and slid his hands down her body to her hips. Her hands stroked the back of his neck as they shared that long, passionate kiss.

"Maybe you should go away more often," Mina said as they released each other. "I could get used to that."

Justin kissed her again. "No. I think I'll stay right here." His hands travelled down her back and she pushed him away.

"We'd better stop," Mina said, but Justin didn't agree and kissed her again. "What did you want to talk about?"

"I lied. I don't want to talk." He planted small kisses on her neck.

"Hello, Mina." A familiar voice came from behind them.

"Justin!"

"Oh, yeah. That's what I wanted to tell you."

Mina punched his chest and walked into his apartment. "Hi, Frankie. How are you?" Mina gave her a hug.

"I'm a little better, now my brother is taking care of me for the week. Would you like a mug of tea?"

"I'd love one, thank you." Mina shot a questioning look at Justin.

"Me too, please, sis." He stood behind Mina, wrapped his arms around her waist and nuzzled her neck again. "I thought it would be better to bring Frankie back with me. She can work from here and I can be with you."

Mina stepped away to help Frankie with the tea. She said to Justin, "You go and sit down. We'll bring the tea over." Her grin was half innocent, half wicked. She was in control and felt empowered, knowing she could make Justin do anything she wanted him to.

Frankie passed the sugar and tea to Mina while she took the milk out of the fridge. "How's work?"

"It's a bit easier. I'm enjoying it now." She added freshly boiled water to the mugs. "If I have a bad day, I have a chat with one of my colleagues."

"Oh, yes. Justin has told me about Daniel."

She hadn't considered how much Frankie knew about her and she wondered what other information Justin might have shared. There was no way she would discuss any of her friends with Rehan. It wasn't the kind of relationship they had. He was an easy-going person most of the time, but he could be authoritative when needed. There was a time when one of his friends made a less than flattering comment about Mina. Moments later, Rehan was on him like a bull in a china shop and the teachers had to drag him off the poor boy. That friendship was never repaired and Rehan was suspended from school. She was curious if, given the opportunity, he would defend her in the same way now they were grown up.

"If I didn't have Dan, I don't know what I would do with myself!"

Frankie said, "Is Justin okay with you spending so much time in another man's company?"

Before she could answer, Frankie was setting the drinks on the coffee table and had taken a seat next to Justin on the sofa. Mina suddenly began to feel like her every move was going to be scrutinised. As she reached for her tea, Mina decided to get out of here as quickly as possible: she hadn't come here to be made to feel like a cheat.

"What do you think? Mina?"

"Sorry, what did you say?"

"I was just telling my brother that I could get used to being looked after like this. I might have to relocate and live with him." Frankie disguised her true meaning behind a sly smile. "I can imagine it...you, me, Justin...and Dan."

Justin frowned and said, "Dan?"

Mina thought, *surely he'll see what Frankie's trying to do.* She was utterly confused by Frankie's behaviour: she had been pleasant, gone out of her way to be hospitable, when they first met. So, either she had been faking geniality, or she had misconstrued something Justin had told her.

"Come on, Justin. When you're not around, it's Dan who looks after Mina, so he deserves to be as big a part of our family as she does." Frankie took up her mug of tea and, without looking at Mina, said, "Don't you think so, Mina?"

"I think I should go." She took her mug to the kitchen and washed it. "Good night, Frankie."

"Good night, Mina. Let's have lunch before I go back to Birmingham."

Out in the corridor Justin reached for Mina's arm. "Hey. What's going on?"

She glanced behind him at the open door to his apartment. He frowned and closed it.

"What have you told Frankie about Dan?"

Justin frowned again. "I told her that he's a good friend to you and I know that he'll look after you when I'm away." He took both of her hands in his and searched her eyes. "Did Frankie say something to you?"

Mina sighed. "You said you had to talk to me."

"I do, but I was hoping we'd be sitting down together."

She shook her head. "I'm not going back in."

"Okay. We'll meet tomorrow. I'll pick you up at twelve and we can spend the whole afternoon together." He leant forward and kissed her once on the lips. She pressed the button to call the lift and then held onto Justin until it arrived.

"Francesca, what did you say to Mina?" He stood in the living room with his arms folded across his chest. "You said something to upset her. What was it?"

Frankie moved slowly to the edge of the sofa and placed her mug on the table. "I asked a harmless question."

Justin didn't move or speak. He kept his eyes fixed on Frankie.

"All I asked was if you were okay with her spending so much time with this Dan, character."

"I can answer that for you. Yes, I'm okay with that because Dan's her friend."

Frankie shrugged. "Fair enough. But you don't know what happens when you're not around."

He dropped onto the armchair, linking his fingers together. He leaned forward and said, "That's something you should have asked me about."

"Alright. So, you trust Dan, do you?"

He relaxed his shoulders and leant back. "Yes, I trust Dan."

Frankie uttered a low sound but, seeing the sadness on Justin's face said, "I want to be sure that you're not going to be hurt again."

After the split from Eve, Justin had tried to cover his emotional wounds by spending every possible waking moment with Frankie; he would meet her for lunch twice a week; call her every night and even invited himself to stay over. She knew that he was hurting, but he had become a recluse. For six months he avoided his friends and declined all invitations. Instead he chose to mope about Frankie's apartment or immerse himself in work. It was only when Justin was commanded by Alex's mum to attend her retirement party or face her wrath that he finally ventured back into the world.

"I thought you liked Mina."

"I do...and then I worry about her being so much younger than you." She perched herself on the coffee table in front of Justin. She lowered her gaze to meet his and said, "I don't want her thinking that by being with you she can put a tick on her to-do list."

He and Frankie hadn't fallen out with each other for months, so he stood up and went into the kitchen, where he quietly made himself a mug of calming camomile tea. As he let it steep in the boiling water, he tapped his fingers impatiently on the counter top and prepared his response.

Back on the sofa, Justin said "I'm going to talk and I need you to hear me." He knocked back the contents of the mug, as if he were drinking shots in a bar on a Saturday night. "For the first time in years, I'm happy. I've found someone who makes my heart race. Emotionally, she expects nothing but offers everything." He started to pace the room. "Mina doesn't have a to-do list. I have a to-do list. Have you even considered that I might be the one waiting to check something off?" He stopped pacing and gave his sister a cold glare. "I'm ready to settle down, Frankie, and I might just have found the person I can do that with. But here's the thing...I haven't told Mina because I'm worried I'll scare her away. So maybe I'm the untrustworthy one." He picked up his keys and left his apartment.

***

He hadn't assigned himself a destination when he started driving, but wasn't surprised where he had ended up. He had no intention of joining the crowd inside, they would drown out the thoughts washing around his mind. He was content with the bench a few feet from the restaurant.

He scrolled the photo gallery on his phone until he found what he was looking for. There were only ever a handful of times when he had felt the need to look at it. It was far better than folding up the original only to squeeze it into a trouser pocket, or worse, misplace it; his mum and dad, taken two years before their death. *I wish one of you were here so you could tell Frankie to stop her nonsense.*

Before she moved out of their family home, Frankie had a habit of talking older than she was. She would get annoyed when Justin refused to do what she told him and then would call him names. The outcome depended on which parent was in the room at the time; dad would scold her but, if their mother was there, Frankie would feel her before she heard her. He supposed he could reach out to his aunts and uncles, but they didn't know him the way his parents did, and what he truly craved was their reassurance and unconditional acceptance of his life choices. *You would both approve of Mina. She makes me happy and I know that's all you've ever wanted for me.*

In spite of his melancholy, he laughed, and then grimaced, as he considered what might have happened if his mother had got hold of Eve. It was bad enough when Frankie dared to bring a male friend home, only to have him run out of the house, followed by a barrage of the sort of insults only a West Indian mother could hurl.

He fidgeted in his seat and looked behind him at the lights, and sounds, emanating from the restaurant. He had wallowed in sorrow for long enough and the company of strangers might help him forget. He collected his jacket from the car and put his phone in his pocket, after switching it to silent. He found a seat at the bar and ordered a bottle of his favourite cider. Looking around, the restaurant wasn't as busy as he had expected it to be. As the ice-cold cider hit the back of his throat, the world seemed not so bad. Someone called his name out and Justin turned around to see who it was. There were hands waving from a small group of people. He tried to get a good look at them before approaching; he didn't fancy bumping into Dan but fortunately he wasn't among them so Justin made his way over to join them. The voice who'd called belonged to a friend of James.

"Charlene! Long-time no see!"

She got up to hug him. "What are you doing here?" She looked curiously behind him. "Alone?"

He nodded. Charlene grabbed a chair from the adjacent table and Justin sat down and she introduced him to her friends. He asked the obvious question. "What brings you to this neck of the woods?"

"Work."

"I know work and this doesn't look like work."

"Damn it." She placed a finger over his mouth and said, "Don't tell my boss or he'll have me back in Liverpool before I've finished enjoying myself."

Justin floated in and out of the conversations, joining in when he felt he could add something, or when Charlene looked to him for an opinion. Sometime later, one of the friends declared it was time for them to get back to the hotel. They said goodbye to Justin; a handshake here and a hug there. Before she walked away, Charlene took a pen from her bag and wrote on a piece of paper. She opened Justin's hand and placed the note in it. She said, "Don't be a stranger" and planted a kiss on his mouth before scurrying to catch up with her friends.

Charlene and Tony

Mina spent her Friday afternoon with Justin, James and Dan, trying not to fall asleep in the car for fear of revealing her secret snoring. The men discussed sport, fashion, movies and music at volumes ranging from *sitting twelve inches away* soft, to *chanting at a football match* deafening, particularly when one of them praised a particular song, sports personality or actor the others disagreed on. She joined in occasionally, but it felt awkward; as though she should be waiting for authorisation before involving herself. She found it bizarre and blamed James' presence; she had never experienced problems in maintaining conversations with Justin or Dan. Her eyes began to flutter, she slipped her shoes off, spread her coat over herself and dozed until she felt the car stop: Justin had pulled into a motorway service station. The men groaned and stretched, the same way her dad and uncles did standing up after long periods of sitting on the floor. Mina walked arm in arm with Justin, behind Dan and James, making the most of being close again.

Before she came out of the toilets, Mina bought one of those tiny, not quite edible tooth brushes, a habit she had had ever since Anisa had become fascinated with them and had insisted on buying one at every service station they stopped at: it was the only thing their parents would spend money on; they always brought enough food for the journey so there was no justification in spending twice the price on something that, ordinarily, would cost far less from the local shop.

They ordered paninis, toasted sandwiches, coffee, tea and hot chocolate.

"Are you sure we'll get back tonight?" Mina asked.

Justin and James looked at each other, both chomping mouthfuls of food. James swallowed first and said, "Yeah, defo. The table's booked for six o'clock, a couple of drinks after and then we're on the way back."

"If, for some reason we don't leave until later, I'm happy to drop you in Birmingham."

"If I had my suitcase with me, and if I hadn't already bought my ticket, that would have been a great idea." Mina was booked on the ten-thirty Bristol to Birmingham train the following morning.

Food and drink finished, they cleared the table and hunkered down for the remainder of the journey. Ninety minutes later they drove past a sign welcoming them to Liverpool. It didn't look much different to Birmingham and there wouldn't be any time to discover anything to the contrary. The men had become silent and Mina's was deep in thought about her family.

She remembered secretly jumping for joy when her mum told her they were going to throw a party for her. It meant they still thinking about her; hadn't abandoned her just because she was out of sight. She had been given no hint though as to the number of people coming or the venue, so she had to remind herself to expect the unexpected. That's when she began to think the worst. *Is the party going to be just her siblings and parents? Is it a simple meal in their favourite restaurant? Or is it a rishtaa to meet a potential husband chosen by her parents disguised as a twenty-first birthday party?* She was torturing herself and had to find out more. She took out her mobile phone.

"Assalam Wailakum," said the voice on the other end.

"Hi, Anisa."

"Mina, baaji! How are you!"

"I'm excited for tomorrow!"

"I know. You're going to love it!"

"Anisa, who's gonna be there?"

"I can't tell you. Mum will shout at me if she finds out I told you."

Mina rolled her eyes, but persevered. "She doesn't have to find out. I won't tell her anything."

There was a long pause.

"I'll tell you one thing...there will be lots of people there."

Mina was disappointed, but it wasn't her sister's fault. "Thanks, Anisa. I'll see you tomorrow."

"Bye, Mina baaji!"

She was still as clueless as before.

"That's very sly, trying to get information out of your little sister."

"Don't worry about what's going on back here. You keep your focus on the road."

"I'd prefer to be back there with you."

She'd have preferred that too, but he had offered to drive first, which meant they could spend the journey back together. He was probably hoping she would fall asleep leaning on him and he could play the role he loved so much, protector, comfort giver, pillow.

"Remind me again why we are travelling nearly four hundred miles in one night?"

"Four hundred?"

"There and back."

"We're going to celebrate James' friend's promotion."

"What's the friend's name?"

"I told you already."

"I know, but I can't remember."

She could see Justin shaking his head.

"I should call you goldfish! Her name is Charlene. And we're here."

Justin parked the car on the drive of a double-fronted Victorian palace - there was no other word for it. Now Mina understood why they had been offered a place to relax and change into their evening gear; this place could house twenty extra guests, never mind the four of them.

They were greeted by a tall, dark skinned woman. Her hair was thick with tight curls and it bounced as she moved. Mina looked around hoping there was a partner or husband about to follow behind and be introduced. They all made their way into the entrance hall and put their cases down.

"James, how are you!" Charlene hugged James who in turn introduced Dan. Then Charlene went straight to Justin. There was no hug but a double cheek kiss on which, to Mina, she seemed to linger a fraction too long.

"This is my girlfriend, Mina." Justin thought it was time to start introducing her officially as his partner, but Mina hadn't given the matter any thought till now. After all, they'd already introduced each other to all the people who needed to know.

"How sweet." Charlene's eyes assessed her from top to toe. "Welcome, Mina." She turned to address them all. "Leave your cases here and come through to the kitchen for a drink. You must all be exhausted."

Dan pulled Mina back. They both watched Charlene link her arm in Justin's as they were left behind. "Bloody hell! Tell me you saw what I saw!"

"Yes, Dan. I saw it." She pushed him forward and said, "Hurry up, I can't let her be alone with Justin for any length of time."

"You need to step up your game, Mina!"

"Shut up and move!"

James had taken a seat at the table, and Justin was still being manhandled by Charlene who was stroking his arm. Mina felt the sudden urge to throw up. *Be brave* she thought. *He's mine after all*. She came up behind Justin and reached up to stroke his cheek. He promptly brought her hand up to his lips and kissed it.

Charlene's attention switched to fixing drinks for everyone and now seemed to be avoiding eye contact with either of them. Mina's confidence soared. She snuggled in to Justin. She had to ward off Charlene, make her realise Justin was unavailable, even if this meant leaping out of her comfort zone.

The interior of the house proved incredible and the garden enormous; it could be accessed either through the kitchen or the conservatory. A decked area with seating for eight led down onto an immaculate lawn surrounded by flower beds and in the middle was a permanent gazebo providing shelter from whatever the British weather might have in store. *Charlene must have a gardener*, Mina thought, *I can't imagine she'd risk jeopardising her pristine manicure for the sake of a few flowers*.

"Mina!" Dan shouted. "Come on. Quick." When Mina reached him, Dan warned her, "Charlene is showing us the upstairs room where we can change."

"Calm down. I'm sure it's just a bedroom."

"Maybe it is." Dan started walking backwards, stretching his arm above his head. "But she's leading Justin up there now and anything can happen in a few minutes."

Mina hurried past Dan, giving him a shove. When they both arrived upstairs, slightly out of breath, Justin and James were looking at a bedroom the size of Mina's family living room in Birmingham. Charlene forced a smile as she walked past Mina and back downstairs.

"Is this the master bedroom?" said Mina.

James shook his head and said, "No, it's one of the guest rooms. Great, isn't it?"

"Well, it's kind of like a person wearing a size eight shoe when really they should be wearing a size four." She was too busy inspecting the decorative features to notice the look James and Justin were giving each other.

"That has to be the strangest analogy I've ever heard."

"Well excuse me Mr Hargreaves. I didn't realise you knew all there was to know about analogies."

"I have to agree with Justin on this one. That's a weird way of describing something that's too big." Dan's voice drifted out from behind a door. "I mean why would anyone ever wear shoes that are four sizes too big?"

"Exactly!"

"I'd love to debate this topic, but I'm shattered." Justin opened his case. "If it's alright with you, I'm going to try and get some sleep before we go to dinner."

"Right, come on Dan, Mina. Let's leave Justin in peace." James ushered them out like a farmer's dog rounding up sheep.

Walking downstairs, argumentative voices floated up to them. Charlene had another guest. They found him sitting at the table, scratching his head and her standing, arms crossed with her back to them.

"Tony! Long-time no see!"

Tony stood to shake James' hand. "I know. Work's been manic! With the senior manager on leave, I've had to step up." Tony looked past James. "Who've you got with you?"

James motioned Mina to step forward. "Tony, this is Mina. Mina, this is Tony, Charlene's husband." At that moment, Charlene turned and the two women locked eyes. Things were starting to add up for Mina.

***

As they pulled up in front of the restaurant, Mina felt underdressed and out of place. It looked unlike anywhere she had eaten before. Inside, one look at the amount of cutlery at each place setting confirmed her initial feeling. She squeezed Justin's hand and said, "Make sure you sit next to me. I might need to nudge you to make sure I'm using the right fork."

Dan walked closely behind them and whispered, "Do either of you know why there's so much cutlery?"

They both laughed. Without turning, Mina said, "Just sit on the other side of me; I'll tell you what's what."

They were shown to a round table large enough for ten people. They were the first to arrive, avoiding any awkward scrabbling for somewhere to sit without being separated from her cutlery etiquette partner. They had barely opened the menu when a waiter came to take their drinks order.

Five minutes later Charlene and Tony arrived, looking as sombre as if the event was a funeral until they spotted their guests and pasted smiles on their faces. Charlene went straight over to one of the waiters and moments later, he was adding another place setting to the table. Over the next ten minutes the rest of the party arrived and dinner began.

When the starters were served, Dan muttered under his breath, "Am I supposed to eat this or frame it?" The food looked like it had been made for one of Mina's favourite cookery shows, *MasterChef*. She imagined contestants, split into groups, each making a separate course, fighting to make it through to the next round, or face elimination. Drawing her plate closer, she wondered why she couldn't spot any judges sampling the creation. Her vegetable starter was dainty, multi-layered, drizzled with sauces in a variety of colours and covered only a fraction of the plate.

"So where do I start?"

Justin picked up the fork furthest from the plate. "This one for the starter."

Mina relayed the message to Dan, on her left. Five miniscule forkfuls later, it was gone.

Waiting for the others to finish, Mina glanced up to see Charlene watching Tony converse with her friends. She seemed to stab her fork into her food with unnecessary force. All was not well in that household and a part of Mina hoped to find out why. Maybe it would explain Charlene's heavy flirting with Justin. Then she wondered why Justin hadn't done more to stop Charlene. As a man of the world surely he was aware of Charlene's attempt to get into his pants? Mina added that to her mental list of things to raise before the journey home.

With the plates cleared, conversation resumed.

"How was that?"

"I'm still hungry."

Justin smiled his *Mina you have so much to learn* smile. She didn't mind because she knew it was true. She hoped the day would come when she could teach him a thing or two and develop her own version of that smile.

"How long have you known Charlene?"

"As long as I've known James. Why?"

"No reason." She lied. "Just curious."

The waiters came back with the next course. There had been no improvement on portion size: maybe the chefs were working to a tight budget. She had learnt all about budgeting since leaving home where her parents provided everything needed without expecting a penny back. At least her hotel employment came with free and substantial meals. Her accommodation, on the other hand, was beginning to make her feel claustrophobic, especially compared to Justin's apartment or Dan's house.

"I never asked you to come!" Raised voices came from across the table. Everyone looked up.

"I had no idea I needed to wait for a formal invitation to celebrate my wife's promotion," Tony responded.

"Well, perhaps I wanted one evening where I'm the centre of attention!"

"Dear, you are always the centre of attention."

Mina thought it was probably a good thing Tony and Charlene weren't sitting beside each other. She could picture Tony's agonised face with a fork driven into his thigh, courtesy of his loving wife.

The whole table was stunned into silence. There was no comeback from Charlene, but she'd stopped eating and was glaring at her husband.

Dan leant in toward Mina. "I didn't know there was a show with the meal."

"I knew something was wrong. I sensed it as soon as they walked in."

Dan laid his cutlery down and held his palm up. "Tell me my future, Lady Mina. What does the man of my dreams look like?"

Mina gently took his hand and said, "Let me see, Daniel." She traced her fingers along the deepest of the lines etched in his skin. "Oh, yes. I can tell you...he doesn't look as good as mine!"

Dan pulled his hand away and said, "That's mean. I want a refund."

Mina put her arm around him. "I'm glad you're here."

A hand settled on her thigh. "What about me?"

She looked round at Justin and said, "I'm glad you're here too."

His hand moved slowly down her leg and back up again. "Are you sure about that?" A cheeky smile spread across his face. "If only there was something you could do to make me believe you."

She knew what he wanted her to do, but could feel Charlene's eyes boring into her. He would have to wait until they weren't surrounded by other people. Instead, she reciprocated, placing her hand on his thigh. "You're just gonna have to take my word for it."

Their moment was interrupted by Tony. "How long have you two been together?"

They both looked across the table, unsure if he actually wanted to know.

"Come on, tell us." He waved his fork around like some sort of magician doing a trick.

"Almost two months," said Justin.

Tony's eyes widened with surprise. He turned to Charlene. "Honey, do you remember our first few months?" He knocked back the whisky in his glass. "Every minute we were alone, we were ripping each other's clothes off. Those were good times."

Charlene rolled her eyes.

Tony looked at Mina and said, "Is he a good lover?"

Justin shot out of his seat and slammed his hands down on the table, making everything shake. "That's none of your Goddamn business."

James stood too, encouraging him to sit back down. Justin searched for Mina's hand and held it tight. "Are you okay?"

She stroked his arm and nodded, although she was a little shaken by the sudden hint of violence in the air.

Justin noticed Charlene trying to get his attention. "I'm sorry Justin." She was barely audible; he had to read her lips.

"I always knew you had a thing for this man here." Tony's voice still angry.

Charlene put her head in her hands. "Just shut up, Tony. You're embarrassing yourself!"

He ignored her protest. "What's your name? Justin?" Tony pointed at Charlene sneering horribly. "She won't admit it, but let me tell you, she'd have you right here on this table if she could!"

Justin swallowed hard, downed the rest of his drink and stood up. He said, "We're leaving." James nodded. Mina and Dan didn't have to be asked.

Before they left, James was the only one who gave Charlene a hug and wished her all the best in her new job.

Outside, Justin breathed deeply, letting his anger pass. "I'm sorry, James. If he'd carried on, I'd have punched him."

James simply reassured him he'd done the right thing. They all got in the car and Justin started the engine.

"Hey, guys." Dan called out. "Is anyone still hungry?" He was pointing down the road to a fast food shop. They all looked at each other and laughed. Once there, their junk food seemed well-deserved after what they'd been through in the restaurant.

"Did you know they were having problems?" Mina addressed the question to James.

"Not a clue. To be honest I was surprised to be invited!"

The three of them looked straight at Justin, which made him stop eating. "What? You think you're here because of me?"

She had to find out what he was thinking. "How do you feel knowing she had a crush on you?"

"What? No, she didn't!"

"Justin, she was flirting with you from the minute she set eyes on you. Tell him Dan."

Dan nodded in agreement.

"It was harmless."

"No, it wasn't. You heard what her husband said."

"He was drunk, Mina." Justin reached to touch her hand but she pulled away.

"Maybe he was, but she apologised to you, not me. She didn't care if I was upset."

James nodded to Dan. "Let's leave these two and get some fresh air."

"Mina, I never had any intention of starting anything with Charlene." He put his hands on the table.

"Maybe not, but she did." Mina poked at her chips. "I don't even want to think about what might have happened if I wasn't here."

"It sounds like you're saying you don't trust me."

She couldn't bring herself to meet his gaze. How she chose to respond could make the next few hours agonizing for both of them. She had nowhere to escape to; she was two hundred miles away from her pokey hotel room, and from the soothing ebb and flow of the evening tide.

"I don't know what I'm saying...maybe seeing her in her perfect home with her perfect hair and perfect skin just made me wonder."

"Wonder what, Mina?"

She couldn't get the words out through her tears. Justin went to her side and put his arms around her. She cried into his shirt and he said, "She's not perfect. We all saw that today. She's got nothing on you, Mina Azad."

The tears ceased and, when she looked at his shirt, she saw the large damp patch she had created. He held Mina's hands in his and kissed them. "I think I might be falling for you...even with your red eyes and runny nose." He laughed and handed her a napkin.

She took the offering and punched him in the arm.

He took her hands in his again. "There's no one I'd rather be with than you, right here, right now." He leant forward and kissed her lips. They walked out of the fast food shop, hand in hand, leaving the smell of oil and vinegar behind.

James was waiting outside, looking worried. "I've got bad news."

"Great. What now?"

James opened the boot of his car. The four of them stood in silence, looking into the empty space then at each other as it dawned on them.

"Oh no!" Mina groaned. "Please don't make me go back there!"

"We don't have a choice," said James. "We've left our cases at Charlene's."

"I'm not going in there." Justin pointed in the direction of the restaurant where the party had been. "None of us should go in there."

"I'll just call Charlene, tell her we need to get our cases and we'll meet her at the house." This was definitely a preferable option. They all watched James pace the pavement with his phone to his ear.

"She's already gone home. She's expecting us."

When they arrived at Charlene's, the house looked even grander than in daylight, lit by an array of spotlights and miniature lampposts dotted along the driveway. James rang the bell and Charlene opened the door almost immediately.

Once inside, Charlene said, "I don't suppose any of you would like to join me for a final drink?"

James said, "We should just get our things. It's a long drive back. Thanks for the offer though." They collected their cases in silence.

"I'll meet you in the car," said Mina, "I need to use the bathroom."

James gave Charlene another hug. "Good luck. It'll work out."

"Drive safe, James." She waited for them to turn away. "Justin, wait."

Justin sighed and faced her again.

"I'm truly sorry for what happened."

"It's not me you should be apologising to." He turned and followed the others out to the car.

Mina dried her hands on one of the soft guest towels and used some of the sweet-smelling hand lotion beside the sink. She walked out of the en-suite, massaging her hands, shaking her head at how an unassuming dinner party with strangers could become such a scriptwriter's dream.

"Mina, can I talk to you?"

She thought about putting her case down on the polished hardwood floor but didn't. She just waited for Charlene to say something more.

"You're lucky to have a man like Justin. When he introduced you as his girlfriend, do you know what I thought?"

Mina didn't respond. Her insides were twisted up in knots.

"I thought...that should be me on his arm, not some immature, little Indian girl who knows nothing about how to treat a strong, successful black man." Charlene's face was inches away from Mina's. "He needs a woman, an independent, successful, beautiful, black woman." She stroked the banister like it was a pet, and said, "This is all mine. What have you got? What could you possibly offer a man like Justin?"

Mina was regretting her last-minute bathroom break. *What does being black have to do with making Justin happy?* In all the moments they shared, race had never been a point of contention. There was no doubt it could be an issue on her side, but to discover the potential conflict it might have in Justin's life, was an unwelcome revelation. She asked herself whether any of his friends were of the same opinion. She didn't have the tools in her arsenal to do battle with Charlene, but she couldn't just stand here like a muppet and be insulted. She started toward the door.

"We shared a moment, Justin and I. A kiss I'll never forget."

Mina dropped her case and strode up to Charlene. "I'll tell you what I've got...self-respect." She felt her heart trying to beat its way out of her chest. "You can keep your fake life and your messed-up marriage. Now if you don't mind, Justin and I are going to share the back seat of a car for the next few hours while you sit in this big house all alone."

She marched out the door with her case. As soon as she closed the car door, her pent-up anxiety came out in tears.

"Mina, what happened?"

Through the sobs, Mina managed to say, "She is one nasty person."

Justin grabbed the door handle to let himself out. "I'm gonna give her a piece of my mind."

Mina grabbed his arm. "No, don't." She wiped her tears away for the second time that evening. "Let's just go. Please."

He released the handle and Mina cuddled into him. With his arms around her, Justin calmed down and James drove away.

None of them said a word. Mina closed her eyes and took comfort in the gentle caress of Justin's fingers on her skin, his steady breathing on her neck. If she could remember anything remotely positive from meeting Charlene, it would be that she had somehow found the confidence to assert herself. She had cried afterwards, but still felt proud for saying exactly what she thought.

A little later and Charlene's last words were echoing in her mind. *When did they share that moment? Why didn't Justin mention anything? Should I ask him about it?* The thoughts spun around in her head. *He told me he was falling for me. He wouldn't kiss someone else if he has feelings for me, would he?* Pushing every other thought away, she drew Justin into a passionate clinch. She relaxed her whole body, didn't flinch when he slid his hand down the back of her thigh. When they finally came up for air, she looked into his eyes, her hand on his chest feeling the strength of his heartbeat, settling her insecurity.

When James pulled into a motorway service station, Mina opted to stay in the car. The opened doors let out the heat so she covered herself with her jacket, and tried to doze. Charlene's words bounced in and out of her troubled mind. *What do I have to offer Justin?* Charlene had accumulated wealth, knowledge, property...but the attitude of a stinky sock! Mina had none of those things. She didn't know if any of them were important to Justin; there had never been any reason to ponder the question before.

Since deciding to move to Weston she had been on a journey of self-discovery. Romance hadn't been on her agenda, not even under the heading *Any Other Business*. She had been ready to focus only on her needs. Now, she was sharing her time, her space, her attention with another person. There had never been any doubt in her mind that was all he wanted – until now.

An indraft of cold air made her shiver. Justin climbed into the back seat and offered her a takeaway cup.

"What's this?"

"Steaming hot chocolate, just for you."

Mina took the cup. Justin was good to her, patient and thoughtful. He touched her arm. "Are you alright?" He sounded concerned.

Her head felt like it was going to explode, but she nodded and forced a smile. For the first time in eight weeks, she wanted to be in her own bed, in the home she had grown up in, with the people she knew better than anyone else. She closed her eyes and silently cried.

Dan was dropped off first. James and Justin said goodbye in the car, but Mina got out for a hug. He said, "Enjoy your party. Call me if you need to talk. Okay?"

"Yes." She sighed and got back into the car.

Mina's hotel was the next destination. She touched James' shoulder and said, "Thanks, James."

"You're welcome. Sorry your night turned out the way it did."

Mina collected her case from the boot. She said to Justin, who had joined her, "I'm going to make my own way to Temple Meads in the morning, if that's alright."

"I was looking forward to taking you, but I understand." He kissed her forehead and watched her disappear inside.

"How is she?"

Justin shook his head. "I've never seen her so upset. "At least she'll be with her family tomorrow which should take her mind off tonight."

"I have to ask, what the hell was going on with you and Charlene?"

He rolled his eyes and said, "Not you as well!"

"Sorry. I just thought if you had something you wanted to say, now would be a good time."

There was no doubt in his mind that Charlene was the type of woman Frankie could picture him with. Both women were zealous and powerful. Charlene's actions from their previous meeting had left him in no doubt of her attraction to him; knowing that, why did he choose to join James in Liverpool? It had been a poorly thought out decision that had, badly, affected the woman he was falling for. The harder he thought about it, the more he had to admit he'd been completely selfish, secretly enjoying the ego boost Charlene's flirting had given him. Only now did he recall how he had felt on discovering Eve's betrayals. *I need to make things right with Mina, reassure her that she's the only one I want in my life.* Not wanting to wait for that to happen, he took out his phone and sent her a text message. It read, *I miss you already. I'll be counting down the hours until you're back. J.*

The car stopped outside the apartment block to let Justin out. He was about to walk away when James called out. "Hey, I almost forgot. When are you making the announcement about the move to the new site?"

Justin froze. He had forgotten all about it! His shoulders slumped. The timing couldn't be worse. He turned back. "Probably by Wednesday." He went in thinking how on earth to reassure Mina about his commitment to her if he was considering moving back to Birmingham.

Surprise!

Mina's dad called just as she disembarked at New Street Station; he had insisted on picking her up and was unusually thrilled to do so. She walked out and saw a hand frantically waving. She squinted through the sunshine and spotted her dad. He popped open the boot of his car and greeted Mina with a bear hug before taking her cases. She stood, gobsmacked, beside the car as her dad opened the car door and waited for her to get in.

"Quickly, Mina beti! We have a busy day!" He ushered her toward the car.

She said, "Are you okay?"

He slapped her back and said, "Of course I am. I am just happy that you are celebrating your birthday with your family, like we always used to. Now hurry up."

Although her dad's behaviour unsettled her, it would make this car journey considerably less stressful than last night's.

She had eventually drifted off to sleep staring into the night sky through the undrawn curtains, wondering if she was being punished for a hurt she had caused someone at some time in her life. It was only when she woke with a pounding headache that she had noticed the text from Justin and sent a short reply. She had only managed to eat a bowl of cereal and some fruit before detouring to the pharmacy to buy some paracetamol and taking the taxi into Bristol.

Her dad was listening to his normal radio station, tapping his fingers on the steering wheel. She shook her head and smiled to herself, glad to see him in such a good mood but puzzled as to the reason. The last time she remembered him being like this was a double celebration a few years ago: Rehan's graduation from university and his upcoming wedding.

Mina was expecting a great big hullaballoo to welcome her home, but the house was empty. Seeing her confusion, her dad said, "Your mother has been asked to cater a last-minute lunch booking, but don't worry. She will be back soon."

"What about Anisa?"

"She stayed at your brother's house last night."

"Oh. If I knew no one was going to be here, I'd have caught a later train."

"So, who am I then?"

"Sorry, dad."

"I forgive you because it's your birthday."

She put her cases in her old bedroom and had lunch with her dad. His exuberance dialled down but he kept checking his phone every few minutes. After lunch, she washed up, excused herself and went up to her bedroom to relax.

She flopped onto the bed and sighed, disappointed that the fanfare she had expected hadn't happened. Memories of this very spot, just over two months ago, came flooding back: it was here she had first discovered Justin's name, oblivious to the impact he was going to have on her life. Keeping her two lives distant from each other should have been effortless because of the physical distance but Tania had almost put a premature stop to that. They had not been in touch since, a lifelong friendship thwarted by jealousy and secrets.

She heard footsteps and then a knock at the bedroom door. "Can I come in?"

It was her mum. She jumped off the bed and swung the door open. "Hi mum!"

"Happy birthday, beti!" Her mum kissed her forehead. "Let me look at you. Twenty-one today! You have grown up too fast." She held her hands and her smile became a grin.

"Why're you looking at me like that?"

"Like what?!"

"Like you know something I don't'."

Her mum shook her head, walking out the door and then shouting back over her shoulder, "That's because I do!"

A few hours later they were dressed up and on their way to a mystery location. She noticed her parents looking at each other whenever they stopped at traffic lights, sharing information without uttering a single word. Worry began to creep in: *there's something they're keeping from me*; she knew they were throwing a party for her and Anisa had let slip that there would be a lot of people there. *What was it?*

They arrived at a banqueting hall adorned with balloons and an enormous banner reading *Happy 21st Birthday Mina*. As soon as she stepped into the main room, she was greeted by an ear-shattering round of applause and cheers. The entire room, which she reckoned could hold two hundred people, was swarming with people, most of whom she barely knew. She smiled as she was escorted to the front of the room to be seated at a large round table.

Anisa rushed over to her sister and squeezed her tight. "You're here! Happy birthday, Mina baaji!"

"Thanks, Anisa. You were serious when you said there'd be loads of people."

Rehan tapped Anisa's shoulder. "I'd like to give my twenty-one-year-old little sister a hug, if you don't mind!"

It became a group hug for all three of them. "It's so good to be home," said Mina and squeezed a little tighter.

"Look at you all! I'm so happy right now." Their mum joined them. "Come Anisa, I need your help with something."

Mina turned to her brother. "Who are all these people?" He simply shrugged. "This is more like a wedding than a birthday party."

Mina saw her sister-in-law on the other side of the table and went to greet her. Then there was a tap on her shoulder and she was interrupted by one of her aunts and uncles, who were rapidly joined by other family members. Mina found herself holding ten envelopes in her hand. Sitting back down, she poured herself a glass of mango juice asking her brother, "Do you know what's wrong with dad? He's been acting seriously weird."

"It must be old age."

Mina disagreed, but didn't pursue the matter. She was opening the envelopes and each one contained cash. She supposed this was the silver lining to celebrating with so many people.

The unmistakable aromas of perfectly prepared Indian food wafted by her as huge platters were placed on her table. These were soon followed by a selection of drinks. There had been no recent opportunities for her to cook her own meals due to her living arrangements in the hotel so she desperately craved home cooking. The last time she had visited home she'd eaten too much and now she would probably eat even more heartily.

Soon the rest of the family sat down to eat with her, with three other people she assumed were mum, dad and son, but they weren't introduced. Whenever she looked up from her food, her parents were talking to their counterparts and nodding and looking in her direction, before turning to look at their son. For a moment she thought they were acknowledging someone behind her, so she turned around to check but everyone was engrossed in their food.

She leant back in her chair, reached behind her sister-in-law and tapped her brother's shoulder. "Who are they?" She used her head to gesture in the direction of the unintroduced family.

He said, "You'll find out soon enough," and went back to eating.

Mina frowned and mumbled, *why can't he just give me a straight answer?* She let the matter of the unknowns go as she tucked into her second helping of food. A few minutes later she took her phone out of her bejewelled handbag to check for any contact from Justin. There wasn't any.

"Hi Mina." Her cousin Rukhsana called, gesturing to get up. She excused herself from the table and headed toward her cousin. Rukhsana grabbed her hand and led her to the ladies' room. Once in there, she shrieked and jumped up and down like a sugar filled toddler. "Congratulations! I'm so jealous!"

Mina frowned. "Jealous of what, crazy girl?"

"You and Riaz, you idiot! He's seriously cute! I wish I was engaged to him!" Rukhsana checked her make up in the mirror. "So, when's the big day?"

Mina stopped brushing her hair and stared at her cousin's reflection. The atmosphere, the lack of straight answers from Rehan, her dad's behaviour: it was all adding up to something. "I'm confused. Everyone's confusing me today."

Rukhsana shook her head. "You must be spending too much time in the sun. Let me ask you again."

"Yes, please." She finished washing her hands.

Rukhsana applied a coat of mascara to her eyelashes, batted them a few times and asked. "When are you and Riaz getting married?"

Mina stared at her cousin blankly. She felt frozen to the ground beneath her, unable to step forward and shake her cousin to get answers out of her, but urgently wanting to. More female members of the family entered the ladies' room and Mina's back was rubbed, her hands were squeezed and she was congratulated on finding such a good boy to marry. Mina was stunned. Rukhsana waved her hands in front of Mina's face. "Hello? Is anybody in there?"

Mina grabbed her arm, her eyes wide with anger. "What the hell is going on here? Tell me everything you know."

***

"Did you see where Mina went?" Rehan asked his wife.

"To the toilet with Rukhsana." She looked at her watch. "But that was fifteen minutes ago."

Just then Rukhsana rushed out of the toilets, and his hope of keeping things calm abruptly faded. He held back and waited anxiously for his sister to come out. The door was thrown open, the handle hitting the wall behind with enough impact to make a dent.

"Mina!"

"Leave me alone."

"Mina wait!" He followed her as she stormed off into the car park.

"Mina! Where are you going?"

"Leave me the hell alone!"

She slowed and finally stopped walking. He could see she was breathing heavily by the movement of her shoulders. He knew she had figured out what was going on. He stood in front of her for a few seconds, the sound of the passing traffic the only thing between them. He had advised his parents not to surprise Mina this way but they had felt it was the only way of getting her here. He felt bad and wasn't sure what to do next.

Her head lowered, she said, "Take me home."

He had met Riaz on a number of occasions and was sure Mina would get on with him. "Just come back inside and..."

"No!" She raised her head. Her voice was slow, exhausted. "You go in, pack some food for me and then take me home."

He smirked a little; at least she still had her appetite.

"Here," he handed her his keys. "Wait in the car for me." He went straight to the kitchen with a plan; he would pack up something for Mina to eat and send Riaz out to talk to her; give them some time alone. Out of earshot of the chosen groom's parents he told him what had happened.

"Nah, mate. I don't think that's a good idea. She hates me."

"She doesn't know you. Talk to her. You know how to talk to women, right?"

"Yeah, but she doesn't want to talk to me."

"Riaz, honestly mate." Rehan shook him gently. "How many women have you talked to who didn't want you to talk to them?" They both laughed at the thought and Riaz took the food and went to talk to Mina.

Mina found solace safely confined in her brother's car. She had been chewing at her bottom lip for ten minutes now, still furious at what her entire family had been plotting. Her milestone birthday was ruined. They were supposed to be adding to the fun and excitement, not using it as an excuse to fulfil a devious takeover of her life. People could be so selfish. Justin had been attentive enough to do something he knew, or hoped, she would enjoy. Their night in Liverpool had distracted her from that and now she remained unsure of her feelings. She had hoped to leave Birmingham tomorrow with a new energy. Instead, she felt like one of those bunnies on the advert for batteries: she was the bunnies whose batteries needed replacing.

"Did mum and dad ask about me?" she said as someone slid into the driver's seat.

The car door closed. "My mum and dad have asked a lot about you."

Mina's head shot up. The voice didn't belong to her brother but he was carrying food and she understood what Rehan had done. "I told him this was a bad idea." He handed Mina the napkin-wrapped package.

"At least I can agree with you on that."

They both stared out at the city in front of them, neither knowing what to say.

Riaz eventually broke the silence. "There are a lot of people here."

Mina huffed. "I should have known something was going on. Even Rehan didn't have so many people at his twenty first."

Riaz tapped his fingers on the steering wheel, which reminded Mina of her dad's behaviour driving home after picking her up from the station.

"Uh, and my dad. He drove me home, he lied to me."

"I hate to intrude on your pity party, but I'm also involved in all this."

Mina gave him a sideways glance. Riaz smoothed out his trousers. They both stared out of their respective windows. He cleared his throat and said, "Let's get out of here." He picked up the keys Mina had left on the dashboard and started the engine.

"What are you doing? I don't want to go anywhere with you!"

Riaz ignored her protest and drove out of the packed car park, leaving their families behind.

"Rehan will be so mad at you!"

"He'll get over it."

Riaz stopped the car a few minutes away, outside a well-known pizza place. "This is the only way I can think of to get you to talk to me."

Arms crossed and still pouting, she said, "I have nothing to say to you."

"Alright." He reached to open his door. "I'll talk and you can listen." Seconds later he opened Mina's door and waited for her to act. She snatched up her bag and stepped out of the car.

Seated at a booth in Pizza Hut, Riaz ordered drinks for both of them. "I'm not the bad guy here. I have things going on in my own life. I don't need to add marriage to that."

Mina was intrigued, but if she got into a conversation she feared her hard exterior shell would crumble. She looked at Riaz sitting opposite her. He was moving the cutlery around the table. He looked up and caught her gaze. He sensed she wanted to say something, and might crack if he continued to talk. "Look, I'm in the last few months of my degree and my parents think I should settle down before I even find a job." He threw his hands in the air. "I haven't told them that I have a girlfriend."

Her surprise was evident and he nodded. They drank in unison, both anxious about what the other might say next. Riaz put his mug down but Mina kept drinking. She was overjoyed: *he has a girlfriend, I've got a boyfriend; the engagement is doomed.* "How long have you been seeing her?"

Mina and Riaz talked for over an hour, sharing stories about their families not understanding the paths they had chosen. He told her about his girlfriend, who was not Muslim, and she told him about Justin. They had now shared secrets very few people knew and vowed never to say a word. They even shook hands on it.

Riaz parked the car in the same place he had driven it away from. Walking back in to face their parents, the guests were eying them suspiciously. He said, "They probably think we've been up to no good!"

One of the on-lookers shouted, "Riaz, your parents have a search party out for you. I told them you can take care of yourself," and raised his eyebrows suggestively.

Riaz rolled his eyes. Mina laughed. "Who's the joker?"

"One of my younger cousins."

"Riaz! Beta! Where have you been?" Both their dads were blocking their way. "Mina! We have been looking everywhere for you!"

"Dad. Mr Azad." He looked at Mina who nodded for him to continue. "Me and Mina wanted to spend some time alone, get to know each other a bit."

Mina's dad said, "I see!"

Riaz put his arm around his father and ushered him inside. "Let's go find mum and we can talk."

"So?" Mina's dad whispered as they followed behind, "He is a good choice, isn't he?"

Their mums were duly located, hovering at opposite ends of the room, and were brought back to the table to discuss the future of their children. Mina and Riaz sat across from each other; the scenario could be managed easier if there was distance between them. Anxious glances passed from one set of parents to the other and then to their children.

"Mum, dad," Mina spoke first, "I'm really upset that you lied to me. I thought I'd be celebrating my birthday with the people I love, but it was all pretend."

Mina's parents lowered their eyes in the face of her accusation.

Riaz said, "Mina and I have had some time to talk about what we both want and neither of us want to get married."

"But..." started Mina's mother, "...We want you to be happy."

"We are happy. It's you and dad who aren't." Mina crossed her arms and looked over at Riaz who urged her on. "Ever since I decided to leave home, you've tried to hold me back. You don't believe I can make a life for myself. Trying to marry me off to Riaz just proves it."

"And I need to focus on completing my degree before I even think about getting married," Riaz said to his parents. "Mina is lovely. She's beautiful, smart and funny." He saw Mina's worry as he drifted off script, but continued anyway. "I'd be honoured to have her as my wife."

At this point both sets of parents were beaming. Mina, however, was biting her bottom lip. Riaz raised his hand and continued, "But that is not going to happen." He grinned at Mina who mouthed a swear word. "I want to have a steady income before I get married and Mina has just moved to a new city. This wouldn't work, even if we wanted it to."

The conversation went back and forth around the table for ten minutes, before silence fell allowing Rehan to intervene. "Keys, please." He smacked Riaz on the back of the head. "Don't ever do that again, mate." His words trailed off as he assessed the mood of the assembled elders and sat down next to Mina.

She said, "Don't ask."

Riaz's dad stood up first, followed by his mother. They embraced Mina's parents, Pakistani style and beckoned for Riaz to join them. He also embraced Mina's parents and then he came over to her. She stood too and he took her hands in his. "It was a pleasure meeting you. Good luck with everything."

"Thanks for listening. Good luck to you too."

The night ended quickly after that. None of the guests seemed alert to the failed engagement or they were saving the knowledge to fuel gossip in the coming days. Rehan took his sisters and wife back home, while the parents tidied up.

"Anyone want a cup of Desi tea?" Mina bounced into the kitchen and took a small saucepan from the cupboard. She filled it with water and reached for the rest of the ingredients.

Rehan came in after her and closed the kitchen door behind him. "Mum and dad are worried about you."

She added three scoops of loose tea to the gently simmering water. "Why? What have I done?"

Rehan put three mugs on the worktop. "I know it was weeks ago, but they still haven't forgotten what Tania said."

"We talked about that." She squeezed open two green cardamom pods and dropped them into the water. "I was with friends." She added cinnamon sticks and cloves.

"Are you seeing someone? You can tell me."

"No, I can't because you'll tell mum and dad."

He spoke gently and said, "You looked out for me when I needed it, all those years ago. Let me do the same for you." Rehan had spent many nights away from home in clubs or bars, getting his kicks from alcohol and women while his parents believed he was studying. When he eventually stumbled home, she had been the one to open the door for him and keep her parents occupied as he crawled into bed.

She watched the tea come to a gradual boil, imagining herself as the cinnamon stick, fighting to stay afloat as the other ingredients crashed around her, trying to pull her down. Opening up to Rehan might alleviate the feeling or it might compound it.

She took a bottle of milk out of the fridge and added some to the brewing tea. "Thanks for the offer."

Decision Made

Although she liked it less with each day, she was relieved to be back in her pokey room, where she could enjoy the fruits of her labour without prying eyes. She had left Birmingham on good terms with her parents, despite their inability to understand why she would turn down a man like Riaz. After a good night's sleep, she would repeat the whole unpleasant affair for Justin, over a quiet lunch. She hoped the time apart had made him realise how empty his life would be without her; there was no doubt she fully grasped the impact on her of a life without him.

The following morning, after using the bathroom, she checked her phone and cursed. She had overslept and not by ten or twenty minutes but by a full two hours. Her normal reaction would have been to sluggishly ready herself for the day ahead. She was annoyed at missing breakfast, but not enough to leave the snugness of her bed. She wrapped herself into a duvet cocoon and stared out through her window. From where she was lying, she could see no sign of any clouds imposing on the clear blue sky, a sure predictor for holidaymakers exposing excessive amounts of flesh. Her musings were interrupted by a knock at the door. She didn't get up, hoping the person was knocking at the wrong door.

"Mina, are you there?"

She opened the door and let Dan past her into the room. She closed the door and slid back under the duvet.

"I'm on a break so I thought I'd come get the goss from you." He took his shoes off and made himself comfortable on the bed. "Did you have a good time?"

Mina groaned. "Honestly? No. It wasn't what I expected." She sat up, still wrapped in the duvet. "I'll tell you everything, but I need to speak to Justin first."

Dan's expression changed from curiosity to concern. "That good, eh?"

"Yeah. That good." She dropped her head onto Dan's shoulder. "Why does life have to be so shitty?" Mina groaned, long and loud, releasing her pent-up frustration.

"Ah, you poor thing. If life was so shitty, I wouldn't be here and you wouldn't have Justin."

"I brought you some food back. It's in the staff room fridge with your name on it."

"Thanks. Never mind what happened in Birmingham, you still haven't told me what went down in Liverpool!"

"Daniel!" She hit him with the nearest pillow and then fell back onto the bed, pretending to cry.

He rubbed her back and laughed. "I'm going to leave you alone now." He slid off the bed and put his shoes on. "What time are you seeing Justin?"

"Twelve," she said from under the duvet.

"Okay. Good luck."

Her hand emerging from under the covers, like something from the Addams Family, searched for her phone to check the time. She needed to get her posterior out of bed. She picked out what she was going to wear - black linen trousers with a white, wide-strapped vest top and white wedge sandals - and had a shower. Hair pinned up, skin baby soft, she stared hard at her reflection and affirmed her suitability to be Justin's girlfriend.

They met outside Beach Food: the best place for ice cream in flavours only a genius could have created; Bakewell tart with almonds scattered through it, strawberry cheesecake with biscuit pieces, toffee popcorn with real popcorn. Mina had spent a fair amount of her hard-earned cash in there already.

She found Justin sitting on a bench with his back to her, a large basket and a cool box beside him. Creeping up behind him, she put her hands over his sunglasses. "Guess who?" she whispered in his ear.

His hands covered hers and he said, "There's only one person I want this to be." He kissed her palms. "You smell incredible."

For a moment they stood in silence, feeling as if they were seeing each other for the first time in weeks. Justin moved first, wrapping his arms around Mina and kissing her the way she remembered. Standing beneath a cloudless sky, the sun increasing the temperature of their embracing bodies, Justin ran his hands down Mina's back. He planted his trademark kisses on her neck. "I've missed you very much."

"I missed you too," she said, only too aware of being in a highly public place. She tried to wriggle away, but he wouldn't loosen his hold. "Everyone's watching!"

"Let them watch." He kissed her one last time. "I think we should go somewhere private."

"No, I don't. I think we should stay right here!"

"I thought you didn't want everyone watching us. You're a dark horse, Mina!"

"I didn't mean that." In an attempt to divert the conversation, she said, "Why do you have a basket that looks like the one I used to take to my home economics class?"

"Ah, yes. I thought we could have a picnic on the beach." He picked up the basket and took Mina's hand. "I found the perfect spot." He led her to space fifty feet from the sea wall, far enough away from promenading onlookers. He spread out a huge blanket and weighed it down at each corner with pebbles. They sat in the middle of the blanket with the basket and a cool box on either side of them.

He lifted his sunglasses onto his head and said, "I really have missed you."

Mina said. "Me too."

He took food from the cool box and placed it in between them. Each item had been bagged and labelled. Everything else was hidden in the basket until needed.

"This looks great." She frowned. "Did you make this all yourself?"

"Yes, I did," he said proudly. "Oh, one more thing." He reached for his phone. "Get your phone out and switch it off. I don't want us to be disturbed."

Mina started with a tuna salad. "Very nice," she said through mouthfuls. "I can't believe you did this all by yourself. You're amazing."

Justin felt his cheeks get hot. "I thought it's the least I could do...after Liverpool."

She was transported back to Charlene's house, being insulted. "I can't imagine why James is her friend; she's a horrible person."

"Did she apologise before you left?"

"Apologise? Seriously?" She poured a drink for herself.

"Well if she didn't, what did she say? You were really upset."

She rehearsed a few ways to tell him, none of them conveying the true unpleasantness of the encounter. She bit into a breadstick and sighed. "She basically told me I can't give you what you need because I'm not black."

The tortilla chip he had just dipped into some guacamole snapped. "She doesn't know what she's talking about!" He wiped his fingers on a napkin. "You don't believe her, do you?"

"Should I? We both know it won't be easy to convince my family, but I didn't think there would be problems on your side."

"I can guarantee you if we were both the same religion there would still be people who'd disapprove."

"Why haven't we talked about this before?"

"Do you want to talk about it now?" He poured himself a drink and topped up Mina's. "When I look at you, I don't see a Muslim. I see a brave and sexy woman. I see a woman who makes me feel like a big kid." He walked his fingers up her arm and around her neck. "I see a woman who gets my pulse racing, a woman who's an incredible kisser." He leaned over to kiss her mouth yet again. One of her hands came to rest on his chest while the other maintained her balance. Justin's fingers played with her hair and stroked her. He could easily get carried away, here on the sand but Mina still wasn't ready to take that step or so he thought before he felt the warm skin of her hand slide under his t-shirt. He groaned and pulled away. "I think we should stop."

Mina agreed. "I still have to tell you about my twenty first birthday party."

They packed away the food residue and Justin pulled out two cushions.

"You're like Mary Poppins with that basket!"

"I've thought of everything, my dear." He rested, his elbow on a cushion and his chin in his hand. Mina remained sitting, cross legged. "Well, where do I begin?"

She told him how it started with her dad's odd behaviour at the station.

"Your dad sounds funny." Justin smiled recalling fond memories of his dad's random, often spontaneous, sense of humour and how his mum would tell him to stop his foolishness and grow up.

"You'll change your mind when I get to the end of the nightmare. Anyway, we got to the hall and it was packed. After I sat down, my parents brought another set of parents and their son to sit with me."

"I take it you didn't know these people?"

"Nope. Me and my cousin, Rukhsana, went to the ladies' room and that's when I found out." She started biting her bottom lip. "There was an engagement party wrapped up in a birthday party." She watched his reaction.

"What?!" He immediately sat up. He shook his head, waved his hands in front of his face. "You got engaged?!"

She reached out for his hands. "No. No I didn't. I was furious. My brother sent the guy I was being set up with to talk to me. I told him, made it clear, there was no way I was going to marry him." She shuffled closer to Justin who was looking concerned. She released his hands and put her arms around his neck, their foreheads touching. "I was scared. I didn't know how I was going to explain this to you, if it would even make any sense."

"For a second I thought I'd lost you."

The sound of the distant waves gently lapping the sand mingled with the far-off hum of the busy promenade. A soft breeze had developed around the couple who were sharing a discovered sense of what could so easily have been taken away from them. They lingered in the moment, their breathing quiet and controlled.

"Before I left, yesterday, I told my parents that I'd started a new life in Weston and I'd be staying here indefinitely. I'm never going back Justin. I want to stay here with you."

Justin knew he had to tell her about the decision he had made, but all he could think of was the distance it was going to put between them. It made him tighten his hold on her.

"Mina, I need to tell you something," he whispered.

"What is it?" She stroked his neck gently and felt him shiver.

The words were stuck in his head, repeating on a loop. He cleared his dry throat and poured himself another drink. The touch of her fingers was distracting, sending signals to parts of his body that had no bearing on his decision to move to Birmingham. He had to focus, so he brought Mina's hand away from his neck and said, "Remember awhile back when I told you the company I work for is opening a new venue?"

She nodded.

"Well, the new place is in Birmingham." He finished what was left in the plastic cup and refilled it. "I want you to understand this was under discussion before you and I met."

"Alright. What is it?"

A family passed by them, the children kicking a beach ball across the sand and screaming to be the first to retrieve it.

"Just tell me."

They locked fingers. "The company asked if I wanted to manage the new venue."

She tightened her grip on his fingers. "Please don't say what I think you're going to say," she pleaded, her eyes desperately searching his for reassurance. "Please don't tell me you're going to Birmingham."

"Mina, I'm so sorry."

She released his hands. "But we're supposed to be staying together." She shook her head, unable to comprehend. "You can't leave. How...? You can't leave!"

"I wasn't going to...but Frankie got really ill. We only have each other. I couldn't live with myself if something happened to her and I wasn't able to be by her side."

She opened a packet of ready salted crisps and offered one to Justin. The sound of crunching crisps grew louder as she considered her future; she had told her parents she was going to make it work in Weston, but her reason for staying was preparing to pack up and leave. She hated herself for thinking it but she wondered how influential Frankie had been in Justin's decision. Frankie didn't trust her. Maybe she had planted a seed in Justin's mind that was beginning to take shape.

"Have I done something to make you want to leave?"

"No, Mina. You've done everything to make me want to stay."

"So why don't you?"

"Come here." They sat side by side, their backs to the world they were trying to escape, arm in arm. "I was no use when my parents died. I can't let that happen while Frankie's sick. She looked after me, made me who I am. I have a responsibility as her brother to do everything I can to help. Can you understand that?"

With her head resting on his shoulder, she mumbled, "Yeah, I can."

"We'll make this work." He had already considered the ways they could maintain their relationship; he would travel to see Mina on his days off and Mina could stay with him at the weekend. It was either that or spend every free minute on the phone to each other.

"When do you have to leave?"

"Sunday."

"Really? We better make the most of it then."

"Don't worry, we will."

They ate a few more of Justin's homemade treats before packing up, leaving the serenity of the beach. Stopping at the bench where they met earlier, she handed the basket back to Justin. "I'll see you tomorrow then?"

"You will." He put the cool box and basket on the ground. "I'm taking you shopping." He kissed her and she watched as he walked away.

Standing alone on the promenade, the sun hot on her head, Mina's thoughts were riddled with Charlene and Tony, her mum and dad, Frankie, Riaz, not being good enough, the threat of having another prospective husband awaiting her back in Birmingham, and worst of all, the distance pending between her and Justin. She slumped onto the bench, her head in her hands. Her breathing came in short, wheezy bursts and she started crying. She lifted her head and tried to breathe slowly. It was as though there was a shortage of oxygen in the air directly around her. She had never experienced a feeling like it, but she was sure she wasn't having a heart attack: there was no pain. She took off her sunglasses, trying again to slow her breathing down.

"Excuse me. Are you okay?" A middle-aged man stood beside her, his family in tow.

She shook her head and tried to speak, but could only manage two words, "I... can't..."

He helped her to recognise what was happening and to calm down whilst his children kept asking what was wrong with the lady and why their daddy was talking to her. A few minutes later, Mina's breathing returned to normal, the way it had been when she had watched Justin walk away.

She thanked the kind stranger and he left after explaining what she should do if another panic attack ensued. She rushed back to the hotel, wiping tears from under her sunglasses. She passed through reception unnoticed, but when she reached her floor, there was a figure at her door.

"Mina! Where have you been?" Dan skipped to his feet. "I've been trying to call for an hour!"

Only then did she remember she and Justin had turned their phones off.

"I need to tell you something!"

"No, please Dan." She walked past him and searched for the key card. "I need to lie down."

"But this is important!"

She removed her sunglasses to reveal eyes that looked like she had recently taken up mixed martial arts.

"Oh my God! What happened to you?"

She sighed and said, "I just need to rest before my shift starts. I'll call you tomorrow."

Dan hugged her. "Make sure you do, it's important." He waited until she had opened the door. "Maybe you should take the night off."

"Work is probably the best thing for me right now."

As soon as she stepped into her room, she dropped her bag on the floor and dropped on the bed, sobbing into the duvet, her whole body shaking with the strength of her sorrow and it was then she had her second panic attack.

When her outpouring ended, she lifted her head to reveal puffy, red eyes and a mess of hair on top of her head. She had created a damp spot the size of a small island, on the duvet: Dan would have told her to change it, would have done it for her, but she couldn't for fear of drawing unwanted attention from housekeeping. She swung her legs down the side of the bed. She had to use the wall to steady herself, her head pounding as though a drummer in a rock band was using it for practice. She crept toward her bag, sat down on the floor and rummaged through her belongings for her phone. She found it and switched it on. Within a few seconds it began to alert her of emails, text messages and missed calls. The three voicemails and missed calls were from Dan, but he didn't drop any hints about what he was desperate to tell her.

"Damn it!"

A rainbow of curse words accompanied her rush to be work-ready. Her challenge to focus became strained when she began to untangle the bird's nest on top of her head. There was no time to wash it, so more curse words shot out of her mouth each time the brush was stopped by a mound of knots. The pulling sensation only served to aggravate her headache, so she swallowed two pain killers before leaving the room.

Any hopes of a standard dinner service were dashed when the staff were told the kitchen were having issues with the equipment. Mina imagined a horde of naughty gremlins pulling wires out and smashing everything that wasn't pinned down. She thought it plausible there were gremlins working to ruin her life too.

Unlike the hotel, she had no contingency plan for her predicament. She had become dependent on her relationship with Justin. She had something to look forward to when she wasn't working and their physical intimacy compounded her anticipation.

Despite the closure of the kitchen, the guests had their dinner orders fulfilled, courtesy of another local business. When Mina had a moment to herself, she took two more pain killers and hoped to feel better in time for her shopping trip.

Countdown to departure

Justin ate breakfast with the balcony doors open, welcoming an ever so gentle breeze into his, soon to be vacant home. He had spent four years securing his employment within the company and achieving an official stamp of approval in the form of his relocation to Birmingham. He had unwavering confidence in his ability to manage a new business. The same couldn't be said about maintaining his personal affairs. In theory, he would devote every spare second to Mina. In practice, past experience reminded him of the inevitable strain their relationship would suffer: he never said it out loud, but he felt partially to blame after he split with Eve. Only time would tell if he was making the same mistake again.

The previous day's conversation with Mina had left him with a more positive outlook and he had returned to work with a little more enthusiasm. The staff had gathered round and announced their plans for a leaving party on Friday night. After consulting some of their loyal patrons, it was decided that Sunset Strip would host it as a public event, an opportunity to thank Justin for creating one of the most popular spots on the beachfront.

He took a bite out of his scrambled eggs and mushrooms on toast and thought some more about the picnic on the beach. When Mina told him about almost getting engaged, the thought of being so close to losing her made him wonder whether their future together was in their control at all. He took some comfort knowing that by staying in Weston she would be out of danger. He knew he was being selfish, but she had become vital to his own well-being. Not only that, but he felt he needed to protect her, especially after hearing the truth about what had happened between her and Charlene.

He had no qualms about the difference in their race and culture; it had always been irrelevant in his relationships, but for the first time, he was encountering other people's discomfort with it. He brought to mind the brief conversation he'd had with Sam on the night of Frankie's diagnosis. He supposed that if they didn't cause outrage because of their race, it would be because of their age gap.

"To hell with them," he said and finished his toast and coffee.

Today was going to be easy and fun - as easy and fun as a shopping trip with a woman could be. He called Mina to make sure she was ready.

"Morning." She sounded groggy. "Is it that time already?"

"Don't tell me you're still in bed!" He was supposed to be picking her up in half an hour.

Mina closed her eyes and rested the phone in between her pillow and her ear. "I've got a pounding headache."

"I'm not letting you stay in bed all day. Take a couple of paracetamol, have a shower and I'll pick you up later - say at eleven."

She groaned through the phone. "What if I still don't feel any better?" She was still recuperating and felt she would need more than a couple of hours to make herself look and feel human.

They only had a few days to enjoy each other's company, so he insisted: "Well, then I'll come with a tub of soup, a bottle of Lucozade and some fruit." Justin smiled when he heard her chuckle.

"That's exactly what my mum would do."

Neither of them spoke for a few seconds, the only audible sound their synchronised breathing. She would be a fool to waste a day in bed; she could do that when Justin was in Birmingham. "I'll be ready by ten."

"Excellent. See you soon."

Mina dragged her body out of bed and straight to the kettle. She needed the best cup of tea she had ever made if her morning was going to improve quickly enough. While the tea bag sat in the boiling water, she drew the curtains apart to reveal what looked like another glorious day beside the seaside, so much so that she opened the window to ease the stuffiness in her room. Unfortunately, along with the fresh air came the noises: commuters, carbon dioxide riddled vehicles and the low hum of the hotel kitchen extractor fans hard at work. She masked the external noise with muted daytime television. After spending inordinate lengths of time in front of the television after leaving college, she had grown to loathe every programme available, especially the ones where people in clear need of professional help chose instead to air their dirty laundry with an audience of total strangers.

Mina was about to step out of the hotel when Dan shouted her name. She turned around and saw him bounding towards her with a vase full of flowers and his trademark grin on his face.

"Look what someone left for you," he cooed.

"These are from Justin? When did this happen?" She took the vase from Dan and tried to name each of the flowers.

"Umm, about ten minutes ago. He said it was crucial I give these to you just before you leave." He made it sound like a covert operation. "I'll keep them in the office until you get back."

"Thanks, Dan." She was about to turn when he called her again.

"Aren't you going to ask what my news is?"

She looked at him, a blank expression on her face.

"I tried to tell you yesterday, remember?"

"Oh yeah. Sorry. I wasn't having a good day."

"Don't worry, we'll talk about it later. Anyway, Michael's leaving to move in with his fiancé."

She searched his face as if a photo of Michael would appear to remind her who he was.

"Michael, my house mate!" He shook his head and rolled his eyes.

"Oh, Michael! So?"

"So, that means there's room for someone else to take his place." He hoped she would be able to read his mind, but the return of the blank expression told him she couldn't. "You can move in with me, you idiot!"

Mina's eyes widened as Dan's words sunk in. "No way!"

"Yes way! We're gonna live together!"

They jumped around and hugged each other in the middle of the hotel reception, getting a few worried looks from guests.

"You don't understand how happy I am right now." She started to cry and Dan hugged her again.

"Stop being silly and go spend Justin's money!"

Her head was swimming with the new information, she was ecstatic, and guilt ridden; was that all it took to get her out of the pit she had fallen into? Yesterday her brain could have caved in trying to make sense of all the drama from the weekend and now...well now she could see a beckoning light in the distance. She was glad of making the decision to see Justin after all.

"You look a lot happier than you sounded on the phone. What happened to change your mood?" He knew she loved flowers, not growing them, receiving them.

"I'll tell you later. Can we get something to eat first? I haven't had breakfast."

"You don't have to wait until later. I know you liked the flowers," he said nonchalantly.

She had briefly forgotten the gift. She leant over and kissed his cheek. "Thank you. They were amazing!"

They ordered food in a quiet backstreet cafe, a short walk from the shopping centre. There were only four other people in the place. The interior walls looked like an exterior: exposed brick, cut off in places, by wooden door and window frames. The pictures on the walls depicted Weston back in the forties and fifties; they held no sentimental meaning for Mina; she was no doubt one of many people who had chosen to build a new life here. Behind the counter was a menu with large enough writing she didn't have to squint to read it.

"You are feeling better, aren't you? I hope I didn't pressure you into coming."

She squeezed his hand. She knew if she began to tell him about her panic attacks they might not get round to shopping, but it was something she needed to share with him. "After you left yesterday...after you left me, I had a panic attack." She told him everything, from the second it happened to the moment she reached her room.

He was helpless to do anything except listen. He noticed how her eyes remained fixed on their intertwined fingers, how she stopped to take a deep breath after every sentence and the beginnings of a tear in her right eye. He didn't know how to protect her, unsure if he even should. Frankie had always talked about distress and anguish being excellent life lessons, the best way to toughen up the softest of hearts. He believed Frankie had been born with the traits of a relentless and unforgiving animal. Mina was the polar opposite.

He could sense she was being hindered from pursuing a life out of the ordinary for a person of her race, but this might just be the start of it. "I'm so sorry I wasn't there when you needed me. I should have stayed and walked you back." He placed his fingers under her chin and lifted her head. "What can I do to help you feel better?"

She forced a smile and said, "Don't worry about me." Her expression altered, revealing a genuine smile. "There might just be some good news hiding in all this."

Justin sat up straight. "What news? Has something happened?"

"Dan's house mate is moving out so I can live there with him!"

In an instant his heart became one hundred percent lighter, Mina wouldn't be alone. "That's great! When can you move in?"

"I don't actually know. I only found out today."

"It doesn't matter. I'm just glad you'll have some company."

They finished what was left on their plates and as they walked outside, Justin said, "Do you want to talk about it?"

She took his hand and held it around her waist. "No. Not today."

They spent several hours walking in and out of a host of women's clothes shops and department stores. Justin waited patiently whilst Mina tried on garments she selected, and a few of Justin's recommendations. He was on hand to swap a pair of jeans or trousers for a different size and then questioned her when that size failed to fit in the next store.

"I don't make the clothes!"

"Men don't have this problem," he shouted to her in the dressing room.

"I'm happy for you all."

Most shops they left empty-handed. When she did eventually decide an item was too gorgeous to leave behind, she kept checking if he was sure he wanted to buy it for her.

"It makes me feel less guilty about leaving you. Are you alright with that?"

"I think I can live with it!"

They went back to the car with four shopping bags; a pair of blue and red trainers, a couple of pairs of tailored trousers, two pairs of jeans and, the sexiest item, according to Justin, an off the shoulder blue and white striped top - when she had stepped out of the dressing room wearing it, he had sounded his approval with what Mina could only describe as caveman sounds.

"Thanks for today. I needed it." She opened the boot of the car.

"My pleasure." He waved the bags in the air. "Every time you wear one of these, you'll remember me."

She closed the boot and said, "I'll be thinking of you even when I'm not wearing them." She grinned and, with her back still turned, Justin stepped forward to kiss her neck. "Now you've got me thinking."

She gasped when she felt him against her. She stroked his arms and tilted her head to the side. Justin kissed her neck again, this time making his way up to her ear. "Come back to my place."

She moaned. He was right; they were in a public place doing private things. "Sounds like a good idea." She turned to face him, her hands moving up his chest. His heart was racing but his breathing was steady, controlled. "Will I get to see what's under here?"

"I guarantee it." He leaned in further and kissed her, groaning under his breath. He wasn't used to being with someone for this length of time without having slept with them, but the anticipation made it even more exciting. He slowed down, savouring the taste of her lips. "Let's get out of here."

Mina wouldn't let go. She had deliberately avoided the sexual advances of her previous boyfriends and here she was, a few years older, encouraging it. When she and Justin were in Weston together, a kiss and a cuddle was enough, but who knew how long it would be before they would be this close again? "One more minute," she mumbled under her breath. Her hands moved to the bare skin under his t-shirt. He groaned again. The sensation of her skin on his was something he had waited a long time for. He tried to pull her hands away and said, "Mina, we should go." He pulled away from her, his breathing still heavy.

She got into the car reluctantly, as though being told off for misbehaving. "Sorry. I got a bit carried away," she said when he started the engine.

"Don't apologise. I like that side of you. Where am I taking you?" he asked, hoping she'd want him to head in the direction of his apartment.

"I wish I could say back to yours, but I need to be at work."

Justin sighed. "Work! It gets in the way of everything!"

"I agree!"

Before Mina stepped out of Justin's car, he told her about the party his team were throwing for him. He used a single finger to trace patterns along her thigh. "I know you'll be working, so I thought you and me could have our own little party at my place on Saturday."

"Would I need to bring anything with me?"

"What did you have in mind?"

"Oh, I don't know...an overnight bag, maybe?"

He stopped in mid-pattern. "You better get out of here, or I'm taking you with me, right now!"

She leaned over and kissed his shocked mouth. "See you soon."

Through his wing mirror Justin watched her walk away; was she serious about staying overnight? He'd have to wait to find out. She may be less experienced than him, but she was already an adept tease.

Dan's shift was about to end when Mina walked into the hotel. She waited for him and they went up to her room together. She tipped the contents of her shopping trip onto the bed. With a few oohs and aahs, he signalled his approval. "Come on," he said handing a garment to her, "Fashion show!"

"What? I start work in forty minutes." She put the clothes back onto the bed. "You still have to tell me when I can move in."

"We can do both." He handed the clothes back to her and pushed her into the bathroom.

Mina went back and forth trying on each item, doing her best to sashay across the fifteen feet of bedroom as if she were on the catwalk for Milan fashion week. Dan told her she'd be able to move in at the end of the following week. His housemate had paid rent to cover the month, but he and his fiancé were keen to shack up together as soon as. They began to plan their first night in the house together; they would order pizza, argue which movie to watch and indulge in a facial or two.

After the exciting news, she gave him a condensed version of the other events in her life, ending with her pending sleepover at Justin's.

"No wonder you looked knackered yesterday!"

"That's charming! You better be nicer to me when we're sharing a house!" They ran to each other and jumped up and down beside the bed. "Did you ever imagine we'd be such good friends when you started working here?"

Mina paused and thought. "I didn't think I'd make any friends, if I'm being honest." Her motivation for leaving Birmingham had less to do with new friends; it had been more about cutting the strings of conformity than she cared to admit.

"Hey, we're both gonna be on the same shift next week. We can go shopping for bed sheets and stuff!" Dan waited for her to change into her uniform and walked her out to the staff room.

The guests hadn't been put off by last night's disruption. It had become a talking point at most of the tables, the customers impressed with how calm the staff had remained and many said they all deserved the night off.

Mina smiled and said, "Oh, well, we do whatever we can to look after you. It's just another exciting day at The Royal Weston."

She watched the minute hand tick away toward the end of her shift and massaged her eyebrows where the throbbing had started. Every time she entered the kitchen, the sound of crockery being stacked and cutlery being piled together, made her wince. She decided against pain killers - the ache was nowhere near as severe as it had been yesterday.

The Replacements

"I think we've covered everything," he said, looking over the new starter induction papers. "I'm in Birmingham on Thursday so just call me if you need anything." Justin smiled at the incoming manager of Sunset Strip, and they formally shook hands. "Welcome to the team." He would leave Shaun to get on with the job of familiarising himself with the rest of the staff, premises and customers. He still had to finish packing the things he could live without until he could unpack them again in Birmingham. Clothes, toiletries and almost everything in the kitchen would be the final items to be stored away. Not only that, but he still had to decide what to cook for lunch and dinner with Mina and, if the night went according to plan, breakfast too. He hadn't ever previously found the need to make detailed arrangements for the first time having sex with someone. She had uncovered in him a level of patience he hadn't known he had, one of many things he was learning about himself.

He hoped he was decoding the signals Mina was sending correctly. There was a tinge of apprehension about spending their first night together; when twenty-four hours later he was going to be over a hundred miles away. It could break his resolve; be enough to bring him back every night for more when he should be spending every free moment in Birmingham proving his worth, again. The impact it could have on Mina worried him still more. Knowing she'd had a panic attack trying to assimilate events outside her control made him question whether it might be detrimental to add a physical element to their relationship.

"I'm going now." He turned to Shaun. "If there's anything this man can't help you with," he slapped James on the back, "I'm only a phone call away."

During the elevator ride up to his apartment, Sam called.

"I heard you'll be gracing us with your presence soon."

"You heard right. I'll be back on Monday."

"You know what that means?" They shouted in unison, "Lad's night!"

"To show you how awesome it is to have you back where you belong, I'm making it my duty to get you laid!"

"Hold on, mate. I'm still with Mina, so you'll have to think of something else."

There was an awkward silence. When Sam didn't try to explain his assumption, Justin said, "Just because I'm in Birmingham, doesn't mean we're not still in a committed relationship."

"Fair enough. I just can't see how it's going to work."

Justin took a bottle of cider from the fridge. Sam had shared his thoughts on dating outside their culture when he first found out Mina was Muslim. Nothing appeared to have changed. He was curious to know where this was going. "What do you think I should do?"

"Jus, there are loads of sexy, black women here. Try your luck with one of them."

He smiled. "When's the last time you dated one of these sexy black women?"

"Alright. I get it. I overstepped the line."

"No, Sam, I don't think you do get it. Unlike you, I have the balls to commit to someone totally different to me." He threw his jacket on the sofa. "No offence, but I'm not in the habit of using women as fuck buddies."

He took a long swig of his ice-cold cider, giving his friend time to absorb the comment and consider a comeback. Instead he heard a deep sigh.

"You're one of my best friends, Sam. We've been through some shit, you and me. Mina is the woman I love and I need you to respect that."

"I didn't know you felt so strong about her."

Neither did he, until now. The words had rolled off his tongue with little effort. Now he was smiling to himself. "Holy shit, Sam. I'm in love."

"It sounds like it. I'm happy for you man. You deserve it."

He wanted to call Mina straight away and declare his love for her, and then remembered she'd be hard at work. He could surprise her, turn up with a bunch of flowers but where was he going to find flowers worthy of a declaration of love at this hour? If he was in a Hollywood movie, he would be able to stroll down the street and find exactly what he needed to execute his idea to perfection. Instead he devised an idea for a surprise on Friday evening to set up their weekend together nicely.

He looked around at the empty cardboard boxes scattered about his lounge and got to work filling them. When he finished, all bar one of his kitchen cupboards was empty and his DVD and music collections were out of sight. He had a shower to wash away the sweat he'd worked up and then had an early night.

Justin's morning began with disappointment. An email from Birmingham; his presence had been requested a day earlier than intended. He called Frankie to let her know and packed a small case. Before leaving he sent two text messages; the first to let James know he would see him on Friday afternoon, the second to Mina.

***

The smell of newness was the first thing he noticed. The finishing touches were still being made before the first event, in a week's time. It was to be an exclusive, invitation only, opening, for business leaders, members of the city council and the media. The doors would open to the public two days later. He spent the entire afternoon discussing guest bookings, suppliers of food and drink and the venue's web presence. Luckily, other people were in charge of those things and all he would have to do is be on their case to ensure they were doing their job in a timely fashion. There would be a meeting with all staff tomorrow morning so formal introductions could take place then. Justin would be expected to give them a tour of the building and hand out their contracts, a task probably involving a slew of queries.

By the time he left for Frankie's, it was dusk. He called to ask if she fancied a Chinese takeaway, but she had already cooked for them. He let himself and heard some funky soul grooves emanating from the living room. She was in the kitchen and had her back to him. She was singing along as she took out plates and glasses. He turned the volume down - better than putting a hand on her shoulder and giving her a fright.

"Someone's in a good mood!"

"Come over here and pour us some drinks." She gestured, still with her back turned.

Justin hurried over, saw they were having chicken and took a bottle of dry white wine from the chiller. "Where do you want to eat?"

"Inside, please. I feel the cold more than I used to."

He put the wine and glasses on the coffee table and went back for cutlery. "Where's my hug?" He turned Frankie around and was stunned to see how much weight she had lost. He hugged her, but for now avoided asking any questions.

She served them a plate of vegetable fried rice with the chicken in a black bean sauce.

"I can't believe you'll be living just a few miles away now. I don't have to tell you how happy that makes me." She was able to maintain control over her self-care, but her movements had become slower and getting physical tasks done more of a struggle. She didn't expect Justin to be able to drop what he was doing immediately, but she knew he would if she needed him. "How did Mina take the news?"

"We're going to make it work, whatever it takes."

"Is that feasible?"

He almost choked on his food. "You make it sound like some kind of business deal. I told you, we'll do whatever it takes." He took a sip of wine and stared at Frankie.

"Remember that as the weeks and months go by." She picked up her wine glass. "Are you ready for opening night?"

"Almost. I have to read through the staff profiles before meeting them tomorrow."

"How is Shaun getting on?"

"He has plenty of experience. I'm sure he'll be okay."

"How's the dinner?"

"Perfect." He finished what was left on his plate and sank back into the sofa with the wine glass in his hand, ready to raise what was uppermost on his mind. "How much weight have you lost?"

"Enough for you to notice."

"Come on, Frankie! Are we really doing this?"

She poured more wine into her glass.

"Top me up too." Justin held his glass out.

"If it helps, I feel better than I look. I have my first follow-up appointment in three weeks, so I'll know if anything has changed internally." She saw Justin ready to reply, so she said, "You're going to be busy, so don't worry about coming with me."

"All I ask is that you let me know when. Will you do that?"

Frankie nodded. "You won't see me in the morning." She kissed her brother on the forehead. "I'm going for a swim before I leave for the office." She started to clear the table, but Justin stopped her.

"I can do that."

"Thanks. I'm going to bed."

***

Justin and his new team got on better than he had hoped. Most of them had worked in hospitality for upwards of five years and so had dealt with every kind of customer imaginable, from the loud, rowdy drunks letting their hair down after a long week, to the subdued characters who preferred to use the establishment during the weekday afternoon for a working lunch. During the tour of their new workplace, Justin showed them the staff room, staff toilets and his office, all of which were located a floor above the main room. Each of them had a full-length locker, so they could keep their uniforms pristine. Justin's office was twice the size of the one in Sunset Strip. He visualised sitting at his desk, in his huge chair, telling Mina how much he missed her and arranging his next visit.

The staff profiles were being uploaded onto the website along with snapshots of the inside of the building. The bar was being stocked and non-perishable foods stored in the kitchen. He was starting to get excited about being at the helm of a brand-new venture, despite the pressure that came as part of the package. He positioned himself behind the bar and looked out towards the main doors. A touch of nostalgia crept in as he fondly recalled the moment he first laid eyes on Mina and how her transparently weak attempts at flirting had been so endearing. A cheeky smile lit up his face as he thought about how she no longer flinched at his touch and her confidence in making the first move. His mind raced back to having her up against the car, his mouth on her soft, sweet smelling skin.

"Nice place you have here." Alex walked in holding a couple of brown paper bags, rousing him out of the daydream.

"Alex! Good to see you!" He hugged his friend. "I hope that's food. I've done nothing but talk all morning and I'm starving!"

"Mexican rice boxes all round!"

"I'll go get cutlery."

"No need." Alex shook the bags until two plastic sets fell out.

"Have you set a date yet?"

"We have, actually. July twenty eighth, next year."

"Congrats. If there's anything I can do, let me know."

Alex nodded and chewed. "There's something I need to ask. Will you be my Best Man?"

Justin's mouth was wide open. When the request had sunk in, he shot out of his seat and hugged his friend. "Oh man! Seriously? I'd love to."

"I can trust you to be sensible and organised, can't I?"

Justin raised his eyebrows and said, "Can you?" He nudged Alex who almost fell off his chair. "This is good food. Where's it from?"

"That new place on Cornwall Street. I forget what it's called."

As they ate and drank, Justin considered asking Alex's opinion on his relationship with Mina, but he didn't know if he'd react well to unsupportive comments. Alex noticed Justin playing around with his food and staring off into space. "What's on your mind?"

"Hmm? Oh, nothing, it's not important."

Alex put his fork down and folded his arms. It was a move he had picked up from Lauren who was adept at knowing when he was plagued by a decision or thought. If he waited long enough, Justin would crack. Sure enough, a minute later, Justin responded to the icy stare. "Do you think I'm making a mistake, coming back to Birmingham for this job and leaving Mina behind?"

"You didn't come back just for a job though, did you?" Alex knew all about Justin's sleepless nights since Frankie's diagnosis; they had spent some of those having deep discussions about the meaning of life. "I know Mina means a lot to you, but Frankie's your sister. You'd feel a whole lot worse if something happened and you hadn't taken the opportunity to be here for her."

"I know, I know. It's just that Mina isn't in a great place herself and I can't seem to figure out how to protect her when I'm a hundred miles away."

"You won't have to. She has a close friend, remember?" Alex pounded the table. Mina's friend's name escaped him.

"Dan."

"Yeah, Dan. Mina will have him to look after her and you can look after Frankie."

"If she lets me. And that's another thing. Frankie might not even want me hanging around her..."

"She will. She just doesn't know it yet."

Talk turned to opening night and Justin told Alex he had secured VIP passes for him, Marvin, Darren and Sam, so they'd better turn up looking sharp. After lunch, he made a few phone calls then headed back to his sister's.

Once there, he got on the phone to Mina. She seemed in good spirits, but she was missing him. He told her he missed her too, but they'd be together soon and would have the rest of the weekend to themselves. She updated him on her moving-in-with-Dan schedule and he breathed a sigh of relief, knowing she was excited by the prospect.

Frankie was late home that evening. After Justin had cooked dinner, he phoned her but his call went straight to voicemail. Instead of worrying, which had become his norm when she was unreachable, he left a casual message to say dinner was in the oven and he was going to have an early night.

The worry he had held back began to manifest itself during his attempt at getting a good night's sleep; he started by trying to sleep on his side and then turned onto his front. Eventually, he kicked the duvet off and spread himself out on his back. With his hands resting under his head he closed his eyes and pictured the look on Mina's face when she opened the door to her room, after work on Saturday morning and saw what he intended to get done. He had lots to do tomorrow. He drifted off to sleep thinking how in love he was and how he couldn't wait to tell her.

***

The door to his bedroom opened, letting in early morning light from the lounge. A blurry figure walked towards the bed, holding a tray. "Breakfast in bed for my little brother." Frankie placed the tray on the bedside table. "A thank you, and an apology, for dinner last night. I was out with a client." She added the key piece of news after that. "My follow-up has been booked for the fifteenth."

He threw his legs over the side of the bed and ate what he could; he had an uneasy feeling in the pit of his stomach, the cause of which he didn't have time to determine. Finishing his coffee, he had a shower and dressed, ready to make plans for the weekend.

Frankie finished her phone call as he loaded the dishwasher. There was a heaviness in the air around him as he searched for something to say. "Alex and Lauren have set a date for their wedding."

"That's good. How long have they been together?"

"Five years. He asked me to be his Best Man."

"That's great."

He idly wiped down the kitchen surfaces. "Frankie, you do know part of the reason I accepted the job offer is so I wouldn't be so far away in case anything happens?"

"Is that why you're moping around?"

"I am not moping. It's just...I want to be useful to you. I won't be here every day but I will want to know how you are and how I can help."

"We talked about this long before you finally decided to accept the job. You should be doing this for you, no one else. Not even me."

He put the cloth down and washed and dried his hands. "I have to think about you, you're my only sister. I couldn't help you when mum and dad died, so don't push me away now." He wasn't one for crying, but if the conversation continued in this way, he might be pushed down that road.

Frankie took his face in her hands and kissed his forehead. "I know how difficult this is for you. I promise I'll keep you up to date on everything to do with my health." When Justin hugged her, he was again reminded of how frail she'd become.

Weekend Bliss

As soon as his feet touched down on familiar ground, he was on the phone to the local florist, and to Dan. He needed someone on the inside to make sure Mina was well out of sight when the bouquets were being planted in her room and somewhere to store them until that time. Twenty minutes later the arrangements had been made; the flowers could be stored in the kitchen store where it would be cold enough to prevent them wilting and Dan said he would feign drunken behaviour, unless he really did end up drunk, after attending Justin's leaving do, to slow her down.

"Are you back yet?" Mina asked hopefully. "Can I see you?"

"I'm not getting back until later this afternoon." He needed to keep up the charade to add to the surprise. "Don't worry," he said, hearing the disappointing sound she made, "We'll see each other in the morning."

"Okay, I suppose. Have fun at your party tonight. Look out for Dan and the rest."

"See you in the morning, Mina."

Back at Sunset Strip, preparations were underway. James and the rest of the staff were keeping hush about the exact details of the night, but warned him he might well change his mind about leaving after they were done with him.

***

At four thirty in the afternoon, half an hour after the start of Mina's shift, four large bouquets of flowers were delivered to the hotel and promptly smuggled out of sight. Meanwhile, the party had kicked off earlier than Justin had anticipated which was good for him because it meant he could leave without missing anything. Unfortunately, those who came to celebrate were determined to fill him with alcohol, so he faked drinking, after the first half a dozen shots.

Sunset Strip had been adorned with Justin's face on an array of banners and balloons that said farewell and good luck. A game of beer pong had been set up on one side of the room and Shaun had managed to hire a full-size pool table. Halfway through the night, there were chants for Justin to get on the decks and play some music, like he had done in the early days. He used the opportunity to get on the mic to thank everyone for making it an awesome four years in Weston. He played a thirty minute set and then checked the time; he would need to leave inside an hour. The excitement had dwindled and so had the effects of the alcohol. He gathered his team around him for the last time and thanked them for the night and their dedication in making this the best place to be, any night of the week. He collected the few belongings he had left and looked for Dan.

"Hold on a sec." Justin rushed into the kitchen.

"What's that?"

"A romantic gesture, I hope. Let's go."

Justin waited in the car, while Dan and another colleague moved the flowers out of the kitchen and into Mina's room. Ten minutes before the end of her shift, Dan snuck Justin in and he waited in the stairwell. Dan found Mina and started telling her about Justin's leaving party. "Oh, you should have been there! I've never seen the place so packed."

"You had a good night then? Did you see Justin?"

"He was around, you know, people were buying him drinks, the girls were chatting him up..."

"What? Who was chatting him up? What did they say to him?"

"I dunno. I couldn't hear them!" He grabbed her hands and made her dance around with him. "Minaaa, it was such a good night. I wish you'd been there!"

"Dan, you need to go to bed, you're drunk. I can smell it on you."

He pushed his face right up to hers. "Nooo. I'm too excited to go to bed! Go get changed and let's go out!"

"No! I need to sleep. I'm spending the night at Justin's tomorrow, remember?" She charged past, hoping he would get the hint, but he followed her.

"Ooo-ooo, let's go get Justin!"

"What! No! I'm going to bed!" Mina thought Justin's leaving party must have been good; she hadn't seen even Dan in such high spirits before.

Justin heard Dan coming and got himself ready for his big reveal.

"Thanks for walking me to my room. You should go home now." Mina swiped her key card and opened the door. She said firmly to Dan, "See you Monday." When she turned back into her room, she saw the bouquets, each arranged carefully into its own vase, on the dressing table. She walked into the room and got a closer look at each one. "Oh my God! How did these get here?"

Dan signalled for Justin to come out of hiding. They watched as she inspected each lily, gerbera, rose and gladioli with her fingertips.

"I take it you like them?" Justin stepped into her room.

She whirled around. "What're you doing here? Are these from you?"

He nodded. "I thought I'd surprise you." He indicated Dan. "I had a little help."

She shook her head. "Justin, these are gorgeous! Thank you!"

He pulled her to him to kiss her. She pushed against his chest. "Not now. Dan's watching."

"Oh, don't mind me. It's nothing I haven't seen before!"

"You knew what was going on, Dan?" He nodded. "And just now, was that set up too?"

"Afraid so." Mina moved past to hug Dan. He said "I'll leave you two alone. Enjoy your weekend!" He closed the door softly behind him,

"Now where we?" Justin pulled her into another deep kiss, his mouth savouring her taste. He pushed her against the door, pressed himself against her. "I'm so glad I'm here."

She guided his mouth back to hers, her hands on his back, pulling him closer even if her words contradicted her actions. "Let's not do this here."

"I agree." He traced kisses across her collarbone. "Get your stuff. Let's start this weekend now."

"I haven't packed anything yet."

"It's already done for you."

"What do you mean?"

"Dan." He kissed her again.

She pushed him away and then saw both a case and a smaller bag on her bed. "Really?" She faced him with her hands on her hips. "You planned it all out, did you?"

Justin said, "Do you mind?" He took her fingers and kissed them. "Shall we go?"

"How long have you been planning this?"

"A few days and when I got back yesterday afternoon..."

"You were here yesterday? So, you lied?"

"Yeah, but I didn't want to ruin the surprise." His brow furrowed. "Am I in trouble?"

Mina was too tired to string him along so she said, "No. I can't be angry with you."

In the car, she cuddled the seat belt and enjoyed the silence. Justin felt her eyes watching him. "What are you thinking?"

"Nothing, just enjoying the view."

At Justin's apartment block, they held each other close as the elevator ascended. Mina was yawning.

"We're here sleepyhead," Justin teased.

"I thought you were moving things out."

He waved his hand around. "Some of this isn't mine to take." He put Mina's bags on the kitchen counter. "What shall we do now?" He kissed her just once.

She put her arms around his neck. "The first thing I'll do is..." She stretched up and returned his kiss. "Get out of my uniform." Her fingers stroked the nape of his neck and their bodies swayed together to music only they could hear.

"That's a very good start." He leant down and kissed her for rather longer. "What will you do next?"

She ran her hands over his chest. "Get into my pyjamas and go to bed." She grinned and left him standing there while she took her bags into the bedroom. "Are you coming?"

"What...?"

Mina took his hand, leading him into the bedroom.

"Are you sure about this?" he said as she changed into nightclothes in the bathroom.

"Course I'm sure," she shouted back. "We're only sleeping. As in close-our-eyes-and-wake-up-in-the-morning sleep, nothing else."

Justin smirked to himself. When they were standing on opposite sides of the bed, he said, "I usually sleep naked."

"Right, I'll be on the sofa then." Mina started toward the lounge.

Justin grabbed her hand. "I have a stash of emergency pyjamas, so you can come to bed." He looked around as if he'd heard an unusual sound. "Woah, that sounded weird."

He changed in the bathroom as she had. When he came out, she was sitting up in bed and had turned back the covers on his side.

"Hang on." He was bare chested, "Where's the top half?" Mina couldn't stop the smile spreading slowly across her face as she watched him. She laid her head on the plumpest pillow she had ever felt and moved onto her side, facing Justin. He got into bed and turned the lights down. He propped himself up on one arm and played with her hair. "I realised something this week." His thumb stroked her lips. "I'm in love with you, Mina."

She lifted her head off the pillow and held his gaze. "You what?" Why was she so surprised? Their understanding of each other had deepened, love was inevitable but hearing the words panicked her; *am I supposed to say it back now or later? Will he be hurt if I don't say anything?*

"I'm in love with you." He leant across and kissed her. "Now let's get some sleep. We've both had a long day."

He switched the lights off and laid down. Mina put her head on his chest, feeling his heart beating. Wrapped around each other, Mina lay awake, smiling to herself; this was everything she hoped it would be. Every time Justin exhaled she detected the faint aroma of an enjoyable party, a celebration he deserved, especially after the efforts he had gone to in surprising her. Then there was the unexpected arrival here, to this moment. Justin's face was in her hair and he squeezed her a little tighter.

Somehow she slept.

***

The sounds of eighties r'n'b drifted in through the bedroom door, along with another indistinct sound. She rolled over to Justin's side to find herself abandoned. *What is that sound?* It was almost an echo, but the key was off. It drew her out of bed and when she peered into the lounge and saw no one, she ventured further on tiptoe and in the kitchen discovered Justin making breakfast and while singing along to the music.

Before alerting him that she was awake, she took a quick look at her reflection in the bedroom mirror; *it'll take at least ten minutes work to turn me into anything resembling a human being.* She decided they would both have to get used to the sight.

In the kitchen her first words to him were, "I thought someone was being tortured."

"Good morning to you too." Relief swept over him at the humour in her words. He buttered two slices of toast then took Mina in his arms. "Did you sleep well?" He felt her nod against his chest.

"Same here. Take this." Justin gave her a wooden table number with a number twelve etched into it. "Have a seat and your order will be with you shortly."

She swivelled the stool from side to side, turning the number twelve around in her hands, running her fingers over the etching. Listening to Justin humming, she placed herself back at Sunset Strip for the first time she'd chosen to spend her there, hoping to meet the cute barman. She remembered sitting on the upstairs terrace, looking out at the sea and being given a table number before choosing where to sit. A table number that looked just like the one she was holding. She stared at the object Justin had given her. "Is this my table number?" she said.

"You mean the table number for a cheddar, red onion and mushroom panini with a side of coleslaw?" His eyes met hers. "Yes, I remembered and the number's been retired. Are you impressed?"

She was speechless. The object had taken on a new significance as did being here with Justin. She began to fully realise the direction their relationship was heading. The simple act of sleeping in the same bed with him topless was inevitable and unfortunate at the same time. In less than thirty-six hours he would be leaving her and she had no way of knowing when the opportunity to really feel him with her would present itself. In her previous relationships she had run as quickly and as far from sex as she could but this time...this time she had tuned in to her body's longing for intimacy with a man who made her whole world complete, and expected nothing but her time in return.

"That's the most romantic thing anyone's ever done for me." She wiped away tears with the back of her hand. "Everything you've done has been more than I ever could have expected." Her pulse quickened when she watched him walk around the kitchen counter to be with her.

"I've already told you how I feel about you." He brought her tear soaked hand to his lips and kissed it, his eyes closing, hiding the strength of those feelings so as not to frighten her. "Everything I've done is because you deserve it. You make me feel like I've found my place in this world." He lifted her chin and bought his mouth down onto hers.

The next thing she felt was being lifted onto the counter. Justin pushed his body in between her legs and she wrapped them around him. She pulled at his top, lifting it over his head. Her hands explored every inch of his muscular chest then moved around to his back. Justin covered her face and neck with kisses, each one sending eager tingles right the way down to her toes. She felt his teeth on her earlobes and then he said, "Oh shit!"

He rushed to the other side of the counter where the scrambled eggs had become crispy and inedible. He turned the burner off under them and did a quick check to make sure nothing else was posing a fire risk.

He returned to Mina. "Are you sure about this because I don't think I'll be able to stop myself once we start." When she nodded, he lifted her up in his arms, her legs wrapped around him once more, and carried her into the bedroom. *Oh my God, am I really doing this?* Her mind raced through all the reasons she shouldn't.

The song playing in the background switched from one artist's struggle as a jilted lover to someone else praising how the angels would sing as he made love to his woman. Justin lay Mina on the bed and slipped off her pyjama top. No one had ever seen her naked before, except her mum, and that was only until she was old enough to bathe herself. First his hands caressed her skin, then his mouth. Instinctively, she groped around for something to cling to, the sensation of his lips, his tongue, almost making her want to push him away but she could feel her inhibitions melting and her head filling with all the possibilities. Justin's mouth was at the waistband of her pyjama bottoms. He glanced up at her for permission. She bit her lip and nodded. He slid off the rest of her clothes and let them fall to the floor. She inhaled sharply as she felt his mouth on her thighs and working right down to her feet. He stood up at the foot of the bed, undid his belt and stepped out of his trousers.

Mina's head was swamped with emotion, she needed to say something before it was too late. Justin manoeuvred himself on top of her, on his elbows. They looked into each other's eyes, Mina held his face and said, "Justin, I love you."

Surprise lit up his face and launched them into a deep, slow kiss. A kiss confirming their feelings for one another. A kiss which led to Mina feeling him inside her for the first time. He was every bit as considerate about her physical needs as he had been about her emotional requirements. He slowed when she asked him to and when he felt her nails bite into his shoulders, he took it as a signal for him to up his pace.

Their fingers were intertwined while her legs supported his movements, pulling him deeper into her. His breathing became heavier, her body arched up onto him and, together, they found the place from which there was no going back.

Justin buried his face in her neck and felt something wet on his face. Lifting up , he saw tears falling from Mina's eyes. His lips absorbed her salty tears. He looked at her but she had her eyes closed, so he kissed each eyelid. "Mina." His mouth was on hers. "Look at me, Mina."

She blinked hard, releasing tears as yet unshed. Her eyes focused on Justin, beads of sweat on his forehead. Sensing what was on his mind, she said, "I can't explain how I feel, but you didn't hurt me."

He moved off her and lay by her side. He moved his hand along her body, making her shudder. "You were amazing." He found he couldn't keep his hands off her now, or his lips. "I wish we could stay like this all day."

She pulled his arm closer around her. "Why can't we?"

"Mmm. Remember breakfast?"

She turned to face him, her inhibitions fading. "We may as well have lunch now. Or what do you call it...brunch."

"Agreed." Justin sat up and said, "I'm going to have a shower. Would you like to join me?"

She thought of what that might entail, nothing she wasn't already used to doing, just an extra body to share her usually private space. "Maybe next time. I just want to lie here a moment longer."

With the bed to herself, Mina pulled the sheets around her. Sensations periodically coursed through her naked body, reminders of how she had given herself to Justin. She didn't want anything to change between them, but it was too late for that. She wondered *Will we start to behave differently now?* Even if they did it would be short lived and, with that thought, she wrapped the cool bed sheet around her warm body and began rifling through the bags Dan had packed for her.

Justin strolled into the bedroom with a towel around his lower half and beads of water clinging to his skin. "I left the shower on for you." He handed her a robe. "I've put a towel in there too."

Justin's bathroom was almost as big as her room at the hotel. A mirror covered one entire wall; *there'll be no escaping bad skin or hair days in this bathroom.* The shower cubicle itself was big enough for four, never mind two.

"Oh my God, Justin!"

Without thinking, Justin sped into the bathroom to check Mina was alright. "What? What happened?"

"It's like showering in a volcano!"

He laughed, unable to stop himself.

"It's not funny! I almost burnt myself! Justin!"

"I'm sorry! I don't know what came over me!" The longer Justin laughed, the more it made Mina want to join him. "Stop it! I'm trying to shower!"

He regained his composure, taking stock of where he was and who he was looking at. As yet, he still had his towel around him, making it too easy for him to slip it off and join his lover in the shower for further foreplay. Justin was starting to see Mina in a different way; sexier, more confident. The combination of his head wanting the same thing as his body made him drop his towel. He prepared himself for rejection, but when his lips touched her wet neck, Mina only shivered and arched her back for more. Her head and heart were in agreement, so she gave herself permission to share her private ablutions with Justin.

Sometime later, they emerged into the bedroom, smiles on their faces. She tried not to watch as Justin applied body lotion, starting with his legs, his calf muscles in particular exhibiting signs of regular gym workouts.

"It's rude to stare," he said, startling her out of her trance.

"Don't flatter yourself!"

"You're biting your lip as well." It was always a give-away that she was deep in thought. "Here, let me help you." He started towards her, ready to massage some of the lotion into her skin.

"I'm finished now!"

"Unless you have stretchy arms, you've missed your back." He squeezed lotion onto his hands, told her to lie down on the bed and his hands applied pressure to the length of her back, while his mind ordered the day ahead of them; brunch had become lunch, then a walk on the beach, maybe a movie and finally dinner and bed.

***

Keys in hand, Justin led Mina out to the lift. She read his face and said, "Behave yourself!"

They ate at Beach Food which meant easy access to the beach straight after. They had both worked up an appetite and ate in silence, each occasionally looking up to see what the other was doing.

"I'm going to miss this." Being preoccupied with the new venue meant Justin had been able to dismiss any thoughts about the day he and Mina would say goodbye. "When will you come and see me?"

"In Birmingham?" *Where will I stay. I'm not going home. Who knows what might be in store?* "I don't know. As soon as I work out where to stay, I suppose." Justin's brow was scrunched. "I'm not going to my parents, if that's what you're thinking."

"There's plenty of room in my new place. Come stay with me." His new job came organised with a three-bedroom detached house, a twenty-minute drive to work. "You could have your own bedroom if it'd make you feel better." Although their relationship had taken a significant leap forward, caution might serve them both well.

"Really? Don't you want to sleep with me again?"

"Of course I do! I just don't want you to think I only want you for your body."

"I don't think that! Thank you, though."

They walked along the beach, arm in arm, talking about Mina's imminent move to Dan's and the opening night at the new venue.

"We know where you'll stay when you come to visit me, but where will I stay when I come to visit you?"

She thought the answer was obvious but supposed she should ask Dan first.

"Alex has asked me to be his Best Man. They set the date for July twenty eighth, next year."

"What does a Best Man do exactly?"

"Helps the groom organise outfits and the stag night." He circled Mina as they walked. "Traditionally, the woman who attends the wedding with the Best Man is also the sexiest woman in the place." He pictured all eyes on them as they slow danced in front of however many guests Alex and Lauren were inviting.

"Well, you better be on your best behaviour if you want me to stick around."

He held her from behind and whispered in her ear. "We should start practising our slow dance." He inhaled her scent, wanting to return to the security of his apartment, the heat of the shower.

For an instant, Mina succumbed, inviting his touch. The once clear visions of people around her became blurry, her eyelids fluttered, fading them out. Sand swirled around her bare feet as she stood, fixed to the spot. She cancelled out the background sounds of excited children, the fainter volume of the pier rides, grandparents calling out for grandchildren to slow down and wait for them, concentrating instead, on her breathing.

"You're good at this." Justin's hands guided her hips to follow his rhythm.

"You're a good teacher."

***

A few hours later, they were on their way back to Justin's apartment.

"I'm sorry for putting you through that! It was the worst movie I think I've ever seen!"

"I know! What made you want to go in the first place?"

"It was supposed to be exciting, edge of your seat stuff."

"Yeah, edge of your seat ready to leave! Look at this." She held up the tub of popcorn and said, "I've never left a movie with half a tub of popcorn left."

Justin put his hand in and snatched a handful of sweet popcorn. "At least it makes a handy snack for the walk back."

Groups of weekend revellers were gathering outside bars and pubs, catching up with friends and family. The humid night meant people wore light jackets or cardigans but three out of every five women adorning their feet with open toed sandals, Mina being one of them.

Cracks in Mina's blissful mood began to make pathways for more solemn consideration; she wanted to tell Justin not to leave her. How could he still want to go after sharing his bed and her body? *If he loves me, as he says he does, he'd stay, wouldn't he?* She clenched her fists, trying to relax. She scolded herself for her part in this predicament; she wasn't supposed to fall in love before achieving independence. "Justin, I need to sit down."

He purloined a chair for her from a bar they were passing and then crouched in front of her, his hands on her knees. She shut her eyes and began to breathe deep and slow.

Justin was talking, asking what he could do to help; *stay in Weston with me* her heart wanted to scream out. Instead she remained in the darkness behind her eyelids. Appreciation of the time she had left with Justin was what calmed her palpitations. Her hands groped for Justin's and she re-joined the present. They drew closer, sharing the same air. He was unmasking a previously dormant, irrationality in her thinking. She had always been proud of being reasonable during times when others were dreaming up worst-case scenarios. This was the first time in her twenty-one years when she found herself unable to reconcile events in her life with the impact they were bound to have. Questions of sex, love and relationships ebbed and flowed whilst her hold on Justin tightened. In their embrace, she opened her eyes to see people going on with their night, uninterested in the person occupying a chair on the pavement. Just a few more moments and she'd be ready to pick up where she left off. She recalled the advice given to her the last time this happened and enveloped herself in the aroma emanating off Justin's skin, the rise and fall of each breath, the security of his arms.

"I'm ready to go now." She kissed his cheek, waited for him to stand and took his hand.

Reaching his apartment, they sat on the balcony with a drink, Mina opting for a mug of tea, in spite of the heat, her legs resting on Justin's. He said, "I want to know what you're thinking."

"I'm not good with things like this. It might not make any sense to you."

"I just want you to tell me what's on your mind. You can help me make sense of it." This was a conversation he could easily be having with Frankie and it worried him. If he made the first disclosure, perhaps she'd follow suit. "I don't want to leave you. It tears me up every time I think about us being so far apart."

She said, "I keep thinking I should ask you to stay, but you'd have to say no. I've never felt this way about anyone and it scares me to be so dependent on you, on us. I know how important Frankie is to you, but I can't help feeling jealous that she'll be closer to you than I will and I'm angry that you're going back to the place I called home only a few months ago." She placed her feet down onto the hot slate tiles. "I thought being in love meant never hurting each other."

"To me, being in love means finding a way to make things work." He settled on the table in front of her. "Even when it seems impossible." He lifted her feet onto his lap. "We can make this work."

Mina reached across him to pick up her mug; like Dan, Justin was getting better at making tea. "I guess we can text each other every day."

"We can have ridiculously long phone calls every week." He bent to rest his chin in the gap between her knees. "And we'll visit as often as we can."

"Oh my God, I'm gonna miss you so much!" She took her feet down so she could lean in to kiss him. She slid onto his lap then and his hands traced a way under her top. After the kiss, he asked where she wanted to have dinner. "What's that face for?"

"I thought you were cooking for me!"

"I was." He moved a strand of hair behind her ear. "But then I thought if we stayed in, we might not get round to dinner."

"Good point. You don't want to see me when I'm hungry!"

***

The restaurant Mina chose was nestled in between an entertainment complex and a gastro pub. It was called Spice of Life and, the closer they got to it, the more apt the name became. The aromas were so familiar to Mina. If she was ever a contestant on Mastermind, spices used in Indian cooking would be her specialist subject.

They were seated at a table in the middle of the room. The lighting sconces on the walls were supported by a single tea light on each occupied table. She relished being the one to lead Justin into a new experience for a change.

"This menu's huge. What do you recommend?"

"You're asking me? I've never been here before. Let's ask one of the waiters."

After an explanation of some of the main course dishes, Justin chose lamb madras, boasting he wasn't afraid of heat, and Mina chose butter chicken. Eating their starters, Mina talked about the shopping trip she and Dan had deemed necessary to make her move complete. The shadows of her earlier distress became distant, no longer hindering her ability to see the contentment right before her. She told herself to keep focused on the things she had control of and to let go of thoughts that could be her undoing.

"Oh, wow!" Justin helped Mina to organise the table for their food; the accompanying naan breads, of which there were too many for just the two of them, were at risk of ending up on the floor. "I think maybe we ordered too much!"

"As long as we don't get rushed out of here, we'll have plenty of time to eat all this!"

Chewing her first mouthful, Mina noticed Justin staring at his plate. "What's the matter?"

He motioned to the cutlery.

"No, don't use those. Get your hands messy!"

"Alright." He tore off a piece of naan and, after some trial manoeuvres, managed to scoop up a chunk of lamb. "There's some serious heat in here!" The intensity of flavour left no crevice in his body untouched and, by the time he was halfway through the madras, it was showing on his face.

Mina dabbed the beads of sweat off for him with a napkin. "My goodness! I wish you could see yourself!"

He gulped down a pint of water and refilled it. "Now I understand what people mean when they say 'This'll put hairs on your chest'!" His mother used to lace her cooking with heat, but this was on another level. After every couple of mouthfuls, he needed to take a drink, astonished that Mina seemed utterly unaffected by the spicy food.

When the dessert menu was handed to him, Mina recommended rasmalai, a sweet milk based dessert, and her favourite. It muted the heat of his main course, much to his relief.

***

"Thanks for that." Justin linked fingers with Mina for a walk back to his place in relative silence, apart from the reverberating music spilling out from packed clubs and pubs into the cool night air whenever they passed an open door. Streetlights cast shadows on the trees lining the walkway and little gusts of wind made the shadows dance, as if wanting to join the party. Justin was conscious of his arm being pulled back, so he slowed his natural walking pace, glad to do so, feeling as though he'd just eaten the equivalent of half his body weight.

Despite moving most personal belongings out of his apartment for shipping to his new Birmingham home, apartment 27 would not be easily forgotten. Two relationships had been subject to major milestones while he had been the occupant; the end of his romance with Eve and achieving an unprecedented level of intimacy with Mina. He eagerly anticipated the milestones awaiting him at 2 Rosewood Drive.

Mina removed her sandals and leant back on Justin as the sofa bore the weight of their overfilled bodies. She closed her eyes, comforted by the rise and fall of Justin's chest. She said, "I think I might fall asleep right here." And did.

Justin placed a pillow under her head, covered her with a blanket and retired to his own bed, sad to have it empty. He lay awake a few minutes, running his hand over the pillow that should have had Mina's head on it. He contemplated waking her up from peaceful slumber to cure his loneliness, but ran the thought back and forth until, eventually, it put him to sleep.

It had been ages since the last time his alarm clock became obsolete, so he didn't get out of bed straight away. He stretched his long limbs, pulled the covers up and turned onto his side. Mina was right there beside him. Now he was certainly not about to rush out of bed. He slipped his arm under her head and she snuggled closer. There would not be another moment like this for a long time, so he stayed in bed with Mina until she drifted out of sleep sometime later.

They managed to eat breakfast together, on the balcony, in the fifteen-degree heat of the morning. Their inevitable goodbye played on both their minds, filling both of them with dread. Mina kept telling herself to stay in control, not to wail as though at the funeral of a loved one, while Justin kept telling himself to lift her into his arms and make love to her one last time. Only one of them would succeed in taking their own advice.

They wrapped their arms around each other in an effort to put their lives on hold, until life itself would give in and declare, *Right, you win. You get to spend the rest of your lives together!*

Justin kissed Mina at last and said, "I have to go."

Her grip on his body reluctantly loosened. "Make sure you call me as soon as you get there - as soon as you step into your huge new house."

"I will." He held her hands and then handed her a tissue.

She had cried with a tighter grip on reality than expected, silent tears rolling down her cheeks. She waited on the street outside the hotel, until the blue Audi could no longer be seen without the aid of one of the telescopes dotted around the beach.

Moving Time for Mina

The start of the working week saw Mina more upbeat than she had believed would be possible. Her telephone conversation with Justin went on longer than expected, and included one or two silences in between when they were content just hearing each other breathing. She maintained rationality by becoming excited about the opening night at Justin's new bar. She imagined the type of invitees, dressed in their sharpest clothes in case they were snapped by photographers. The press would sing the praises of the team behind it and then, of course, Justin's photo would be everywhere, making him an overnight city celebrity.

Wednesday came around, and Justin could only talk for a few minutes before being dragged away to ensure no detail had been overlooked before the event. Mina did her best to remain calm. *It isn't his fault; he has a job to do.* Then early evening, Justin called her.

"Hi! I didn't think I'd be hearing from you." She wondered if he could feel her smile across the ether.

"Yeah, me too! I'm getting ready, so I thought I'd call." He intended to make the most of the forty-minute reprieve. "What are you up to?"

"I'm writing in my journal." She had started to keep one since moving to Weston, but entries had been sporadic until the weekend of her twenty first birthday party. She closed the notebook and said, "Describe what you're going to wear."

Justin detailed the bespoke suit ordered for him. "I'll send you a photo when I'm dressed."

One question weighed heavy on her mind, but she delayed asking, not wanting to put any pressure on him. Instead they shared what had become an expectation during each phone call, until Justin said, "I really miss you."

Tears formed in Mina's eyes. "I really miss you too. When can you come and see me?"

He had asked himself the same thing, and didn't like the answer. "I won't be able to leave here at least until after the weekend. We open officially on Saturday, so hopefully sometime after. Is that okay?"

"Not really, but I understand."

In an attempt to lighten the mood, he said, "I've taken some photos of the house. I'll send them in a bit." A further silence filled the gap. "I have to go."

"Good luck and don't you forget the photos!"

"Thanks, and I won't."

The next day, the day before she moved in with Dan, she showed him Justin's photos.

"The ladies are gonna be all over him!"

"Oi!" Mina snatched the phone away. "I didn't show you so you could make me paranoid!"

He put his arm around her and said, in his most apologetic voice, "I'm sorry. What I meant to say was no woman is going to go near him because they'll look at him and see straight away that he's Mina's man."

"More like it."

"Anyway, big day tomorrow! Have you got everything packed up?"

"I'll finish up after work. Have you got my key?"

Dan tapped the pocket of his trousers. "See you after work tomorrow!"

After finishing her shift, she changed out of her uniform and went for a walk along the beach. She bought an ice cream from Beach Food and let the tiny grains of sun-baked sand slip in between her bare toes. She had put off the phone call for a few days now, telling herself it made no difference when she told them, but the fresh air and radiant heat changed her mind.

Thank goodness, she thought, when her dad answered. "I thought I should let you know that from tomorrow evening I won't be staying at the hotel."

"Oh, right. Where will you be then?"

Mina thanked her lucky stars he didn't ask if she'd be coming home. She explained her new living arrangements, omitting the part where about her work friend happening to be male. They had the briefest catch-up and then she found a quiet spot on the sand, laid out her blanket and tried to call Justin. After two failed attempts, she lay down and closed her eyes.

She dreamt of living in Justin's Birmingham house, falling asleep with him every night and waking up with him every morning. She dreamt of having breakfast together in his immaculate garden and then going out for dinner to all their favourite eating places. She dreamt of how engrossed they would become in each other, only to turn her head and spot a family friend watching them from the other side of the room. She dreamt at that exact moment, a cluster of spiders surrounded their table and began to clamber onto her legs. Some were on her chest and she heard a familiar sound. She swiped each of the spiders away with a napkin and heard the sound again. When she glanced up, Justin had disappeared, but the spider onslaught was continuing. She felt something on her face and woke with a start. A frantic shake of her clothes and blanket revealed no sign of a close encounter with the spindly-legged creatures. She looked around to get her bearings and when she realised she was still on the beach, she heard that sound again. It was her phone. Justin had sent her four texts while she'd been dreaming.

Checking the time on her phone, she found she'd lost half an hour. She dusted off the blanket and made her way back to the hotel. She responded to Justin's messages by telling him not to worry: *I'll call you tomorrow evening, once I'm settled in.*

She packed everything she could and spent her last night sleeping in the tiny, claustrophobia-inducing room.

***

Mina's new home sat in the middle of a street of semi-detached houses. Dan gave her the key and, with the grin of a child who's been told she can stay up past bedtime, she unlocked the door to her new abode. She marvelled at the simple things anyone else would likely take for granted; the sight of a long corridor, with doors that led to other living areas, a bedroom ceiling so high she could jump on her bed and still not reach it and, the one fixture creating a sense of space unlike any other, a staircase. It was like having her very own time machine where she could live out different parts of her day in different parts of the house: who knew what her future self might get up to!

They took Mina's things to her bedroom and started finding homes for everything. She didn't own enough to fill all the available drawers, so they were enjoying a mug of tea, in the kitchen within half an hour.

"Look what I got us!" Dan revealed two mugs, both slate grey with a single, large white letter engraved into them, D for Dan and M for Mina. "I couldn't resist them!"

"Dan, these are lovely!" She ran her fingers over her engraved letter and then thrust the mug into Dan's hand. "Well, put the kettle on then!"

"Listen here young lady," he wagged a finger. "Don't go getting too big for your boots now!"

"What's the plan for tonight then?" She wanted to stay in, but decided not to make a fuss if Dan wanted the opposite.

"Tonight we celebrate with pizza and a movie."

"I'm choosing. The last time I watched a movie recommended by someone else, it turned out to be the worst I'd ever seen...or heard!"

"I'm intrigued."

"No way, I'm not going through that again! Come on, let's see what's on."

They scrolled through a complete list of Netflix movies before narrowing the search to two categories: romantic comedy and superhero action. Mina had the final say, and with a film chosen, they ordered from the best pizzeria this side of the beach - according to Dan anyway. He described the long search process for outstanding pizza in such detail, anyone would have thought he'd been after his prince charming, not a nine-inch mozzarella, mushroom and chicken covered dough.

The last time she and her family had enjoyed a cosy night in front of the television had been the week Anisa caught chicken pox; she'd insisted the only sure-fire way to make her feel better would be for all of them, Rehan included, to watch her favourite animation with a tub of sweet popcorn apiece. Before the film had ended, she'd fallen asleep.

Mina noted the dramatic changes in her life since then. For a start, the regular thrice yearly celebrations hosted in her home had dwindled to nothing. There had been no warning; everyone just stopped coming. She'd hoped it was temporary, that as soon as her relatives had dealt with whatever they were coping with, her parent's home would, once again, come alive with the lip-smacking aroma of food and the chatter of voices. Six years on and she was only now realising those times would never come again; not as they used to be.

To live in Weston, she'd made the bold decision to leave home and now bold decisions had become the norm in her life.

She was biting into her third slice of pizza when Justin called. She signalled to Dan to keep watching and took her phone into the kitchen.

"I couldn't wait for you to call, so here I am. How was the move?"

"It went well. We're just watching a movie and eating pizza. How are you? How was Wednesday night?"

"It was perfect. Everyone had a great time. Take a look at the website; the photos have been posted."

She had already browsed the website. It was her way of keeping close to Justin. "I wish you were here with me. There's too much space in my bed." She had grossly underestimated the impact sleeping with Justin would have on her when he left.

"I have a suggestion...get a smaller bed!"

"Very funny! I thought we were having a moment!"

"Sorry. What are you up to tomorrow?"

"Not much. Dan's got a family thing to go to, so I'll have the house to myself."

"You should jump on the train; come see me."

"You'll be too busy getting ready for opening night. I'd be a distraction."

"I could do with distraction. Think about it."

If the night wasn't so important for him, she knew she definitely would travel to Birmingham. "I'll think about it but don't get your hopes up."

"Too late for that! I'll let you get back to your movie."

Dan quizzed her over choosing not to rush into Justin's arms at the first opportunity. "He's gonna be busy. People will need to speak to him. He'll need to be everywhere getting things ready. We won't get quality time together. It's kind of a big day for me too." When Dan looked confused, she explained, "It'll be my first weekend in my new place."

Dan said, "The novelty will soon wear off. I still think you should go see him."

The movie ended with the female lead realising the male lead was the man she should have been with a hundred and thirty-five minutes earlier. "Thanks for watching it again." Dan had seen her chosen movie before. "Still good third time around."

He stood and reached for the pizza box. Mina took it from him. "I'll tidy up. You go to bed." She discarded the empty box, cleaned the table and washed the glasses and cutlery before turning off the lights and ascending to her new bedroom. She had bought two duvet sets in colours to match the bedroom wallpaper and Dan had accused her of being a plain Jane. She liked the colours anyway and chose to use the sky-blue set first.

She climbed into bed and called Justin, wanting to make sure he understood her reasons for not visiting. Their conversation took a few different turns over the course of twenty minutes and, when she said goodbye, the images of their first sexual encounter came flooding back. She didn't find it easy to sleep after that.

Family Ties

The management team were buzzing, as were the press and media; the invitation only event had been a roaring success. The marketing team had already taken bookings for a number of high profile events in the run up to New Year. Ongoing success hinged on social media hype filtering out to the nocturnal inhabitants of the city and a handful of fresh faced, bright-eyed youngsters had been hired to distribute special offer promotion leaflets to entice revellers away from their competitors.

Justin had a light breakfast and drove to the gym for an early morning workout. He was glad the week had flown by, but not fast enough though; he'd still found snippets of alone time which he filled with thoughts of their last weekend together. A look at his schedule for the week ahead reminded him of the futility of even thinking about trying to organise his life into categories. He'd informed his line manager of Frankie's situation and was reassured they would allow him time off when he needed it and now he was working full-tilt to get ahead of things.

When he got into his car, he entered Dan's address into his navigation system. The voice told him he could be there in one hour and forty-five minutes. He stared at the screen. A few minutes later he picked up his phone, sent Mina a text message and drove home. He knew it was the right decision for both of them, but that fact did nothing to appease his heart. This was the longest time he had spent away from Mina. He was no stranger to difficult moments in a relationship, but not usually in the honeymoon period. He'd been seeing Mina for no more than ten weeks and, as far as he was concerned, they could do without the distance between them. Mina had said she'd be a distraction if she visited him and he agreed but the mammoth task of managing a new venue, after the success of Sunset Strip, saw Justin searching for something to distract him, and Mina was all he wanted. Their paths had crossed at a point in both their lives when neither of them had any inclination to look for a life partner, but now they were being kept apart by an invisible power, forced to live individual lives, under the pretence of still being in a relationship. He couldn't quite put his finger on the reasons why he had to have Mina in his life, but she'd become part of his being and he'd do whatever he could to keep it that way. He would be with her even if only for a couple of hours; time enough for a walk on the beach or a snuggle on the sofa. He laughed at the last one; the thought of snuggling had never appealed to him until Mina came along and told him it was because he'd been doing it wrong.

He sat in the kitchen and pored over numerous emails of checklists, supplier details and memos. In spite of the impact moving to Birmingham had already had on his love life, Justin couldn't deny the hit of adrenaline that poured into him when looking over his new domain. The thrill of being responsible for laying the foundations of an establishment that, he believed, would still be standing strong in ten years, had been good enough reason to grab the opportunity when it had presented itself. He switched off his laptop; work would have to wait until after he'd seen Frankie for which he was driving six miles to a house he'd not visited in far too long.

He rang the doorbell and a stout, sixty-odd year old woman greeted him with a hug. "Boy, why you don't ever come round see me and your huncle dem?"

Then she smacked him over the head. "You not too big to get a good beating!"

His Aunt Jo and Uncle Hector were the most active couple he knew. They took part in weekly tennis and swimming sessions at the local leisure centre and made regular trips to the gym; his love of being in the gym must have come from them. When Aunty Jo hit you, it reverberated through you like the aftershocks of an earthquake.

"I'm back in Birmingham now, so you'll see me more!" He put his arm around her and they walked into the living room. Everything about the décor had changed since his last visit. Even the television had gone, replaced by a large bookcase. They walked through to find Frankie making lunch in the kitchen.

"Something smells good!" Justin inspected her creation. "I hope there's enough for me too."

"Oh, so you come and see me after all dis time and hexpect to be fed!"

Justin used Frankie for cover, expecting another smack. "How are you, sis?"

"I'm feeling good at the moment." She was mixing ingredients in a large wooden bowl. She covered it with cling film and set it in the fridge. "Let's sit." She led Justin into the conservatory and eased herself with care into a chair.

"How are you really feeling?" He was the only one who knew the full extent of her health issues and she wanted it kept that way as long as possible. She'd been staying with her aunt and uncle for a week, wanting the company. They didn't interrogate her and she settled in as if she'd never left. Their company of people meant less time to dwell on unspoken things.

"I'm glad to be here." She put her hand on his and said, "It's better for the time being, even if you've got other ideas."

"I'll agree with whatever's best for you. You know that."

"Are you ready for tonight?"

"I'm rearing to go. I don't know about anyone else."

A shout announced Uncle Hector. He grabbed Justin's hand and said, "Here's the man everyone's been talking about!" He looked Justin straight in the eyes and said, "Your parents would be proud of you, son."

"Thanks, uncle."

"Things to do..." he said. "...But me and your aunty will be coming to your opening!"

Justin and Frankie looked at each other and smiled, neither one of them having the courage to argue the point.

Lunch was served at the dining room table, an excuse for reminiscing on the good old days. Afterwards their aunt and uncle excused themselves as they were meeting at their local church to help with a fundraising event and Justin prepared to say goodbye too.

"Don't forget we're meeting my consultant on Tuesday morning."

He hugged his sister and said, "I won't. I'll see you tomorrow for Sunday dinner anyway."

The Trouble with Tania

A quick glance at the external CCTV cameras showed a queue of people, curving around the railings and passing round the corner and out of sight. He gave his team talk and the doors were opened to the public.

The three bars situated in different sections of the club were soon surrounded by people taking advantage of the drinks promotion leaflets handed out earlier in the week. The surroundings were a stark contrast to Sunset Strip; there were no podiums or stages for dancers in Sunset Strip and in the new place, there were three separate rooms, four if you included the VIP room, each playing a different genre of music; hip hop and r'n'b, pop and house music.

A text from Marvin landed to say they were all on the way in and Justin headed towards the entrance to greet his friends and their partners. A hand on his arm brought him to a halt. It was someone he hadn't seen for some time.

"It is you! I so hoped we'd bump into each other! I saw your face in the paper and I had to get myself in here!" Tania beamed.

Now this will be a story to tell Mina, he thought. "Hi, how are you?" He hoped to get a quick reply and then be on his way to find his friends.

"I'm doing much better, now." She stroked her neck and said, "Isn't Mina here with you?"

This could get very awkward, very quickly, so he answered carefully. "Why would Mina be with me?"

"She was with you the last time I bumped into you in Birmingham. Remember?"

Justin's mind raced back to the time Mina first met his friends wearing the dress he'd bought for her. "I was out with friends that night. Anyway, I'm just on the way to meet some people and I've got loads to do, as you can imagine!"

"Alright. I'll find you later." Tania let him rush away from her.

He wondered, with a frisson of fear, why she wanted to see him later. He hoped to avoid any backlash, for Mina's sake. Tania had given him nothing but a negative vibe ever since her first night in Weston with Mina and he was well aware of how much trouble she had instigated with Mina's parents and brother.

"Marvin!" He waved to catch their attention.

"There he is, the man of the moment!"

He was greeted by slaps on the back and hugs from each of the lads and cheek kisses on the cheek from their ladies. "So, what do you think? Pretty amazing isn't it!" He showed them to a reserved booth and before long their table was covered in Dom Perignon, Grey Goose Vodka and Jack Daniels. Justin joined them at intervals throughout the night and was pleased to see they were all having a good time. So far, he had avoided further run-ins with Tania, but the night was young and, from what he recalled, she didn't give up easily.

His night consisted of serving drinks to customers, being photographed with them for the website and other publicity tasks. He made sure to sneak away into his office for a few minutes, after the first rush of the evening had slowed. From there, he exercised his role of guardian and protector of the club, with CCTV his loyal sidekick. The intermittent crackle of walkie-talkies filled the quiet room, another way for him to stay in touch with what was happening while he hid away. He began to miss the bellowing bass lines and flashing lights, so finally he left the serenity of his office and prepared to let his very short hair down with his friends.

In the VIP room, most of his friends had been enticed onto the dance floor. There were less people up there than in the rest of the club which meant less likelihood of injuring innocent bystanders in the throes of their latest dance moves. Justin had to be careful not to over exert himself; he only had one set of clothes and presentation was key, especially on opening night. Eventually, he realised the others were outshining him, so he bowed out gracefully and sat down for a few minutes with Alex's fiancé Lauren, Chloe, Marvin's partner and Darren's girlfriend, Hazel.

"Are you alright ladies? Can I get you anything else?"

"No, we're fine, thanks. I think I've had too much already!" said Hazel.

Lauren leaned over and said, "How are you and Mina dealing with the change?"

Justin sat back against the sofa and said, "We haven't seen each other for a week now and we both have things going on, so it hasn't sunk in yet."

"I can't imagine how difficult it must be for you both. You looked really happy together. Don't let that go."

"I don't intend to."

Voices over the walkie-talkie alerted him to a spot of bother in the pop room, so he excused himself to see what was happening. He reached the room just as security were escorting two women out, followed closely by their respective groups of friends, the aftermath of a fracas over a spilt drink. He checked none of his staff had been caught up in the situation then made his way back towards the VIP room. His route took him along the wide corridor serving all the three main rooms. A female group came out of the hip hop room as he passed and before he could register who they were, Tania was upon him.

"Here he is, girls!" To friends she said, "May I introduce Mr Justin Hargreaves, the manager of this club." She turned back to him, a wicked grin all on her face.

For a moment, he had to forget how much he despised Tania. "Ladies, I hope you're all having a great time!" Before he could protest, they had flanked him on both sides, their arms were around him and Tania was taking photos.

He forced a smile but then Tania said, "Now it's my turn." She pushed her friends aside and stood as close to Justin as she could get. She let her hand slide as low down his back as she could and said, "Smile Justin."

They cackled and clustered round each other's phones to see the results and Justin seized the opportunity to be on his way. "It's been great, ladies, but I really have to go!"

He didn't manage to shake off Tania who, keeping pace alongside him, said, "I suppose things didn't work out for you."

Justin didn't respond.

She had another go. "Now that you're in Birmingham, maybe we could try again?"

He stopped, looked her straight in the eyes and said, "Try what again?"

She tilted her head and walked her fingers up his chest. "I'll ask you out again and this time you can say *yes*." She was good. And so self-confident, he could tell she'd done this many times before.

He had to protect Mina at all costs. He held her wrist and said, "The answer will still be *no*. I have no interest in starting anything with you, so if you don't mind, I'd like to get back to work."

Her expression switched from flirty to pissed off, in the blink of an eye. She straightened her shoulders, lifted her chin and said, "I don't know what game you and Mina think you're playing, but it won't end the way you want it to!"

"I'm just trying to get on with my life. I suggest you do the same!"

As Justin walked swiftly away down the corridor, the impact on Tania's ego had the force of a dart thrown directly at the bullseye. A number of options coursed through her mind; she could defend herself, she could become a thorn in his side for the rest of the night or, a rare occurrence, she could leave with her self-respect intact. The unfortunate thing was he was so damn alluring; his caramel-honey skin good enough to eat off. Letting him go meant she'd have to live knowing at least one member of the opposite sex couldn't be persuaded to sample what she had to offer.

"Justin, wait!" Having made up her mind, she raced after him. She reached for the bare skin of his arm, forcing him to stop.

He looked down at the hand on his arm and said, "I've nothing else to say to you."

"Well, I'm not finished. You've met me a couple of times and you think you know me. I can be your best friend or your worst enemy."

"Which one are you to Mina?" Perhaps that was a misjudged barb, but too late to retract.

She recoiled in astonishment. "Mine and Mina's friendship has nothing to do with you, unless there is something going on between you."

Justin's phone began ringing. "I haven't got time for this. I've got a club to manage. You should get your priorities in order and realise the world doesn't revolve around you."

This time as he stormed off, Tania let him go. She scrolled through the photo gallery on her phone, found the one of her and Justin and sent it to Mina.

Justin Needs a Time Out

Her grip on Justin's hand grew tighter with every word the consultant uttered. Frankie's body had been battling itself to stay strong and, up until now, she'd believed she was winning. The slower pace at work, staying at her aunt and uncle's and constant support from Justin had all given her a false sense of improvement. She felt her resilience crumbling and hated her own weakness; it was the facet of her personality she kept hidden, but she no longer knew how long she'd be able to maintain it.

The consultant left them alone, giving them time to absorb the latest update on Frankie's health. For a long while they sat in complete silence.

"Can you take me home, please?"

Not a word passed either's lips all through the drive back to their aunt and uncle's house. Frankie stared out of the window, expressionless, picturing her own demise and realised, in doing so, she was preparing for an emotional meltdown. Her resolve was being stretched and, instead of snapping, it would hang limply around her like a pointless piece of string, leaving her to meander through whatever remained of the rest of her life.

They reached the house and before there was any opportunity to be asked how it went, she excused herself to her room.

Justin went into the living room and answered the questions posed by their elders. His uncle poured generous servings of Jamaican dark rum as the conversation came to a head. From their faces he could tell they were just as devastated as he was.

"We'll do everything we can to help."

"I know. She just needs some space right now."

A few hours passed and Justin needed to get ready for work. He went upstairs and knocked on her bedroom door. "How are you doing?"

Frankie patted the bed and Justin sat down beside her. "I don't want the surgery."

He exhaled deliberately slowly. "Are you sure? Maybe you should sleep on it."

"I know the risks. I'm not willing to put myself through that."

He wanted to shake her and tell her to stop being selfish and to think about what she was putting him through, but instead he nodded and told her he'd respect and support her decision.

He cancelled his plans for the following day; it would be selfish to leave Frankie now, even though she'd probably scold him for putting his life on hold.

He suggested she stay with him for a couple of days, or as long as she wanted. Having her own space in which to be as contemplative or as sullen as she saw fit did wonders for her overall outlook. She became more active, returning to the gym and she was in touch with the office letting them know she wanted to resume work. They even managed to discuss his pending birthday. Frankie mooted a larger gathering, but Justin was content to go out for dinner with Frankie and his friends instead, and he had his heart set on time with Mina too.

***

Whilst most inhabitants of the city were comfy in their warm beds, Justin drove down the M5 eager, with every inch of his body, to be beside the woman he loved. The last few days with Frankie had started to take its toll on his ability to maintain focus. He needed to escape somewhere, to something else.

Music emanated from the speakers and a smile crept over his face; the exact songs he'd played on his sound system the morning after he and Mina first slept together. He turned the volume up and put his foot down on the accelerator.

When he arrived outside Dan's house, it was four in the morning. He called Mina's phone three times before she answered.

"Justin? What's going on?"

"Not much, except I'm here." He gave her time to wake up and realise what *here* meant.

"Where?"

"Outside Dan's, actually." The phone went silent and he stepped out of the warm car, into the cold morning.

A minute or so later, Mina opened the door looking shocked and tired.

"Come in, quickly. It's cold!"

Justin stepped inside and as soon as the door had been closed, swept Mina into his arms.

"I can't believe you're here." She noticed afresh how good he smelt, in spite of having been at work for hours before.

He kissed her in the hallway, letting his hands refamiliarise themselves with the curves he remembered. "Good morning."

"Good morning." She realised he wasn't an apparition. "Do you want a tea or coffee?"

He shook his head and said, "I want you."

"Smooth talker. Have you come straight from work?" When he nodded, she said, "You must be shattered." She stroked his face and kissed him. "You should sleep." She took him by the hand and led him upstairs to her bedroom. There they both fell quickly asleep, Justin's head resting on Mina's chest.

She awoke a few hours later and noticed neither of them had changed position. She stroked his arm and he stirred. "Good morning, again."

"What time is it?"

"Nine." She slipped her arm out from under him. "I'll make us tea and let Dan know you're here."

She talked to herself as the teabag sat in the boiling water then she reached for a teaspoon from the drawer.

"Morning!"

The teaspoon in Mina's hand flew across the kitchen counter and onto the floor. "Jeez Louise! You scared the living daylights out of me!"

"Oh. I'll just go back to bed then, shall I?"

"Sorry. I was in a world of my own." She poured milk into each mug.

Dan looked over her shoulder. "You've made two mugs of tea. I don't drink tea in the morning. What's going on?"

"Justin's here. He got here at like four in the morning."

"No way! He's such a romantic!"

"You'll see him later; you can tell him yourself."

She set the mugs down on the bedside table unable to take her eyes off him, sitting up, bare chested in bed. She had a sudden urge to climb on top of him and make up for lost time, but they weren't in an apartment, on their own. This was Dan's house and she should respect that. Still, she couldn't see any reason why she should completely deny the impulse; in moderation of course. She sat across his lap, her legs either side of him, her hands absorbing the texture of his skin. *Oh, this is so good.* Her pulse quickened as she took a long look at the only man she had given herself to. Justin sat upright causing her to lock her legs behind him. His mouth on her skin made her whisper his name and she tightened her grip on him. His hands under her top made her shudder and then rested on her hips, pulling her even closer to him.

He started to lift her pyjama top over her head and that's when she stopped him. "We really shouldn't, not here," she said, in between his kisses. "Even though I really want to."

"If we were in Birmingham we wouldn't have this problem." Determined not to let the moment slip through his fingers, he continued his onslaught on her skin. "You feel so good." He slipped her top off, exposing her nakedness.

167

"Just imagine, we could be in any room in my huge house, with no one to disturb us." His hands rested under her arms, his thumbs caressing her breasts. Then he let his mouth take over.

She was finally beginning to appreciate how desperately she needed Justin in her life but her anxious anticipation of his next departure was getting in the way of letting her body succumb to his demands.

She felt herself rolling over, Justin now on top of her. "I don't think I'll be able to let you go now," she said

"I've got ages before I have to leave, so don't think about that now." He searched behind him for her pyjama top and climbed off her.

Mina handed him his mug of still hot tea then sat up and reached for hers. "Now you're here, what do you want to do?"

"The thing I miss the most, after you of course, is the beach!"

"Okay. Get dressed and I'll fix breakfast."

What should have been a short visit to the kitchen for a quick bite to eat, turned into a forty-five-minute affair to include a catch-up with Dan. He wanted to find out everything about Justin's new place and whether it was anything like Sunset Strip *which, by the way, is not the same without you.* By the end of the conversation, he'd invited himself to Birmingham on Mina's next visit.

Justin and Mina strolled along the beach as they had done many times before, but now when they shared stories of their week, the feeling of separation intensified. Mina was missing out on important events in Justin's life and the longer they lived separate lives in different parts of the country, the harder it would become to deny an ever-decreasing connection. She should have been thrilled knowing he missed her so much it justified an impromptu one-hundred-mile journey in the midst of an important week at work, but as she pieced together the events from his week and a half in Birmingham and it became clear the extent of what was happening to him, she felt even more out of the picture. *Just remember*, she said to herself, *he is where he needs to be.* That left her wondering whether she was where she needed to be. She was proud of how she had coped without him, re-discovering the independence that brought her here in the first place, but sensed this surprise visit would leave a Justin-shaped hole in her existence, twice the size of the one left last time.

They returned to Dan's house to find him in the kitchen. "Drinks for both of you?"

"Well," started Justin. "Are you both going off to work at the same time?"

"Yeah, we are. Why?"

"Well I was going to take Mina out for lunch, but I can make something here for all of us." He looked to Mina for approval and she nodded. "Great! Let's see what we've got to work with."

After her initial disappointment at the prospect of having to share Justin with Dan, Mina started enjoying the scene they were acting out together. Justin assigned each of them a different task; he prepared the chicken fried rice, Dan was on vegetables and Mina grabbed any fruit she could find for a refreshing dessert.

She recalled Dan's fondness for Justin when she had joined him and other colleagues on her first night out, but they had only spent time together once before. She took a chopping board and the fruit she had gathered onto the table, leaving the men with their backs to her. She listened to the banter between Dan and Justin with a hint of melancholy; if there was any justice in the world she'd be able to introduce Justin to Rehan and they would have the same kind of opportunities to bond and get to know one another. As it was, Justin was still a secret and now, after the Tania situation, he felt obliged to maintain the ruse. *Would it actually be so earth shattering to come clean about our relationship?* Prior to the confrontation in Birmingham, Mina's answer might have been *No*. However, Tania had a score to settle and with the texted photograph of her and Justin, it was clear she wouldn't go down without a fight.

Mina put the chopped and sliced fruit into a large glass bowl, added some sparkling elderflower and blackcurrant water, covered it and put it to chill in the fridge. "I'm all done. When do we eat?"

Dan said, "You can't rush perfection."

"You took the words right out of my mouth. Well said!"

"It's like that now, is it?" Mina washed her hands, took her mug out of the cupboard and proceeded to fill the kettle. "Excuse me," she said squeezing in between them for teabags and sugar.

Dan put his knife down in horror and looked from Mina to Justin. "Do you see what she's doing? She hasn't even offered to make us a drink and here we are slaving away so she can eat!"

"I didn't want to ruin your quest for perfection."

"This is what I have to put up with when you leave!"

In her bedroom Mina took out her journal, returning to the kitchen with it to finish her tea and compile her thoughts. She wrote about being woken up in the early hours of the morning by Justin's arrival. She wrote how conflicted she was remaining in Weston, pursuing her chosen path. Reading the words on the paper brought out a reality she would need to confront; *if I changed her mind, where would I live? Am I honestly considering moving back to Birmingham? What happened to the pleasures of independent living?* The answer to the last question was one word – *Justin.*

"Can you get the plates, please Mina?"

The words on the page, and the solution to the problems she had posed, were ingrained in her mind.

"Mina! Can we have the plates, please?"

"Hey!" She flapped her hands about to stop Justin tickling her ear. "Stop that!"

"We're ready to serve." He put his hand on her shoulder and said, "Are you alright? You seem miles away."

She kissed his hand and then fetched three plates. "I hate to say it, but this smells good."

Silence descended as they savoured the well prepared delights. They glanced at each other and smiled.

"We make a good team, Dan."

"I agree. That was better than any takeout!"

Mina cleared the table and took the fruit salad out of the fridge. "The best saved till last!" She served each of them a bowl of fruit salad with whipped double cream.

Dan chose to wash up and told Mina and Justin to put their feet up.

"I'm glad I decided to come. I needed a change of scenery." Justin looked around the living room. "How do you like having your own space?"

"It's fine, but I'd much rather live with you."

"Really?" He inched closer. "You know that can be arranged."

She pulled his arm around her and each fell to imagining being a more permanent part of the other's life.

***

Justin convinced her not to pull a sickie from work because it wasn't as if he was spending the night. Dan walked ahead, giving them some privacy. She locked the front door behind her and walked down to the gate where Justin was waiting. They wrapped their arms around each other for, what neither of them knew, would be their final embrace on the streets of Weston Super-Mare.

Mina caught up with Dan a few minutes later. She walked alongside in silence, before saying, "I need to be with Justin."

"Duh! Any idiot can see that!"

"I mean, I need to wake up with him and fall asleep next to him. I need to have breakfast, lunch and dinner with him by my side."

"Oh. Well, that's a different story altogether."

His visit had left her wanting more, much more. The minute his car was out of sight, she was booking a return train ticket to Birmingham and the next twenty-four hours became Mina's most productive hours at work; even torrential rainfall on the walk home couldn't dampen her spirits.

She packed a small case for the weekend and let it comfort her as the last thing she looked at before closing her eyes to sleep.

The following night, Dan accompanied a group of co-workers to Sunset Strip after their shift, but Mina abstained and chose to get some rest before her trip. She spoiled herself with musings on how ecstatic Justin would be to see her and how they would fill their time together. Sleep found her easily.

Seal of Approval

She skipped breakfast in the morning, said a quick farewell to Dan and rushed to the station. The smell of freshly baked pastries and coffee made her clutch her stomach; perhaps missing the most important meal of the day had been a mistake. She selected some unhealthy options from the shop and cursed the expense.

On the train, Justin sent a text telling her Frankie was going to their aunt and uncle's for the day, giving them space to be together. She settled into her seat, her excitement dwindling, but deep in thought. She was coming to terms with knowing how close her family would be to her destination and how clueless they were about what she was doing there.

Hidden junkyards and the neglected, overgrown gardens of abandoned houses rushed by the passengers on the train. The world on this side of the track exposed the attitudes of the people who lived there or whose job it was to maintain a good impression of the city. Fortunately, for the city of Birmingham, commuters didn't have the need to work, or play, in any of these awful areas. Mina was acquainted with a few of these places through trips to adopted aunties' houses with her mum. There was one auntie in particular who Mina looked forward to visiting; she made taste bud-exploding food, the highlight for Mina, and she had young children for Mina would play with. The frequency of these visits had lessened as Mina grew older, but she always remembered the flavoursome food especially as her mum produced similar dishes.

Whenever her mum complained about her lack of interest in the kitchen, Mina would say, "But mum, I'll never be able to cook as well as you!" Her mum would call her a silly girl and tell her to watch how she made the chapattis or the careful preparation of lentils for the tarka dhal, or cooked a variety of vegetable dishes and rice in all its variations (with potatoes, chickpeas, mincemeat). Measurement was a thing for Westerners. Authentic Pakistani home cooking consisted of a handful of this and not too much of that and Mina found herself marking the cooking spoon with an invisible line for later reference. The end result was nothing short of perfection.

These thoughts warranted half a smile. She had been given everything she could ever have needed and that was what she grew up believing. What she wanted, however, had revealed itself when she had made the decision to leave home, and was the reason she was on this train. She wanted a companion, someone to share her experiences with. Someone who accepted her foibles and irrationalities, who would embrace the person trapped inside. She had found that someone and now she wanted to strut down the streets of Birmingham arm in arm with him, showing the human race two people from opposite ends of the cultural spectrum could find common ground and share their worlds with each other.

She was the first one out of her seat and poised in position at the train's doors as it left the penultimate station. Her body rocked side to side with the rhythm of the train and she loosened her grip on the handles of her luggage. She glanced to her left and wondered what her fellow passengers were hoping to accomplish after disembarking and whether their lives were any less complicated than hers. She almost leapt onto the platform when the doors slid open. She had never been this excited to see him, ever, so, when she reached the concourse and couldn't pick out his gorgeous face from the crowd, she dropped her luggage in exasperation. Her heart raced. She second guessed herself, checking the messages she and Justin had exchanged. She verified the time on her phone against the overhead screen detailing the day's arrivals and departures and looked around one final time before walking outside to where the taxis queued.

Gone was the mass of cars parked in diagonal rows, devoid of people until the meet and greet had been completed. In its place, the city planners had opted to smooth over the rough edges with an expansive silver-grey walk-through to the indoor concourse, perhaps to complement the enormous, shiny metal eye perched above all comers. On a dry day, people would sit atop the double-decker length sections jutting out of the approach, dedicated to the year-round addition of colourful plants and foliage.

Mina's calm exterior became a little more frantic when she still couldn't see her beau. She mumbled words to help calm herself; *he might be stuck in traffic, he's probably parking now*. If she had turned at that moment, she would have foiled his attempted surprise, but she didn't and she only knew he was there when he said "Hi, Mina!" and then, "Ow!" as she swung her hand bag at him.

"You idiot! Why would you do that?" She was giving him what for with both hands. "You frightened the bloody life out of me!"

"I'm sorry," he said putting his arms around her.

She knew he wasn't really. His voice carried a hint of devilment. "Well you'll have to make it up to me," she said as she let his strength envelop her.

"I thought you might like to see the club before we go to my place. You can leave your luggage in the car and we can walk."

"Then we'll have to walk back too." She thought about how exposed they would be to unwanted scrutiny and suggested, "Can't you just drive there?"

"I don't mind."

They were able to park less than a minute away and Mina felt foolish for being so afraid of walking with him. He unlocked the huge double doors and turned on the lights.

"It's a bit different to Sunset Strip, isn't it?"

He took her by the hand and gave her a tour of each room, pointing out the exact spot where he and Tania had *bumped into* each other. Then it was the turn of the VIP room with its lush, oversized furnishings. Mina let her hand glide over the velvet coverings, a huge smile on her face as she twirled around to take in the rest of the room. "Is this the sexy room?"

Justin admired her from afar, stroking the fabrics, copying her actions. "It is now you're here."

"I've missed you, too. A lot," she said.

He resisted the urge to close the gap between them, keeping the anticipation growing. "I wish I could switch the cameras off, just long enough to show you how much I've missed you." Hearing a sharp inhalation from Mina, he began to move towards her.

"Stop right there!"

"Why?" He continued closing.

"What you said. There are cameras everywhere! We're being watched!"

"We're being recorded, that's for sure."

She walked around a sofa, putting an obstacle between them. "Exactly! Imagine if someone decided to watch this back!"

"Nothing's happened." He loved these moments when he could play with Mina's words. "But if something did, I might want to watch it back."

She stared at him, unable to find a reply. He propped himself up on a stool at the bar and she noticed how the muscles in his arms tensed. He sat with his thighs apart, looking pleased with himself. "You could watch it with me."

"Right!" She threw her hands in the air. "That's enough! I think we should go." She headed for the door. "Come on!"

"I'm not moving until you kiss me."

"I'll kiss you when we get back to your place. Now let's go."

He shook his head.

"Oh my God! You're acting like a big baby!"

"Just one kiss. That's all I'm asking."

Her heart raced. She knew if she went over there her resolve would disappear. Just look at him; she'd be a fool to refuse him. She wanted him as much as he wanted her. She released her hold on the door. *One quick smack on the lips*, she repeated in her head. She came to a halt when his legs were either side of her. He closed his eyes and pouted his lips. She shook her head softly at his antics.

The instant he felt her lips on his, he wanted to grab her, pull her into him and make love to her on the counter where, later that night, guests would be ordering drinks and perhaps brewing their own flirtations. He occupied his hands by keeping them steady on the stool and let his mouth do the work. The kiss was soft and slow and the feel of Mina's hands resting on his thighs excited him. She was right; they needed to get back to his place.

Their eyes met as the kiss came to an end and he whispered, "We can go now." He took her hand and led her out of the building.

While Justin drove, Mina stroked his neck. "Mmm, that's nice. Tickles, but it's nice."

"I hope you've got food in. I didn't have a proper breakfast."

"Don't worry, I'll throw something together for us after."

"After what?" It took a few seconds before she realised what he meant. She closed her eyes and for the rest of the journey imagined what they would get up to.

She opened her eyes when Justin told her they had arrived. She wanted to get a good look at the surroundings, but Justin ushered her straight inside.

"This is lovely. Where shall we start the tour?"

Justin pulled her along. "We'll start up here."

"You've got stairs!" she said, remembering how excited she was when she moved in to Dan's house.

He led Mina past a bathroom and a smaller bedroom. The room to the door he opened had been decorated in grey with hints of blues and greens in the accessories.

"Wait. Where's my bag?"

Justin turned around and pinned her against the wall. "It's just you and me. Now I can show you how much I've missed you." He kissed her slowly, pressing himself against her. He let go of her hands and she wound them around his neck, increasing the pressure of his mouth on hers.

All of a sudden he stopped and stepped back, his chest rising and falling rapidly as he soaked in the view of the young woman standing before him and wondered when he would lose the feeling of astonishment at Mina's part in his life.

Inching forward he lifted her t-shirt over her head. His fingers stroked along her shoulders and down her waist. His hands stayed there as he let her unbutton his shirt. He couldn't get over how amazing this woman was. His head told him to take it slow and steady but his body commanded him *be assertive* and, heeding that advice, his mouth moved along her bare skin as he undid her bra. The sounds she made boosted his confidence and he lifted her off the floor, laid her down on the bed and finished undressing her. Mina began to undo his belt and Justin reached for the foil wrapped protection in the bedside table drawer. Then he felt her mouth on his neck and forgot why he had opened the drawer.

***

Justin set a tray down on the bedside table. He opened a window and got a pleasant chill on his skin. "Wakey, wakey sleeping beauty." He kissed Mina's forehead and lips. "I've made something to eat."

She rubbed her eyes with the back of her hand and sat up. She had fallen asleep after their lovemaking and hadn't put on any clothes, so she held the covers close to make herself comfortable.

He handed her a glass of orange juice and said, "By the way, I told my aunt and uncle I would bring you over for Sunday lunch."

"Oh. What! Why would you do that?" Her first meeting with Frankie had not been what she had expected, but at least she knew it was happening. *His aunt and uncle?* She presumed they were like guardians to the siblings, making them heaps more fearful than Frankie. Would they put her on the spot, ask her too personal questions? They might already have formed an opinion of her. Echoes of Charlene's final comments swirled in her head. Sensing her hesitation, Justin sat on the bed and placed his hands on her legs. "You'll be fine, don't worry. Frankie will be there too."

"I know." She shifted upright, moving from under Justin's hand. "That doesn't exactly fill me with relief considering how we parted the last time." Mina started eating the cheese, mushroom and onion omelette Justin had made and pondered Frankie's insinuation that Dan might be more than just a friend. To change the topic rather than over thinking things, she said, "Don't you think this house is too big for just one person?"

"Compared to the apartment, yeah, it's huge. But you have to admit the garden is awesome."

"I haven't seen anything other than this room yet, remember?"

Justin thought, his eyebrows drawing together. "Oh, yes." He laughed as he recalled leading Mina straight to his bedroom. "As soon as you're ready, I'll show you round."

The garden was indeed both awesome and low maintenance. A few large pot plants dotted here and there added splashes of colour, a concrete path led around a medium sized strip of freshly trimmed lawn to a decked seating area from which you could see the back of the house, and across to the neighbouring houses. "This would be good place to eat our evening meals before you have to go to work".

"Today's been so good. I wish you were staying permanently."

Mina wished the same but stayed silent. She imagined every day like the one almost at an end. She rested her head on his shoulder and an arm around his waist and admitted to heightening her attachment to Justin by making this visit. *I should have been pottering around Dan's place for forty-eight hours until work on Monday. I should be looking forward to hearing Justin's voice on the phone, instead of wanting his hands all over my body. I should be congratulating myself for holding onto my independence, not dreaming of giving it all away.*

"I better get ready. Are you sure you don't want to come with me?"

"I'm sure."

She had prepared for spending the night alone by bringing the book she had started reading a week ago. There was also the option to surf the internet on Justin's desktop computer. She watched him go into the house and stretched her legs out on the wicker sofa busying her mind with a contingency plan.

***

Male and female perfumes battled for dominance in the air of Justin's bedroom. They were both getting ready for lunch at Justin's aunt and uncle's house. Mina went from a pair of grey trousers to a pair of blue jeans. Then she decided on a short sleeved green jumper.

"I'm so glad I bought a few extras with me," she said, slipping on a pair of trainers.

"You'll look incredible no matter what you wear," said Justin and he kissed her.

"You're only saying that to get yourself off the hook."

"For what? I haven't done anything!"

She glared at him then started on her hair. "I think I'm going to cut a few inches off this when I get back." She brushed it and then pinned it up into a loose bun.

"Are you sure about that?"

Looking at him in the mirror she said, "It's beginning to get on my nerves so yes, I'm sure."

"Be sure to send me a before and after photo for a keepsake."

"I'll get the hairdresser to save a lock of hair for you."

"No thanks. I love your hair but that would be a bit creepy."

Mina let out a sigh and said, "I'm ready."

***

Justin pressed the doorbell with one hand and Mina tightened her grip on the other. He gave her what he intended to be a reassuring kiss just as they were greeted by his Uncle.

177

"Hi son!" Uncle Hector grabbed Justin's hand with a force Mina believed should have pulled his arm out of its socket. Then he locked eyes with Mina beaming at her. "This must be the woman Justin spends half the day day-dreaming about." He reached for Mina's hand with both his own. "Welcome to our home."

They were led into the living room and Justin whispered, "See, I told you."

"I still have to meet your aunt."

"Ladies," bellowed Uncle Hector, "Our guests have arrived!"

Frankie looked up over the rim of her glass. "Mina! How are you?" She got up slowly, steadying herself on the counter top.

Mina rushed to her side. "I'm well, thanks." Shocked as she hugged Frankie's frail body she asked a question she felt obligated to ask, "How are you?"

"Not as well as I hoped to be, unfortunately. We can talk about that later."

Justin was next in line to give his sister a hug whilst Mina was approached by Aunty Jo who held both Mina's hands in hers for what seemed like ten minutes and Mina thought she saw tears in her eyes. "I have to say, after everything Justin has told me about you, I don't like you..."

Oh, no, here goes. I knew this was going to happen. I hope Justin hears me silently calling for help. Get me out of here'

"...I don't just like you, Mina, I love you."

What did she say? She loves me? She doesn't know me; how can she love me? These were emotions far beyond Mina's comprehension. In her family it was assumed you were loved by your aunts and uncles, heck even by your parents, but the actual words never left their mouths. Justin's breath on her neck startled her out of her confusion.

"If he ever hurts you, come and see me."

All Mina could do was nod. With her panic out of the way, at last she smelt the aromas from a lovingly prepared lunch.

"Go sit down. We'll be eating in few minutes."

Mina looked around to see Frankie moving into the conservatory. Turning to Justin she said, "Are you coming?"

"I'm helping with a few things here. You'll be fine," he said.

Mina ran through all the things she wanted to say to Frankie and then realised she would say something totally different. In the beginning they had got on amicably, so ending the way it did came as a shock. Now, sitting across from Justin's dominating older sister, Mina saw how much her physical appearance had changed and hoped a similar, less destructive, change had occurred with her personality.

Frankie said, "I haven't seen my brother this happy in a long while." She turned to face Mina. "I underestimated his feelings for you...and yours for him."

Even though these were the words Mina had hoped to hear, she remained on guard. "He moved to be closer to you, Frankie."

"I know and I can't tell you how grateful I am. I know what it feels like to be parted from the person you love." She came over to sit by Mina and said, "He needs you in his life and I don't just mean weekly trips back and forth. I mean he needs to have you by his side, every day. To know, no matter what life has in store, he can turn to you for comfort and support."

"Isn't that why he moved here in the first place? So, you can do that for each other?"

"Justin supports and comforts me, but the motivation I have for an active life slips away from me each day. It's Justin who takes me swimming twice a week. It's Justin who makes sure I leave the house every day, even for a ten-minute walk around the block." Their eyes met. "Who does he go home to after he's spent time with me?"

A small spot on Mina's blue jeans turned darker as she listened. "I'm sorry," said Frankie, "I didn't mean to make you cry."

Mina shook her head and accepted a tissue. "I never looked at it that way before." She cleared her mind to tell Frankie something she hadn't mentioned to Justin. "I think I'm going to move back to Birmingham too."

Bye, Bye Weston Super-Mare

The Royal Weston was a stand-alone, so any hopes of a simple relocation from here to there vanished. The three choices left were to look for a job in a different hotel, enrol at a local college on a hospitality course, or do both. Option three would no doubt mean less time loved up with Justin, but maybe a weekend job would be manageable. It would be nice to hold onto an ounce of self-reliance by earning some money while living with her parents, her way of showing she had spent her time in Weston wisely.

The speediest way to get back to Birmingham would be to enrol on a college course; she might not be as lucky landing a job this time and then she'd have to go through an interview process - the whole thing could take weeks and, with a notice period to give of just a week, she hoped to be able to leave Weston within ten days.

Dan had mixed emotions about the news; he was devastated to be losing Mina's company, but he was just as thrilled to see her following her heart to someone of Justin's calibre. "Have you spoken to your parents yet?"

"Nope. I'm checking out enrolment dates at UCB first."

"Have you told Justin?"

"I'll speak to him after my parents."

"Oh, I nearly forgot, I've got you an appointment at the hairdressers on Thursday at four in the afternoon."

After two days of looking into college courses, the time came for making the phone call home. She tapped the contact photo on her mobile phone and waited.

"Assalam Wailaikum."

Hearing the voice gave her butterflies. "Hi, dad."

After a brief pause, he said, "Mina! Hello, beti! How are you? We thought you had forgotten all about us." The guilt-inducing comment had arrived, as expected.

"I know. I've been busy." She waited for a response. When none came, she continued, "I've decided to come back home."

"Really? Your mother will be so happy. When are you coming?"

"Next weekend."

"Don't worry, beti. Everything is just as you left it. Do you want me to pick you up from the station?"

It was all becoming a little too real. The longer her dad talked, the greater the sense of constriction binding her. She had shifted things along at such a rapid pace since her weekend with Justin, that she hadn't planned for the negative impact the move would have on her confidence. There would now be four other people to take into consideration when leaving the house to meet Justin, instead of just the two of them.

"No, dad. I'll make my own way."

"Okay, no problem. I'll let your mother know as soon as she is back. We will see you next weekend."

As she waited for Justin to answer his phone, she told herself how difficult this was going to be. "Hey, you. How are you?"

"Better now I'm hearing your voice. How are you?"

"Are you busy?" She sat down on the sofa and said, "I'm moving back to Birmingham."

"No, you're not! Are you serious? Why? When did you decide this?"

She slipped her shoes off and pulled her feet up onto the sofa. "I wanted to tell you face to face, but there was just no time."

"Okay, hold on, let me sit down."

The thirty-minute conversation was honest and hopeful and at the end she suggested spending Thursday and Friday with him before finally going home on Saturday.

"Absolutely, yes. I love you, Mina. You know that, don't you?"

"I do. I love you too and I can't wait to see you again."

***

"Now are you sure that's how much you want off?" Dan's hairdresser friend, Josh, had never lopped off so much hair from one person's head. He looked at Mina in the mirror and showed her how much she was asking for.

"I'm sure. It's not a big deal." *Until mum finds out.*

The scissors began cutting away four, five, six inches of hair and within twenty minutes, she had been blow-dried and straightened. "Oh, wow! That's incredible!" She ran her fingers through her shortened hair and admired her reflection. She paid Josh and then remembered. "Would you mind taking a photo of me? I told my boyfriend I would send him one."

All the customers in each of the shops she walked past caught an unexpected glimpse of Mina who used every display window as her personal mirrored catwalk. She bounced back to Dan's, amazed at how much lighter she felt. As soon as she settled down, she sent the photo to Justin who immediately called back to tell her how gorgeous she looked.

Her last weekend in Weston consisted of supper out with Dan and a select group of co-workers, at a Mexican restaurant and then back to Sunset Strip for a few drinks and a dance or two.

"Can you believe it, Dan?" Mina said looking around, "This is where it all began."

By this time Dan had acquainted himself with three shots of Tequila, two whisky and cokes and two more shots of Tequila. "Stop talking, Mina! Come and dance!" He dragged her onto the floor she had shied away from during Tania's visit. She allowed herself to become his puppet as he pulled, pushed and waved her arms about to get her moving. A few more of their group joined them and she began to relax.

When a break presented itself, she hurried to the bar and spotted James. "Hi."

"Hi, Mina. Long time, no see."

"I know. Listen," she beckoned him closer, "I'm moving back to Birmingham, so this is probably the last time you'll see me."

"Well, say hi to Justin when you see him."

That should have been the end of their conversation, but something pushed her to ask, "How's Charlene?" She didn't care, at least not consciously, but the words somehow found their way out.

"She and Tony are getting divorced and, so far, it's not pretty."

Mina feigned concern and hoped Charlene didn't have plans to make another move on Justin. She took her drink out into the cool night air and found somewhere to sit. She allowed the calming effects of the lapping seawater to help her drift back in time, back to the moment she'd learnt the name of the cute barman who had handed her a note. She had watched countless Bollywood movies where two people fight to be together against all the odds and, until now, it had never occurred to her she might well have a struggle of her own. She had enjoyed these movies for their over-the-top melodrama and exquisite costumes, believing these things only happened to other people. Yet, here she sat, on the verge of leaving behind a self-made, autonomous life to follow her heart and be closer to the man she had grown to love. With the romance part covered, the drama was bound to come sooner rather than later.

"I knew you'd be out here!" Dan charged towards her, trying not to trip over a chair or table leg in the process. "This is our last night out so I'll be damned if I'm gonna let you sit out here being all sad and stuff!" He hoisted her out of her chair causing her to miss the incoming phone call from her mother.

This time, when she returned to the dance floor, she made more of an effort to join in, for Dan's sake. This night was in honour of their friendship. He had kept her mind distracted when she was in need of both support and friendship.

Their relationship oozed honesty and laughter, significantly more than her relationship with Tania had ever done. Dan wasn't someone who picked and chose the moments in his life to share with her, he talked to Mina about everything that was happening. Dan was indiscriminate, and the very opposite of vindictive.

Tania's friendship stemmed from their joint attendance at the same junior and senior schools. Back then, and Mina would only admit this to Justin during one of their reflective conversations, she had been just like Tania; loud, abrasive, unpopular. However, unlike Tania, Mina mellowed, became easier to get along with, especially during her last two or three years of full time education. How they managed to maintain their friendship for all the years that followed, was something now beyond Mina's understanding. Returning to Birmingham meant she would have to muster all the strength she could to keep her distance from Tania.

Dan's drunken face was momentarily hidden behind a mass of waving arms. When he reappeared, she found she had an urge to hug him, so she did. He reeked of a cocktail of rum, whisky and beer, but she found a source of comfort in his arms, even though he didn't hug her back and said, "Hey, you. No soppy, floppiness from you," and then carried on dancing.

She had enjoyed her last weekend in the company of a bunch of people she had grown to like and respect, but she looked forward to spending a whole Sunday with just Dan.

***

Dan's phone rang at nine o'clock the morning after the night before. It rang five more times before he answered. "You're mean." Ten minutes later, while Mina checked the sautéing mushrooms and buttered two slices of toast, Dan dragged his feet into the kitchen. "Dim the lights already!" he said, dramatically covering his eyes with his hands.

"Oh, stop exaggerating. Now get over here and hand me two plates."

Mina was right; he was being theatrical and today was supposed to be all about Mina. He got out of his seat and unscrewed the lid of the coffee jar. He took a long inhale and said, "Okay, let's have breakfast!"

He outlined his plans for the entire day; they would start by shopping, Dan's treat, they would lunch at a super swanky restaurant reserved only for last lunches with friends, then bowling, a sport in which neither of them had any noticeable skill, and an evening topped off by a movie and takeout.

They walked arm in arm through the city centre, stopping only to decide if the shop they were standing in front of was worthy of their presence. Shopping with Dan was strikingly different from shopping with Justin; Dan pulled clothes off the rails because of the colours, the style and the fabric, before Mina even had the chance to change from one item to another. It was speed-dating with clothes; a quick glance in the changing room mirror and then onto the next. If she spent any longer than ten seconds admiring her reflection, Dan pointed out what was wrong and shoved her back into the changing room with a different outfit. The process was repeated in at least five different shops. Her protests went unheard. "I know what looks good on you, so stop whining."

"But I don't like words on my clothes!"

"Listen, I'm buying for you, remember? So, whenever you wear it you'll be thinking of me!"

"Yeah and I should have just asked for a gift voucher instead!"

"Listen to us! We're going on like an old married couple. I hope you don't stress Justin out like this."

Mina accepted a checked cotton shirt and a deep red vest top. "Now this is more like it."

They both left the shop with smiles on their faces. Famished, after a hard morning, Dan introduced her to his favourite eating establishment.

"How did you know about this place?" She said, as they were escorted to their table.

They were each handed a menu and, as soon as the waiter had left, Dan said, "An ex. If you think I'm spoiling you today, imagine feeling that way every day."

"Really! So, what happened?"

"Turns out, it wasn't his money to spend."

Mina's eyes widened and her mouth hung open. "You didn't get into trouble, did you?"

Dan shook his head and Mina understood his non-verbal response as a request to move onto another topic. Her questions would have to remain unanswered, for now.

When their meals arrived, Dan's warning glare helped deter her from taking a photo with her phone. After her awe at such pristine culinary presentation dissipated, her thoughts turned to how hungry she would be if the rest of her food came out the same. Somewhere in the back of her mind it reminded her of the fancy dinner in Liverpool, but there she never got past the first course before it all kicked off.

Dan picked up his glass of bubbly and held it in the air. "Thank you for coming into my life when I really needed someone."

Mina lifted her glass of juice and said, "I was gonna say that!"

They brought their glasses together and proceeded to eat a highly civilised lunch. Their foray into the world of bowling, however, saw that mask slip. She approached the computer to enter their names onto the overhead screen. "What do I do?"

Dan stood next to her. "Start typing our names in, duh!"

She pressed the buttons with force and said, "I'm trying."

"Not that one! Move over, let me do it. I can't wait to see you bowl."

"I'll have you know, you're going to need the sides up if you want to beat me!" Mina tightened her shoes hoping to make good on her threat.

"Choose a ball already!"

She turned and glared at him. "I'm finding one I can hold. Wow, you're so impatient." She chose a medium-sized ball and walked with conviction toward the lane. Before releasing the ball, she turned to Dan and said, "Get ready to lose." She let go and closed her eyes. Dan shouted disbelief from behind and she opened her eyes to see only one pin still standing. "Yes!"

"Beginner's luck, that's all."

All at once, the life she was going to leave behind became apparent; lack of restriction on her movements would soon be replaced by questions to which she would have to give reassurances. She could only hope her return home would be taken as something other than weakness, an inability to retain her sense of self without the unconditional support of her family. At least she still had time to kick up her heels before coming down off the high she had experienced.

With a mere three points between them, they agreed to call it a draw and head home, even though Dan would later recall no such agreement. During their shopping trip they had bought two scrapbooks and decided to spend the evening compiling these instead of watching a movie. They printed a selection of photos from each other's phones and stuck them in the exact same place in each scrapbook, along with written descriptions of each event. They pondered over the photo Dan's hairdresser friend had taken after lobbing off a fair amount of her hair.

"Your mum's gonna freak out when she sees what you've done."

"I'll just keep it pinned up for a few days. It'll be fine."

"You can't keep it pinned up forever."

"I said a few days, not forever! OH MY GOD!" She snapped his scrapbook closed and said, "Make yourself useful and go put the kettle on."

He snatched the book away and retorted, "You make yourself useful and decide what we're going to eat tonight!"

Their eyes fixed on each other, their lips pressed together, unusual sounds building up in their throats, until they were laughing. They wiped the tears from their eyes, hugged and each went to carry out the other's request.

Mina was still perusing a bunch of takeaway options when Dan came back into the living room five minutes, later holding their mugs with their choices of hot beverage. "I've done my bit. Have you done yours?"

"Yeah, yeah. I'll ring an order in now."

"Fab, what are we...you haven't chosen yet, have you?" He shook his head and sat down on the beanbag.

"You should know by now how long these things take me." She offered a menu for Dan to look through, but he shook his head.

"Not this time, missy."

"In that case, you might starve before bedtime."

Dan observed her childlike expression over the rim of his mug before giving in. "Fine. Hand me a menu."

Mina smiled in triumph and gave Dan a pizza and curry menu whilst she looked through a Chinese selection. "There's nothing interesting on here."

"I don't fancy pizza."

"So Indian it is! Thanks, Dan."

They agreed on the lamb jalfrezi, saag chicken, two servings of pilau rice, two naans and two rotis.

The night drew to an end and the friends slouched on chairs with no attempts to exert more energy than needed. The silence in the kitchen was agreeable, with a hint of the almost sombre. Mina's eyes fixed on her mug, resting upside down on the drying rack, alongside Dan's. She gulped down the lump in her throat, at least until she was alone.

"Dan," she said and touched his arm, "Go to bed. I'll clean this up." He stood up then stretched and yawned. "Thank you for today. I had a really great time." She hugged him and sent him away before he noticed her teary eyes.

Her work colleagues had chipped in to buy her a leaving gift and presented it to her at the end of her final shift. Dan followed Mina into the office when she returned her uniform. Rachel thanked her and wished her all the best and Dan followed her back out.

"Dan," she reached for his hands, "Thank you for everything." She hugged him and he squeezed back. "You better come and visit."

"You too. I'm gonna miss you, but only until I find someone else to rent your room!"

"You won't find anyone better than me. Take care of yourself."

Mina took a final look back at the place she had called home for three months, Dan standing at the hotel entrance, waving like a crazed lunatic. She blew him a kiss and stepped into the taxi.

The Whole Gang's Here

Mina had been trying to scan each of the three open tabs on the desktop computer to find course details and enrolment dates, but had also been trying to fight off the distraction of a half-naked Justin. They had only been able to spend a few hours together the previous day, before Justin had to leave, so they made up for lost time by spending the entire morning in bed. Now as the clock ticked closer to question time, she had no concrete answers.

Justin placed a mug of tea beside her. "Is there anything I can help with?" He sat down next to her and watched helplessly. "Are you sure you're ready to move back in with your parents?"

Mina studied his face before saying, "I'm not moving back to Weston! That would be madness!"

Justin shook his head. "You haven't even considered it, have you?"

"Haven't considered what? You mean me moving in here...with you?" She returned her attention to the computer screen. "I thought we were going with the flow, seeing where each day takes us. You know, not rushing into things."

"You're right. I'm just so happy to have you all to myself, I don't want you to ever leave." He kissed her cheek, her ear and the hollow of her neck. His right hand moved along her shoulder and brushed her face. "I don't know what I was thinking," he said as his mouth lingered on her skin.

She mustered all the strength she could, determined to continue her search for answers even though every inch of her physical being cried out to turn and kiss him; he was the reason for her return after all. She absently scrolled the mouse around the screen. The internet wasn't going anywhere; she could do this later when she was alone. She turned to meet his mouth, her worries drifting down her mental to do list. *Is this how it would be if they spent twenty-four hours a day, seven days a week under the same roof? If so, wouldn't that be a good thing?* With each physical experience they learned things about each other's bodies that heightened their pleasure. Life would be so easy if people only had to worry about their next sexual encounter and nothing else.

Mina needed to regain some of the control she had forfeited by leaving her independence to spend her days wrapped around a semi naked masculine body. She pulled away from Justin, moved his hands and took a deep breath. Their heads touching, her heart beating rapidly, she whispered, "I really need to get this done."

"I know. I'll make myself scarce and leave you to it."

A moment later a sudden gust of wind blew through the kitchen as Justin opened the doors leading out into the garden. She found solace in the sound of the breeze disturbing the leaves, the uplifting scent of the lavender planted in the garden floating in her direction.

The placebo effect of the lavender came on with speed. She closed all but one of the tabs, confident the answer had been staring her in the face all along. She clicked on the link to download the course details for the level two and level three in hospitality at University College Birmingham. According to the entry requirements she qualified to move straight onto the level three, which was a year-long module. Minimising the screen, she looked for those all-important enrolment dates; just over a week from today. She bookmarked the page and stretched with a groan.

She looked out at Justin who was lounging in the garden with his laptop open. He had put on a pastel green, short sleeved shirt and every few seconds the breeze exposed smooth, taut skin.

She walked outside and stretched. "I'm going to enrol on September fourth."

"Great! Come sit down here." He motioned to the space beside him. "I've got a few more emails to respond to," he said as he typed, "Then I'm all yours."

Mina sat next to Justin and slipped her sandals off. While she waited for him to finish she amused herself with a game on her phone. Ten minutes later boredom began to set in. She put her phone down and cuddled up, her head on Justin's shoulder, nuzzling into his neck. "This is taking ages." She put one arm around his waist and closed her eyes. "You smell nice."

"Are you falling asleep?" He moved his shoulder up and down.

"Nah, not me...I'm waiting to be ravished by you again."

He clicked send on his final email and shut down the laptop. When he looked at Mina, she was indeed fast asleep. He placed her head on a cushion and fetched a blanket to cover her. He moved a few strands of hair out of her face and stroked her cheek. Looking down at this beautiful woman who had sacrificed everything she had built for herself, the freedom she had tasted, to be close to him, he felt like the luckiest man alive.

***

The lovers were in each other's arms, engaged in a kiss without end. The leisurely pace of mouth on mouth would soon be halted by the arrival of a taxi to take Mina home.

"You're spoiling me, you know." She cradled his head, encouraging his lips onto hers. Justin's hands moved slowly under her shirt and he whispered, "I don't know when we're going to see each other like this again."

His phone buzzed, giving them a five-minute warning. Mina brought his hands to the fasteners of her bra strap, but for once he failed to oblige. "We haven't got enough time for that."

"We can pretend no one's home when the taxi gets here." Her fingers played with the waistband of his jeans.

The sound of a car horn commanded their attention. Justin drew away slowly. "Just in time."

As they approached the front door, Justin hugged Mina and said, "I love you so much."

Mina held onto him as though a hurricane was threatening to pull them apart. "I love you too. I'm gonna miss you loads. I'll call you every night."

Justin helped Mina with her luggage then stepped back into the doorway of his house to watch the taxi pull away.

***

Waiting for the taxi driver to remove her luggage from the boot, all Mina could think was *no matter what challenges I'm going to face, no matter how constricted I might start feeling, it's necessary to make this new arrangement work.* The mere thought of what her life would look like started the flutter of butterflies in her tummy, or perhaps she was coming down with something.

Before she even had a chance to put her key in the door, she heard the unmistakable sound of her younger sister, Anisa, shouting her name from somewhere inside. Mina put down the bag she was holding, the door was flung open and Anisa jumped into Mina's arms. The sisters whirled around, Anisa overjoyed at their reunion.

"I can't believe you've come back home! I thought mum was playing a trick when she told me."

"Anisa," she said as her sister's grip tightened around her neck, "You're strangling me."

"Sorry, Mina baaji. I'm just sooooo happy to have you back!"

"You've grown," Mina said. "I haven't been away that long, have I?"

"Yeah."

Mina stood startled. "Since when do you speak like that?" She followed her sister into the house. She could hear muffled sounds coming from the living room. "Who's here?"

"Just us lot, innit."

"Innit?" She shot a confused look at the back of her sister's head. "It looks like I've been away too long." Anisa rushed down the long hallway, into the living room. "Hey, what's the hurry?" she shouted after her.

Mina rounded the corner into what should have been a furnished living room and was met with darkness. She fumbled for the light switch.

"Surprise!"

"What the hell!" It took a few seconds to register all of the faces in front of her. "Wow."

"Hi, Mina!"

"Think we got you!"

"Hey, cuz!"

Greetings were shouted across the room and she was surrounded by many more people than she'd expected. Her first thought; *is this another attempt at fixing me up for marriage*. That would be unbearable. She would be so angry she'd blurt out that she was already in a relationship. *No way, not a good idea.* Composure was key, and of course finding out the truth.

She found her mum and gave her a bear hug. "Hello, mum." Then it was her dad's turn before greeting Rehan and his wife. She pulled Rehan aside and whispered, "Is this a set up? Coz if I see someone I don't know, I'm heading for the door."

"Relax. It's just family."

Rehan helped her take her cases up to her room. "How are you feeling, being back?"

She looked at him, slumped onto her bed and sighed.

190

"That bad, huh." He sat down next to her and nudged her with his arm. "You'll be fine. You'll have to make some adjustments, but you'll be fine." He put his arm around Mina. "I know what it's like leaving your freedom behind. It's like coming down off a big high. Enjoy today and give yourself a few days to recalibrate." He stood up to leave and placed a hand gently on her shoulder. "If you need to let some steam off, call me."

She wiped her eyes with the back of her hand and lay down on her bed. A second later her phone alerted her to a text. It was Rehan. *Someone's here to see you. Mum's sending her up.* Her? Mina shot out of bed and busied herself with unpacking. *This could turn ugly.*

There was a knock at the door. "Can I come in?"

Mina opened her bedroom door. "Tania!"

"Hi, stranger!"

"Come in! Excuse the mess."

Tania sat down on the bed and surveyed the cases. "It didn't work out then. What happened?"

Mina knelt down beside her open cases, copping Tania's failed attempt at concern. "There's not much to it really."

Tania thought, *she can't honestly believe I'll fall for that*, so she pressed, "Are you sure it's not because you got lonely?"

Mina shook her head a little too enthusiastically and said, "Actually, do you remember Dan?" Tania looked puzzled, or disinterested. "Well, we became really close. We ended up as housemates." She began taking clothes out of her case and hanging them in her wardrobe. She would have to forbid her family throwing any more surprise parties for her, or at least to let her vet the guest list beforehand.

"Let's cut to the chase, Mina. I know all about you and Justin Hargreaves."

Mina turned her back to the wardrobe. "You don't know anything. How could you? I did all the hard work trying not to lose touch with you!"

Tania rose from the bed. "That's not fair! I had a lot of shit going on here and you left me to deal with it!"

"Wait a second. We spent loads of time together, even before I made the decision to leave, and you never said a word."

"It was awkward stuff. I didn't want you to feel bad for me."

"We've known each other a long time so don't give me that and you've never had a problem with people feeling bad for you." She picked up a clothes hanger and draped a jumper onto it. With her back to Tania she said, "What did you want me to feel when you sent me that photo of you and Justin?"

Tania sat back down, lost for words. From the bottom of the stairs Mina's mum called them down to eat. Mina continued to empty her cases, feeling a shift in the dynamic of their relationship. She was no longer an accessory like an umbrella or a pair of sunglasses, but a principal in her own right.

"Can't you see how bad it would look if you hooked up with a black guy?"

"You seemed happy enough in the photo." She zipped up the empty case and started on another.

"It's not the kind of thing you do, you know? You've always followed the rules, kept people happy." Tania smoothed down her skirt and continued, "Me, on the other hand, I'm a non-conformist. Pretty much anything goes with me."

"Are you saying that black guys are reserved for you?"

"Not all black guys. Only Justin Hargreaves." Tania knelt beside the case Mina was unpacking and handed her some clothing. "So, if you're not seeing him, it won't matter to you if I make a serious move on him."

Mina thought *The girl is delusional. I can't wait to tell Justin the good news that he's still got a chance with Tania.!* "Just how non-conformist are you?"

"What do you mean?"

Mina was ecstatic to have the spotlight on Tania rather than herself. "I mean would you show him off to your friends and family?"

"You're not serious, are you? I wouldn't leave the bedroom! Can you imagine how amazing the sex would be? Not to mention he owns a nightclub!"

"He doesn't own it, he manages it."

"Either way," Tania continued, too caught up in her own fantasy to have noticed Mina's slip, "I wouldn't be able to keep my hands off him!"

Mina smiled to herself, knowing that feeling all too well.

Another summons interrupted the showdown. "Mina baaji, mum said come and eat."

Mina closed the wardrobe door and rubbed her stomach. "I'm ready to eat. How about you?"

Tania smoothed down her skirt and examined her reflection in the mirror. "No, thanks. I think I'll go home. I've got some planning to do."

Oh, God help Justin! Mina tried to think of a way to change Tania's mind. "There are probably thousands of available black guys in Birmingham. You shouldn't limit your options."

"Maybe. Anyway, I need to go." She hugged Mina and disappeared downstairs. Mina grabbed her phone and dashed off a text message for Justin.

Back in the throes of the living room, the men had somehow managed to separate themselves from the women and were glued to a sports channel. Her stomach started rumbling when she caught sight of the enormous piles of food on the dining room table.

Every Spare Minute

Who would have thought it would be so easy to slip back into college life? Although it wasn't without its annoyances like waiting to cram into a lift with fifty other students. It was a college spread over eleven floors and, at some point, every student would have a reason to travel all the way up or down. Despite this, after her first day, Mina blended right in.

She spent far too much money eating in the college cafeterias and in the ground floor bakery and, whenever she presented her parents with her latest purchase, she would always be reminded not to throw her money away. The best thing about college was having the opportunity to sneak away to spend time with Justin. Her lectures were distributed across the week in such a way that they gave them a full day and a half to be together. In an effort to alleviate some of the guilt over deceiving her parents, on her day off she would go into college at eight in the morning to study for a couple of hours before being whisked away for hours of lovemaking and food. For their half a day together, they tended to have lunch at an Indian restaurant a short walk from the college.

Mina lay in Justin's arms, staring out the window. This was their third escapade since she had returned to study. Each time felt like the first and she prolonged the journey home a little more every time. It was getting to the point where she was returning home at six or seven in the evening and dreading the inquisition. It hadn't come yet, but she still felt bad.

Her skin tingled, feeling the warmth of Justin's mouth on her neck and she stroked his arm. "What are you thinking?" he asked.

She filtered out everything going through her mind until only one thought remained. "I love being here with you, like this."

"And I love having you here like this." His hand caressed the length of her body. "I've got some time off next week, Thursday, Friday and Saturday." He nibbled her ear, and whispered, "Do you think you might be able to spend the night?"

Mina's brow furrowed. "I'm already pushing it by staying out longer than I should."

"You have a point. We'll still see each other anyway, won't we?"

"Just try and keep me away!"

He squeezed her tight and said, "Let's get ready for lunch. I'm taking you to an understated pub in Worcester." He pulled the sheets away and walked into the en-suite.

"Worcester? That's miles away!" She sat upright.

Justin appeared from behind the door, brushing his teeth. "Twenty-seven, to be exact."

***

Mina opened the front door to her empty house at seven thirty that evening. She left her things in her room and checked on Anisa. In her little sister's room, everything was perfectly tidy, as though Anisa had rolled out of bed, clicked her fingers, Mary Poppins style, and was ready without lifting a finger. After making herself a mug of tea Mina flopped onto the sofa. She wished she wasn't home alone. She wished she hadn't been in such a hurry to leave Justin's. Then and there she resolved to try to get out of the house more, with some of the new friends she was making at college.

Without any warning she began to feel like her tea was about to make a surprise reappearance. She covered her mouth and made a dash for the bathroom. She put her head over the toilet bowl, expecting an almighty spew of her insides, but all that came back was a long string of spittle. She rinsed her mouth and stared at her face in the bathroom mirror. She took a pro biotic drink out of the fridge and gulped it down. It had worked when she'd felt nauseous before. She poured the rest of her tea away down the sink and got herself a glass of water instead.

Sitting on her bed she called Dan and asked if he fancied spending the weekend in Birmingham. She told him Justin had offered him a place to stay, as long as he promised to behave himself. He agreed and they both expressed their excitement about the possibilities Birmingham could offer them.

***

"Mum, I'm going now." She gave her a hug. "Thanks for letting me stay over at my friend's tonight."

"You are a big girl now, but don't get into any trouble, okay? Oh, and take this." Her mum handed her two twenty-pound notes.

Mina looked at the money in her hand and thought, if you knew where I was really going you'd be giving me something else. "Thank you." She hugged her mum extra tight.

She took a taxi to Justin's then, after leaving her bag, she and Justin drove to New Street Station to collect Dan. "I can't wait to see him! Thank you for having him to stay."

"He looked after you. I'm just returning the favour."

At the station, twenty minutes later, Mina said "You wait here and I'll go and find him." She checked the overhead screen to find the platform for the train from Bristol just as Dan texted her to say he was at the station. Screwing her face up, Mina tried to see past the throngs of commuters. She spotted a strawberry blonde head looking frantically from left to right and then down to what she suspected must be his phone. She was able to stroll right up to him before he noticed her.

"Oh my God! It's you!" Dan and Mina hugged with such obvious enthusiasm that people around them were smiling as though they understood how it felt to see your best friend after five weeks apart.

"Come on, hurry! Justin's waiting for us." She carried Dan's bag, fighting off his protests, and led him outside.

Justin greeted Dan with a firm handshake. "Hi, Dan. Welcome to Birmingham!"

"Thanks for having me."

"It's the least I could do."

Later, after Justin left for work, Mina and Dan prepared for drinks with Marvin and the gang, partners included, before heading down to Justin's new club. For the first time since her return home, she put aside all concerns about her responsibility to her family and how her actions might impact on the stability she had maintained so far. The time had come for her to let her hair down and party with her best friend, her boyfriend and his friends, and she had no need to worry about getting home on time either.

Justin met them at the entrance to the club, taking care to make any watching, less special, patrons envious. The sounds of house music ripped through the main room where, hands aplenty in the air, the party was in full swing. Dan mouthed "Wow" to Mina. They stopped off in the VIP room where they could hear themselves think.

"What are you all drinking," Justin asked. "The first round's on me." When everyone had a drink in their hand, Justin raised his glass and said, "A toast. To love," he held Mina's gaze, "And friendship."

"And a damn good Saturday night!" added Dan.

"I need to attend to a bit of business" said Justin. "I am at work after all." He stood and looked over the small group on the sofas. "Go explore and enjoy. I'll catch up with you soon." He took Mina's hand and led her away a few yards away from the others. He kissed her softly, his fingers entwined in her loose locks. "I can't wait to have our first dance together."

She smiled against his lips. "Oh, didn't I ever tell you? I can't dance."

"That's alright. I'll just hold you against me, like this." He slid his hands down to her waist and pulled her into him. "No one will ever know."

Leaving the comfort of the VIP room, the gang headed back into the main room. Now and then Mina listened to dance music on the radio, but what she heard here was unlike anything on the radio. The bass coursed through her body, challenging her heartbeat to keep up. Dan, Mina, Alex, Lauren and Sam channelled their way, hands in the air, onto the packed dance floor until they found a spot large enough to enable them to stay close together. Mina had no idea if what she was doing could be considered dancing but she copied everyone else, adding a few of her own moves. By the time Lauren and Sam talked Dan into getting more drinks, Mina was so into it she refused to leave her space, so Alex stayed with her.

When the both of them eventually returned to their friends, Justin was back with them. "I saw you dancing," he said, taking her hand and whirling her around. "We're going to slow down the tempo a bit and head to the r'n'b room."

There Justin pulled Mina into him and guided her movements as the pace of the music developed its own deliberate sensuality. Around them, other couples danced with passion and measured energy. Justin turned Mina around so she had her back against his chest, his breath on her ear. His hands had moved down to her hips and he pressed himself against her, hoping she understood what he was thinking. Unable to resist any longer, he turned her to face him and lowered his mouth onto hers. Against her better judgement she wrapped her arms around his neck, savouring the sensation of being watched.

He drew away from her, breathing hard. "We need to stop this. Or, we could lose this crowd and go to my office."

"Let's stop," said Mina, pulling away from him, grinning.

Marvin and Chloe and Alex and Lauren called time out on the party before midnight. Dan, Mina and Sam stayed until the last song played and the house lights were switched on. Mina took out her phone to call a taxi, but Dan told her Sam had invited him out to another club and, if she didn't mind he thought he'd go with him. She almost asked why she hadn't been invited but then realised it meant she could wait with Justin and they could go home together.

When the last door had been locked, Justin and Mina raced back to a night of passionate lovemaking, neither of them aware of the approaching bump in the road which would challenge their future together.

Crisis Point

Despite the fresh autumnal atmosphere, the lecture room seemed to be heating up. There was a lack of air the higher up the building you were and Mina was on the eighth floor. She had trouble keeping her eyes open and had to excuse herself to use the bathroom. She took two steps out of the room and her head started spinning. She leaned against the infinite corridor wall and waited for the feeling to pass. The lecture ended and Mina hadn't moved.

Some of her classmates gathered around, asking if she was okay. The lecturer came out to see the commotion. "Mina! What happened?"

The tears flowed and she said, "I don't know. I've been feeling lightheaded and so tired."

"Okay. We have a nurse in the building. I can take you to see her if you like."

Mina nodded. The lecturer took Mina's belongings and made her way up to the tenth floor. She knocked on the door marked *medic's office* and entered. Mina waited outside, drying her eyes. Her lecturer motioned her inside and left her at the mercy of a woman with thick curly hair and glasses. "Come sit down, dear. Tell me what's the matter."

Mina explained her nausea, dizziness and how she had started feeling more tired than usual. The medic asked a few more questions then said, "When was your last period?"

"Oh, that was..." When the answer didn't come as rapidly as it should have, she closed her eyes to concentrate. Her eyes shot open and she said, "I haven't had a period since I left Weston!"

"When was that?"

Mina forgot she wasn't alone, talking to herself. "Shit! This can't be happening!"

"I think you should either visit your GP or pop into the Brook Centre, they offer free pregnancy tests."

"But I can't be. What am I going to tell my parents?"

"If it helps, there's a counsellor on the third floor. I can call and book you in for an appointment."

Mina stared at the posters on the walls, the information blocked out by other, more pressing, concerns. *What now?* She answered that one by telling herself the only way to be sure would be to take the test. Until then, worrying would do nothing except give her headaches.

"I've made you an appointment for ten o'clock tomorrow morning. Is that alright?"

Mina sighed and nodded.

"The Brook is open until six this evening." She stood up to open the door for Mina. "Good luck."

She walked down ten flights of stairs, past the ground floor bakery and straight into the city centre. After fifteen minutes of walking, she stopped outside a building and fished her phone out to check if her feet had brought her to the right place. She went to the reception and, in a hushed voice, told the lady behind the desk why she was there. A moment later, the woman returned and showed Mina to the bathroom.

Refusing to allow herself any emotional response to her situation, Mina peed on the stick. She handed the sample in and waited. All around her were posters with advice relating to disease and illnesses alien to her. *Why worry about sexual health if there's no sexual activity?* Perhaps she should make a mental note of the information. On the other hand, doing that would mean acknowledging the mess she had created. Instead she closed her eyes and rested the back of her head against the wall. She pictured lying on a blanket at the beach, her feet sinking into the cool sand, Justin lying next to her planting kisses on her face and neck, children building sandcastles and eating ice cream. *Wait*, she thought, *why did children interrupt my sweet daydream?*

Riding the bus home, she plugged in her earphones, determined to stave off all negative thoughts. It was when she finally reached home and stood in the living room, watching her dad flick through the channels, complaining of nothing decent to watch, that she let every forlorn eventuality gush over her. There was no way she could continue living in this house, not when her body would be changing with no way to hide it.

The subject of starting a family had never entered hers or Justin's consideration. *How will this affect our relationship?* She dropped the bag from her shoulder and ran into the bathroom. This time her body had more than just a trickle of saliva to shed. She filled the gaps in between throwing up with deep sobs, her tears falling into the bowl with the rest of the mess. The bathroom mirror had nothing nice to tell her, so she washed her face, downed a mug of peppermint tea and went to bed.

Her restless body swayed back and forth as if on a tugboat sailing through a choppy sea. She mumbled protests, waving her hands about, until she felt an arm.

"Mina, wake up. Dinner's ready."

"Anisa? What are you doing here?"

"This is my home too, duh!" She grabbed her sister's arm and pulled her into a sitting position. "Why are you sleeping? It's so early!"

Mina swung her legs off the bed, her head in her hands. "I'm not feeling very well today."

Anisa wrapped her arms around her big sister. "All you need is a cuddle from your favourite sister."

Grateful for the innocent presence beside her, Mina freed an arm and reciprocated. "Thanks, Anisa." She planted a kiss on her head.

"You're welcome! I'll tell mum you'll be down in ten minutes."

Mina fumbled for her phone. While sleeping, Justin had called her four times and sent one text asking her to call as soon as she could.

"Mina! I've been trying to get hold of you!" She heard the urgency in his voice.

"What's happened."

"It's Frankie. She's in the hospital. I... I don't know what to do. She's in there by herself and..."

"Justin, listen to me. All you can do is be there for her. You know that's all she wants."

Mina listened to his unsteady breathing, knowing that if she had her hand placed on his chest it would be pounding.

"Oh God!" he started, "I won't be able to see you tomorrow. I'm sorry."

"Don't be silly," she said, remembering her appointment with the college counsellor. "Frankie needs you more right now." She breathed a sigh of relief.

I'll have a bit more time to think about the next move before I see your gorgeous face.

"I love you, Mina."

"I love you, too. Keep me posted."

He hung up and she looked for a moment at the photo she'd selected for his caller ID. She wished she could be with him now, but it seemed as though each of them had more than enough to deal with in their own space. She trudged downstairs, her legs unwilling to exert any more effort than absolutely necessary.

"Mina, Anisa said you weren't feeling well, so I made you something." Her mum pushed a mug in Mina's direction.

Oh no! Another one of those ancient concoctions. She sniffed the contents and grimaced. "I'm too scared to ask." Sipping the liquid medicine with about as much enthusiasm as having a blood test, Mina realised she really needed her counselling session; she had a desperate need to talk, unreservedly, about what was best for everyone involved.

MINA'S FIRST COUNSELLING SESSION

The wait seemed to go on forever. There wasn't even a private waiting room where someone could contemplate the conversation that was soon to be had. People were periodically walking past interested in nothing but the person next to them or the content of their next lecture, but they still made Mina feel as though they were noticing her and silently asking themselves the reason why she might be sitting there waiting at this particular time.

A woman wearing a navy-blue ankle length skirt, a patterned navy and white blouse and white loafers called Mina's name. She stood to follow the woman. They exchanged smiles. Mina's was more forced.

They entered the consulting room and the woman softly closed the door behind her.

As Mina walked into the room she noticed that one of the walls was adorned with three landscapes each framed in the same style but each of them quite different. The nearest picture was of a group of people holding hands and looking toward a scene of apparent destruction but beyond the destruction there was a sunrise and green meadows with strong trees growing in them. The next picture was a simple quote, *Someday everything will make perfect sense. So, for now, laugh at the confusion, smile through the tears and keep reminding yourself that everything happens for a reason.* The last picture was of a windy day in the park with nobody in it. Mina was certain that the first picture summed up her current situation, but without the calming sunrise and the implied happiness that came with it.

The walls of the consulting room were painted cream. Mina noticed the skirting boards were painted a slightly darker shade. There was a long desk at the opposite end of the room with a stationery organiser and paper tray on it. Mina felt a little more at ease when she spotted a colourful arrangement of gerberas, roses and chrysanthemums in a long glass vase on a smaller table in between two soft chairs on one of which Mina was invited to seat herself.

"Hi, Mina. I'm Charlotte." She waited for Mina to get comfortable. "What's on your mind?"

Silence fell as Mina hugged herself. She bowed her head and said, "I've been seeing someone for a few months and I've just found out I'm pregnant."

"How do you feel about that?"

Mina wondered why she was being asked a question to which the answer should be obvious. "I don't know. I just need to figure out what to do to stop anyone from getting hurt."

"It sounds like you feel responsible for other people."

Mina poured herself a glass of water whilst she considered this statement. She did believe she had a responsibility to fulfil the expectations set by her family not only to be a role model for her younger sister, but also to maintain the status quo. Then there was Justin, who deserved nothing but absolute honesty and the chance to tell her what he wanted.

The ice-cold gush of water flowing down her throat returned her voice. "I don't know how I'm supposed to feel." Her fingers clutched tighter around the glass. "It's like they've only just accepted me moving out, that was enough of a struggle. Now I'm back and everything should have been returning to normal but..."

"When you say *they* who are you referring to?"

"My family." *Of course Charlotte can't be expected to know that.*

Charlotte rested her hands on her stomach and said, "You said your family struggled to accept you moving out." When Mina nodded, she continued, "What made you move back home?"

A small smile broke through Mina's sadness. "I met someone in Weston Super-Mare; that's where I moved to. He had accepted a job here, before we met, and he needed to be closer to his sister, who's not well." She placed her glass on the table. "I managed a few weeks without him but in the end, I missed him too much."

Mina began to think that if there ever was such a thing as an odd couple, it would be her and Justin. Justin towered over Mina at six foot two whereas she was almost twelve inches shorter, they had an age gap of more than ten years between them and, perhaps the most controversial oddity, they were from different cultures. She started thinking about where she would be able to break the news to Justin; *over dinner at their regular restaurant; or out on a walk after college, or maybe during a cuddle on his sofa?*

"I'm afraid we've reached the end of our time."

Mina, who had just begun to feel at ease, took a gulp of water and picked up her bag.

"It might help if you came to see me again next week."

Mina agreed. She made a beeline for the nearest toilets. This time it wasn't nausea; she needed a private place to cry. Emerging fifteen minutes later, eyes bloodshot and exhausted, Mina headed to the eighth-floor cafe; it would be quieter and she would only end up in bed if she went home. She bought a toasted sandwich, fruit juice and a packet of crisps and found a seat as far as possible from the front.

Half an hour later, a mass of students filled the cafeteria, buying lunch and hot drinks, looking as happy with themselves as she would have been if she was in their shoes. Following that train of thought led her to consider if she would even complete her course. This time next year she would be a parent. Some would be concerned about her ability to look after the needs of a small child when she couldn't even look after herself. One set of fingers tapped on the table while the other absently picked crisps out of the packet and into her mouth.

Unable to spend her free day with Justin, Mina began to contemplate what she would do for the rest of the day; she could indulge in some retail therapy - she had been after a new pair of ankle boots for ages; or she could walk the city streets in a daze, heightening her anxiety levels. In the end, neither option made the cut, but she did perk up enough to delight in some baked goods from the ground floor.

Arriving home, she changed into a pair of wide legged, grey trousers and a baggy t-shirt. She then proceeded to create an edible array of snacks, sandwiches and liquid refreshments. She selected some of her favourite movies, put one in the DVD player and snuggled down to veg out.

***

"Oh no, not this one again!" Anisa had just got home from school. "You're crying! How can you cry? This is the most boring movie ever made!"

Mina grabbed another tissue and wiped her tear strewn eyes. "You're just a kid, you wouldn't understand."

"Well, I don't want to." She looked at the bowls of food and said, "You are gonna share this, aren't you?"

Mina snatched a bowl of Bombay mix into her lap and gave her sister a sideways glance. "Maybe, if you're nice to me."

"Hmm. I'll have to think about that." She picked up her school bags. "I'm going to get dressed. I've got tuition at four."

The second movie came to an end just in time for her to catch a phone call.

"I really need to see you. I miss you." Justin's voice was heavy and slow.

"How's Frankie?"

"We'll talk when I see you." He paused and said, "Can you get out to meet me?"

She looked down at her lounging clothes, and the uneven distribution of crumbs in their deeper creases. "Give me forty-five minutes."

Mina stood on Justin's doorstep and he came out to give her a long embrace. "I wish you could stay...and never leave."

"I'll make us some tea and you can talk it out." She kissed him and closed the door.

The Lovers Lunch

She recognised the car straight away and felt her stomach do somersaults or flutter with butterflies, whatever the physical feeling was, she knew she felt nervous. She wasn't sure if today would be the day, but she knew at some point this week she would be telling Justin her news. He parked the blue Audi alongside her and she opened the door to get in. She could tell it had been recently cleaned, "I see you've been busy since we last met."

As she turned to face him and their eyes met, her stomach started feeling funny again. Justin placed his hand on Mina's cheek and pulled her towards him. She rested her hand on his thigh and felt his lips touch hers.

He pulled away and cheekily said, "Hello to you too."

They shared another short kiss and then Mina asked, "Could we stop somewhere to eat? I feel like I haven't eaten since breakfast!"

"Me too, even though breakfast was only four hours ago!"

"Don't make fun of me. Sitting in lectures is hard work you know." She gently nudged him with an elbow.

"Waiting for you to leave the lectures is hard work for me."

Mina's whole face lit up as she imagined Justin waiting patiently until he could finally see and hold her.

Justin undid his seat belt and told Mina, "There's a nice place we can go a short walk from here."

She stepped out of the car groaning. "I've just walked all that way from college." She gestured in the direction of the building she'd left a few minutes ago. Justin tilted his head quizzically. "Well, can I at least leave my humongous bag in the car? I've been carrying it all day!"

After putting her bag away, she rubbed her shoulder as if to make the point clearer to Justin. He placed both hands on her shoulders. He leant in and whispered, "I can help you with that later if you like."

Her heart started beating faster at the thought of Justin's hands on her bare skin, but decided not to play his game. "Well, it depends on how far you're making me walk." She turned to face him, trying to look serious.

With her back against the parked car, Justin put his hands on the roof either side of her and she realised again how much taller he was than her. She noticed his eyes moving over her and she remembered the secret she hasn't shared with anyone, except Charlotte. "I'm getting hungrier the longer you take."

"Me too." Justin grinned and moved his hands away. "Let's hurry!"

He took her to a quiet bar. "It gets quite lively at the weekend," he said. They would have chosen to sit near the doors opening out onto the beer garden had it not been such a chilly afternoon. Instead they opted to sit in the lounge area among an assortment of armchairs, wooden chairs, small sofas, and coffee tables. Mina wanted to sit in an armchair, despite Justin's assertion that it would be difficult to reach food on the table from there. He placed their order at the bar and got them two soft drinks. He liked not having to drink alcohol when he was with Mina; it made a change from his usual habits.

His memory drifted back to the time he first set his eyes on Mina. He had seen her twice on consecutive days. On the second meeting, he decided he really shouldn't waste any time, and so made the first move. He smiled to himself as he pictured the look on her face when he handed her the piece of paper that, unbeknown to either of them, would change the course of their lives. He thought about what came after; an almost unbearable wait for his phone to ring so he could hear the voice he so desperately wanted to hear. He had surprised himself by how much he wanted to be with this complete stranger to find out everything about her.

Justin set the drinks down on the table and moved his chair next to Mina's. He took her by surprise kissing her with a passion that she was usually uncomfortable allowing in public, but on this occasion, knowing what she knew, she wrapped her arms around him, returning the kiss.

As they pulled away from each other, Justin whispered, "I'm so lucky to have you."

This prompted her to pull him in for another kiss. At that moment they were able to forget their worries and immerse themselves in positive emotions. Justin felt there was nothing he and Mina couldn't achieve together and he was in need of someone who would stand by his side. When they pulled away from each other, for the second time, his eyes were still closed and he was holding her hands up to his face. She suddenly felt the urge to tell him exactly what he meant to her and that he was going to be the father of her unborn child, but she wasn't ready, despite what her heart was telling her.

He finally opened his eyes to see Mina with tears in hers. Seeing his reaction, she wiped the tears away and told him, "Don't worry. I'm just a little surprised by how intense we just got."

They both took long sips from their drinks and then Justin moved his chair to sit opposite her. He watched her fidget with her napkin and the cutlery on the table. He wanted to soothe her nervousness so he said, "How was college?"

Mina was expecting a different question, but replied, "It wasn't too bad today. I only had one lecture and it was an interactive one, thank goodness. So, I've had a decent Friday, so far."

They were interrupted by the waiter approaching with their food The first plate he proffered was a vegetarian lasagne with cheesy garlic bread which Mina took from him. Justin had ordered a spaghetti Bolognese with garlic bread.

"It smells lovely," Mina said and prepared to tuck in.

Justin could see how awkward Mina was finding it to reach the food on the table, but didn't comment. What he couldn't help was the small laugh he couldn't choke back when she went to eat a mouthful of lasagne and it dropped back onto the plate.

She stared at him and said, "Don't you even think about saying anything."

Justin held his hands up and said, "I'm not going to. I wouldn't dare!" He picked up his garlic bread and, before he could take a bite, it slipped out of his hand and onto the floor! He lowered and shook his head whilst Mina laughed uncontrollably.

"Serves you right," scolded Mina, and then made him an offer. "Here, you can have some of mine." She held a piece of cheesy garlic bread out for Justin. He took a bite and all the while their eyes remained fixed on each other.

They enjoyed the comfortable silence that followed. Justin thought back to the last time Mina had visited Frankie and he started to worry, not for his older sister, but for his girlfriend. Physically, Frankie had changed and, after coming to terms with that, the impact of the sickness on her personality was already proving more difficult to handle. He wasn't aware of Mina having a physical reason for the heightened emotions she was displaying and the last thing he needed was to have to manage someone else's issues whilst trying to keep himself cool, calm and collected.

He looked down at the hand he had intertwined in his and then at his watch; they had been talking and eating for just over two hours now.

He looked at Mina and asked, "Are you ready to go?" She nodded and they both rose up from the seats and brushed themselves down. He took Mina's hand in his again and led her out of the quiet bar and back to his parked car.

She couldn't remember the last time that they had had such a difficult conversation, but she knew the next one would be even more problematical. Unconsciously, she squeezed Justin's hand. He felt it but still didn't know what was actually bothering her. His gut instinct had been telling him all afternoon to be a little more relaxed than he usually was and at least the gentle squeeze on his hand confirmed that he was taking the right tack with her.

When they reached the car and Mina saw Justin was about to open her door for her, she held up her hand and, with her first proper grin of the day, said, "Stop right there. I think I can manage a door."

Justin grinned back and said, "Umm. When did you get so bossy? But I think I still like Bossy Mina," He made his way round to the driver's side and added, "I can't wait for my next orders!"

Mina made herself comfortable in the passenger seat while Justin got the car started and said, "Your place or mine?"

Mina replied, "Your place, please. I don't think my parents will be there!"

"Well, they haven't replied to the dinner invitation I sent out to them, so you're probably right,"

Mina punched his arm. "That isn't funny."

Justin retorted, "It is actually."

She knew he wasn't looking at her and recommenced biting her lower lip. Her insides were twisted up and not because she had eaten too much. "When we get in I need to talk to you."

"Is everything alright?" he said, keeping his eyes fixed on the road.

"I don't know yet."

Justin, anxious to hear what Mina had to talk about, pushed harder on the accelerator and they reached home in record time. He raced to the front door and almost pushed her inside. "Tea?" *Anything to get her to talk and put me out of my misery.*

He returned to the living room five minutes later to place two steaming mugs on the table. "So, what do you need to talk to me about?"

Her cheeks burned up, reminding her of the first presentation she ever had to make in front of her classmates at school. She cleared her throat, took a sip of burning hot tea, almost scolding her tongue and cursed out loud. Then she took hold of his hand and said, "I've been having counselling at college."

Justin squeezed her hands tighter, covering them with both his own. "Why didn't you tell me? What are you seeing a counsellor for?"

She took a deep breath out and placed his hand over the stomach in which she was carrying his baby. "I'm pregnant."

"Oh, man. You had me worried there. I thought you..." He stared at his hand still resting firmly on Mina's stomach. He removed it only to take hold of her chin while kissing her deeply.

"We're having a baby?" He didn't seem at all put out at the prospect.

She nodded as the tears flowed freely and Justin held her in a passionate embrace.

Mina's Big Break

"Why are you doing this to us, Mina?" Mina's mum had stopped her before she'd been able to make another trip to Justin's with her belongings. "Once you leave, don't think you can ever come back. You're bringing shame on our family."

"You wouldn't understand why I need to do this. I hope maybe one day you will."

"I'll say this one time...if you leave your family to shack up with this, this, whoever he is, don't think you can come running back when it all goes wrong."

"He's not like that mum."

"I don't understand why this is happening. You came back, you started going to college."

"I need to go." Mina unhooked her front door key and placed it on the dining room table. Without another word, she left the room.

"What are you doing?"

She turned to find Anisa standing on the driveway beside her. "Oh, damn." She had hoped to sneak away like a coward. "I can't explain it all right now but, I'm moving out to live with someone else."

"Oh. You mean like a friend?"

"Yeah, exactly like that." The taxi driver closed the trunk of the car, a signal for Mina to hurry her explanation. She hugged her sister and said, "Mum and dad aren't happy with me. You might hear things that upset you."

"But why wouldn't they be happy if you're only moving in with a friend?"

Mina wished she had more time to warn Anisa how her life would change as she got older, how her every move might be dictated and depend upon validation from people who were family but had no idea what was really best for her and how, one day, she might be faced with a decision that could tear apart the life she had grown accustomed to.

All Mina could think to say was "If you've got any questions, call me." She planted a kiss on Anisa's head and stepped into the taxi and her new life.

FICTION FROM APS PUBLICATIONS

(www.andrewsparke.com)

Davey J Ashfield: Footsteps On The Teign
Davey J Ashfield Contracting With The Devil
Davey J Ashfield: A Turkey And One More Easter Egg
Fenella Bass: Hornbeams
Fenella Bass:: Shadows
HR Beasley: Nothing Left To Hide
Lee Benson: So You Want To Own An Art Gallery
Lee Benson: Where's Your Art gallery Now?
Lee Benson: Now You're The Artist...Deal With It
Lee Benson: No Naked Walls
TF Byrne Damage Limitation
Nargis Darby: A Different Shade Of Love
J.W.Darcy: Ladybird Ladybird
Milton Godfrey: The Danger In Being Afraid
Jean Harvey: Pandemic
Michel Henri: Mister Penny Whistle
Michel Henri: The Death Of The Duchess Of Grasmere
Michel Henri: Abducted By Faerie
Hugh Lupus An Extra Knot (Parts I-VI)
Ian Meacheam: An Inspector Called
Ian Meacheam: Time And The Consequences
Stoppa O'Reilly: Gainful Employment
Tony Rowland: Traitor Lodger German Spy
Andrew Sparke: Abuse Cocaine & Soft Furnishings
Andrew Sparke: Copper Trance & Motorways
Phil Thompson: Momentary Lapses In Concentration
Paul C. Walsh: A Place Between The Mountains
Paul C. Walsh: Hallowed Turf
Michael White: Life Unfinished
AJ Woolfenden: Mystique: A Bitten Past

www.ingramcontent.com/pod-product-compliance
Lightning Source LLC
Chambersburg PA
CBHW061134200626
46817CB00016B/1399